SOMEON ✍ S0-CGS-169
AT THE WATER'S EDGE . . .

It was a man, half in the water, half out of it, on one side. An arm and hand moved sluggishly. Dixon said, "Who is he?"

"It's—it's the gardener," Sarah said. "Costellani."

The body lay nearly submerged in the shallow water; it moved a little in the rock of the water, giving it a grisly semblance of life.

"How long . . . ?"

"I don't know. Some days, I should think."

"Was he—drowned?" Even as she asked it she knew that Costellani, who swam as easily as he walked or raked or pushed the mover, had not drowned.

Dixon said, "He was stabbed."

It was very hot and still. She whispered, *"Like Arthur . . ."*

MIGNON G. EBERHART

"A GRAND MASTER OF MYSTERY AND SUSPENSE."
--*Mystery News*

"ONE OF THE MOST POPULAR WRITERS
OF OUR ERA."
--*San Diego Union*

Also by Mignon G. Eberhart

Alpine Condo Crossfire
Another Man's Murder
The Bayou Road
Casa Madrone
Danger Money
Family Affair
Hasty Wedding
Hunt With the Hounds
Man Missing

Murder in Waiting
Next of Kin
The Patient in Cabin C
Postmark Murder
Run Scared
Unidentified Woman
The Unknown Quantity
Witness at Large
Wolf in Man's Clothing

Mignon G. Eberhart's Best Mystery Stories

Published by
WARNER BOOKS

MIGNON G. EBERHART

THE UNKNOWN QUANTITY

WARNER BOOKS

A Warner Communications Company

DEDICATION

To Bernice Baumgarten Cozzens

to mark with gratitude a friendship
which is twenty-one years old on this date
but which came of age long ago.
February, 1953

All persons and events in this book are entirely imaginary.
Nothing in it derives from anything that ever happened.

WARNER BOOKS EDITION

This Warner Books Edition is published by arrangement with
Random House, Inc.,
201 E. 50th Street, New York, N.Y. 10022.

Warner Books, Inc.
666 Fifth Avenue
New York, N.Y. 10103

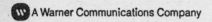 A Warner Communications Company

Printed in the United States of America

First Warner Books Printing: June, 1985

Reissued March, 1990

10 9 8 7 6 5 4 3 2

1

There were flowers on a table. Arthur's large suitcase, already closed and locked, stood beside the door. Otherwise there was nothing to testify to his presence, no penciled notation, no magazine or half-emptied package of cigarettes. He was finically neat. He had arrived in San Francisco Sunday morning. It was then late Tuesday afternoon, but the absence of small signs of his presence gave the hotel suite an air of having been tenantless for a long time. Even the air seemed lifeless and still.

She went to the table where the great vase of red roses stood. She saw then a note addressed in his fine, neat handwriting. "Dear Sarah, I'm sorry I couldn't meet you at the plane. I'm tied up with conferences. If I don't get back to the hotel before six, meet me at the Top o' the Mark. It's across the street. I hope you had a pleasant trip." It was signed "A."

Sarah read it again, unconsciously trying to read something into the sparse lines which was not there, and put it down.

She looked at her watch, mentally rearranging its tiny hands to suit west-coast time. She had left La Guardia Field only that morning and it seemed much later than, in San Francisco, it actually was. She'd have time to freshen up and have tea before she went to meet Arthur.

There was not a word in his note to explain why he had

5

wired, the day before, asking her to meet him in San Francisco. She had had a feeling of urgency, mainly because he had specifically said: "Be here Tuesday night. Take the morning flight." He had wired, too, to Rose Willman at his office who had seen to the tickets. Rose's efficiency in seeing to it that Sarah got off at the time Arthur expected had added to the sense of urgency. Yet it would not have occurred to Sarah to hesitate. In five years of marriage to Arthur Travers she had grown accustomed to the exigencies of his business. The fact was, Sarah could not have avoided knowing that such a chore pleased Rose. It emphasized her status as Arthur's confidential secretary for many years, long before Sarah had thankfully accepted a job Arthur had offered her, as a typist. Far down in the office hierarchy from Rose Willman's height, Sarah, so short a time later, had become Mrs. Arthur Travers. Rose was devoted to Arthur and to her job. They comprised her life. She had placed Arthur on a pedestal and it was difficult for her happily to accept Sarah, the little typist who had run errands for her, as Arthur's wife.

Sarah opened her bag, and while water was running for a bath, strolled idly around the spacious suite. Arthur always traveled as a prince is supposed to travel and seldom does. His bedroom was as bare of the signs of occupancy as the living room. A small suitcase and a dispatch case which, together with the big suitcase, always accompanied his many journeys were not anywhere in the rooms. It struck her, seeing their absence, that he had already packed and sent them somewhere—an airport or a railway station. Was he, then, going on from San Francisco? Where, there was no way to guess. She ordered tea sent up.

She was getting into her gray traveling suit again when the telephone rang and she hurried to answer, thinking it was Arthur. A man's voice said, "Is this Mrs. Travers? My name is Dixon. I have an appointment with your husband."

"I'm sorry, he's not here."

"Oh. . . . He said to meet him at his apartment at 5:30. I'll wait then. Will you tell him in case I miss him? I'll be downstairs in the lounge."

She had been well-trained by Arthur in the most minute courtesy to any and all of his business acquaintance. "Will you come up here, Mr. Dixon? If he said 5:30 he'll be here in a few minutes."

"Thank you."

She put down the telephone, zipped up her gray skirt, fastened the cuffs of the fresh white blouse she had taken from her bag, ran the comb through her short reddish-brown hair, fluffing it high above her temples, and reached for lipstick. The door buzzer sounded as she slid into her trim gray jacket and she went through the living room, scented by the red roses, to open the door.

"*Arthur* . . ." she said, and stopped, staring at the man who stood there.

"Yes, I know," he said. "It surprised me, too. . . . I'm Dixon."

"You look so much like him! I thought—I didn't expect . . ." It was so extraordinary and unexpected a likeness that she was taken aback and confused. "I'm sorry! Do come in."

"It's not so close a resemblance when you take a second look." Dixon put his hat and Arthur's initialed dispatch case on the table by the door.

"N-no." He was not as tall as Arthur, and broader. His face was broader, too, with a generous width of temple and jaw, his dark hair was crisp and thick, his mouth was fuller and just then half-smiling, amused. He was younger than Arthur, too. Nevertheless the resemblance was startling. His strongly marked features, his strongly curved black eyebrows emphasized it. He could have passed for Arthur—except, of course, with people who knew them well.

She realized that he was staring, too, and looked also a little surprised. "Please sit down. Arthur will be here in a minute or two—he's always prompt. Will you have tea or—" she glanced at the remains of her own tea, on the table by the window, "—or you'd rather have a drink at this hour, I expect. I'll phone down . . ."

"No, thank you." He hesitated, then as she sat in the armchair near the table he sat down opposite her. She said, "It's a remarkable resemblance. But as you say, at second glance . . ."

"Like the advertisements. Which is the real Fred Murray? Which is the real Alan Ladd? But you can always see the difference." She had a quick impression that he didn't really like looking so much like anybody else.

She said lightly, "But think of all the people in the world. Mother Nature must get tired of inventing new patterns."

"And resort to duplicates?" He laughed shortly. His laugh was not at all like Arthur's. As a matter of fact Arthur rarely laughed. "It amused your husband, too. He said he was going to try to get me to make public speeches for him."

"Yes, he hates public speeches."

He took out cigarettes, glanced at her and said rather gravely, "Do you mind if I smoke?"

That too gave her a quick impression, this time of a woman in his background, old-fashioned and gentle, someone perhaps like her own Aunt Julia. "No, of course not."

"Will you . . ."

"Thank you." He rose, offered her a rather battered leather case, lighted her cigarette and returned to his chair. He had an air of concluding polite conversation and getting down to business. "I brought the power of attorney for you."

"Power of attorney?"

"I've got the plane tickets, too. Travers said to get them in his name."

"I don't understand . . ."

His eyes were not like Arthur's, either; they were a dark, blue-gray and not so narrowly spaced as Arthur's rather hazy brown eyes, and just now he had a very direct look of inquiry. "I thought you knew . . ."

The telephone rang again. She made a gesture of excuse and lifted it and this time it was Arthur.

"Sarah? . . . I'm sorry I couldn't meet you. Did you have a pleasant trip? Is young Dixon there?"

"Yes . . ."

"Put him on, will you?"

She turned to Dixon. "It's my husband. He wants to talk to you."

He came to take the telephone and she strolled to the window, looking down into the cavern of the busy street far below. Arthur had sounded hurried, but, as usual, cool and precise. She listened absently to Dixon's replies. ". . . yes. Yes, I've got them. Yes, in your name but . . . The dispatch case is here. I thought you might want it. . . . Oh, I see." He listened for a long time then and when he replied sounded rather reluctant. "Why, yes, I'll tell her about it if you want me to. But I . . ." he listened and then again said in a tone of surprise, "*Where?*"

Arthur seemed to be giving detailed instructions. They were instructions which Dixon did not seem particularly to like. He said reluctantly, "Well—all right, but it seems a little out of the way for . . . No, I don't understand. Oh, well,

8

of course . . . Yes. Yes, I'll be there." He looked at Sarah. "He'd like to speak to you again."

She took the telephone, warm from the pressure of his hand. Arthur said, "Sarah, my dear, something has come up rather suddenly. Dixon will explain as much as he can to you. He's a lawyer and I've retained him to do a few chores for me. I can't explain from here, but he'll tell you. I'll see you in half an hour or so at the Top o' the Mark. Right?"

Arthur was always secretive and guarded in any business affair; probably he was speaking from someone's office. "Yes . . . All right."

"See you then." He rang off promptly.

Dixon had moved to the door and had his hat in his hand. She said, "He told me you'd explain. . . ."

"Yes. Well, there's not much really. He—perhaps he told you I'm a lawyer."

"Yes."

"He—the fact is he's got to go on a trip. It's something very hush-hush, for the government. They want his opinion about something as an expert. But it's all got to be kept very quiet."

"You mean he's leaving soon?"

"I don't know when he leaves. That is, he'll not know himself until barely time to get to the airport. I don't know where he's going, of course. But what he asked me to tell you is—" he looked rather troubled—"he asked me to get plane tickets for tonight's plane. For you, that is, and for me. In his name, I don't know why but—at any rate he wants me to take the same plane to New York. It's a rather long trip for you since you've just got here. I—he was sorry to have to ask you to go back tonight."

That, she knew, he had invented: Arthur was never tired himself and never expected anybody else to tire. "Oh, no, that's all right. It was an easy flight today. When does the plane leave?"

"Nine o'clock. It doesn't give you much time."

"I didn't unpack." Something he had said before Arthur's telephone call returned to her. "You spoke of a power of attorney."

"Oh, yes. He had me draw up one for you. He's to take rather a long trip, I understand. He wanted you to have a power of attorney, but it's—only a matter of routine."

"I understand. My husband is very exact about such things."

He took up Arthur's dispatch case. "I'm taking this to New York for him. He asked me to bring it here with me, but I'm to meet him later." At the door he hesitated, "I'll see you tonight, then, at the plane."

"Nine o'clock. Thank you . . ."

He nodded and looked so like Arthur again as he walked away from her down the corridor toward the elevators that it was as if it was Arthur himself, carrying Arthur's dispatch case, but a younger Arthur, rather as she remembered him five years before. He rang for the elevator and she closed the door. Arthur's projected trip, then, was the reason he had summoned her so urgently across the continent to meet him.

She wondered where this journey was to take him. If he had ever acted as advisor to any government agency before that, she had not known of it. But he was an expert. He was indeed rather a legend in the oil industry, for he had risen almost to the top very swiftly and remained there, fabulously successful.

She repacked the few things she had taken from her bag, replaced powder and perfume in her cosmetic case. She put on her small gray hat. Probably Arthur would go from the cocktail lounge direct to dinner. There would barely be time to collect her two bags and get to the airport—and meet Dixon.

She looked at herself in the mirror, struck suddenly by a sense of dissatisfaction. She tilted the gray hat forward, over one side, straightened it again. She looked, she thought with exasperation exactly what she was, a girl from a little college town, a nice enough face, direct blue eyes, a nice enough figure and a good carriage (Aunt Julia had seen to that) and that was all. A girl who had been plunged into the great world with her marriage to Arthur and had never been a part of it; a girl who still had habits of thrift and economy. Her gray suit was just a suit, simple and well tailored and nothing that anybody would look at twice. Her white silk blouse was just a white silk blouse. She took out a small sapphire pin Arthur had given her and fastened it at her throat. She pushed up her brown short hair and wished the red lights in it were brighter. She added more lipstick, took her handbag, went to the door and opened it and a man was standing outside, in the corridor. He was standing there, as if waiting, facing the door.

He was dark and swarthy, with small dark eyes, wore a

rather wrinkled brown tweed suit and a bright tie. It was the bright tie that awoke Sarah's recognition. He had been a passenger on the plane that day, he had been in fact a late comer, sprinting for the runway with the bright tie flapping.

She drew back involuntarily and he stepped toward her. There was a coy, inviting simper in his face. "Now, little lady, don't be scared. You look lonely." He had a slight and untraceable accent. He sidled closer. "Lonely little lady in a big city. How about having dinner with me? Here . . ." he fumbled in his pocket and drew out a card. "I'll introduce myself. All proper. Robinson's my name. Robinson. How about it?" He held out the card.

A pickup! He had seen that she was traveling alone. By chance he had stopped at the same hotel. Nonsense!

She didn't back into the room and close the door; there wasn't time. She walked briskly past him toward the elevator and rang. She knew that he hadn't moved to follow her. Nevertheless she was pleased when the elevator came almost at once and had several other passengers. When she stepped into it she had a fleeting glimpse of the man in the corridor, philosophically putting his absurd card back in his pocket.

The sun was lower when she emerged from the hotel into the street. She crossed it and entered the Mark Hopkins and went up, up, up in the elevator there, to the wide room, enclosed in windows, the Top o' the Mark. Arthur had not yet arrived, so she waited for a moment or two at the elevators, and then walked past the huge circular bar to a table at the back beside a window. She sat down there and looked out and down, down upon the city, down upon the bay.

The sky was brilliant with yellow and pink, and the bay reflected its colors with tranquil clarity. Blue shadows were gathering in the busy caverns of the streets and lights were beginning to glimmer there like stars in sapphires. The room, with its great windows from floor to ceiling, was like an island set about by the sky, an island of lights, gaiety, people. She leaned her chin on her hand, lost in a survey of the wide panorama of bay and hills and city. Unexpectedly and gradually, waiting for Arthur as she had waited so many times, a kind of sadness and loneliness came from the very beauty and tranquillity of the blue bay and rosy sky and twinkling lights. It was as if she surveyed, too, the small panorama of her own life, but found by contrast an important, a basic beauty and tranquillity lacking.

It was not the first time she had looked at herself with a

11

sense of futility, but she had never before then surrendered to it.

Arthur would come and would greet her politely. He would tell her, politely, of his trip. She would agree politely to any instructions he wished to give her.

There would be no shared recognition of the beauty of bay and sky. No shared small jokes. No shared delight in eyes meeting eyes, hands touching hands. Nothing shared between them alone, shutting out all others.

It seemed to her in that queerly sad and lonely moment that she had built a house without a foundation. Out of stubbornness, perhaps out of gratitude to Arthur for his generosity to her and to Julia Halsey, out of loyalty to him, to herself, to what Julia had taught her of marriage, she continued to dwell in that uncertain house.

Yet she had once been in love with Arthur. She had been dazzled, certainly; she had been a little bewildered and spellbound—but she had been in love, she was sure of that.

In a bright flash of memory she remembered Arthur, smiling at her across a tennis court. The sun had been in her eyes so she couldn't see him clearly, but in that flashing memory the face that smiled at her across a sunny court was the face of the young lawyer, Dixon.

A waiter was at her side. She ordered something, anything, and told him there would be another person. It dispelled the swift illusion.

Her mood of sadness was due to fatigue. Obviously the young lawyer so resembled Arthur as he had been five years ago—perhaps Arthur as she thought he had been five years ago—that the likeness had touched a wound which lay resolutely concealed within her controlled routine of life. It was a life which she had chosen; she reminded herself of that. She wondered and had wondered many times, why Arthur, even then the great Arthur Travers, had chosen her.

She looked up and Arthur was coming toward her.

2

Something, somewhere had changed. It was so marked a change that it drew her from Arthur, tall and rigorously slender in his precisely tailored brown business suit, threading a delicate and catlike way through groups of people, past waiters, to look out the window beside her. The sun had dropped beyond the edge of the Pacific. The rosy light had gone from sky and bay; a dusky twilight had fallen like a curtain upon the city, upon the bay, surrounding the lighted, gay room. Voices seemed louder and shriller as if in unconscious defiance of the advance of night.

Arthur came to her side, kissed her cheek lightly, sat down opposite her and smiled. "What a day I've given you! You look well. It must have been an easy trip. What will you have?" The waiter appeared again. She said, "I've ordered," and Arthur said, "Oh—a double martini, please." The waiter hurried toward the bar and Arthur leaned back and smiled. He was, she saw at once, in a pleasant and exhilarated mood.

The lawyer Dixon came irresistibly again to her mind, but this time because he was so unlike Arthur.

Arthur, smiling at her across the table was strikingly handsome in a rather elegant, finely articulated way. His narrow face had strongly marked and rather sharp features, with high cheekbones, a high and narrow forehead and a thin mouth. It was a face which might have looked out from above a starched white ruff and velvet doublet; he might have posed for the portrait of a Spanish gentleman of medieval times. His hair was black and sleek. There was a half-excited gleam in his eyes, a definite exhilaration in his face. It was a look she had seen before; he looked like that when he was launched upon a big and a risky business deal which might go wrong but which, he was certain, would be successful. It was perhaps the exhilaration of a gamble against danger.

"Arthur, where are you going?"

"We'll talk about that later. I've got something for you." He took a jeweler's box from his pocket and put it on the table.

Another present!

"Open it. It's from Gump's. Gump's," he repeated, savoring the fine and rather aristocratic name a little, as he might have said, and probably had said in her hearing, Cartier's, the St. Regis, Worth Avenue.

The white wrapping paper rustled as she drew out a long, slender box. She opened it and a jade bracelet lay upon a couch of white velvet.

"Touch it," he said.

13

She did and the pieces of jade were as cool and smooth as the depths of the sea.

There had been other gifts, many of them. She thought, irresistibly, there's something he wants me to do. Something he knows I'll not want to do.

The waiter put down her cocktail and Arthur's. He took his glass and drank two-thirds of it quickly, which was unlike him. "Put it on," he said, eyeing the bracelet.

The pieces of jade were linked together with diamond-set bars; she pushed the glittering little heap of green toward him and said, unexpectedly, not intending it, "What do you want me to do?"

Arthur's strongly arched black eyebrows drew upward. "What do you mean? Sarah, surely you didn't mind—I'd have met the plane if I'd known you would mind. But you see, this is really an important kind of thing." He glanced around them. By chance the nearest tables were vacant, but he lowered his voice. "I don't like to talk about it here, but there's not much time. The thing came up very suddenly and from such high places, a request like this. . . ." He shrugged. "I can't refuse. In fact I wouldn't want to refuse. It's—well, the fact is it's a patriotic sort of thing. I'm very grateful to you for coming out here. I wanted to see you, of course. And besides—I've got to ask you to help me."

She looked at the green, sparkling bracelet. "How?"

"It isn't much, but it's important. I only want you to go home and stay there, and I want you to tell everyone, anyone who asks, that I'm there too. That's all." His voice lowered so it would have been inaudible except to her ears. "It's a rather dangerous sort of thing. There'll be, they told me, people who'll want to stop me. The point is to keep anyone from knowing that I've gone." He watched her. "Surely you don't object to helping me."

Go home, to the house on the lake, give the impression to anyone who might ask that Arthur, too, was there. Who would want to stop him?

Arthur said, "I don't want to frighten you, but it is really important. It has to do with the possibility of oil wells. I can't tell you about it, not even you. But you understand how very important it is."

"Is it dangerous?"

"So they say. It's their idea, not mine, to give me this kind of—call it protection. Security for the mission itself and for me. They feel that the whole affair must be kept very secret.

14

They don't want anyone to know of our interest and consequently of my trip. I'm—well, not an unimportant figure in the industry. My absence at this time would suggest government interest in it. Besides we have enemies within our gates—everybody knows that. They believe that they might . . ." He shrugged again. "Frankly, I don't think all this hush-hush business is necessary. On the other hand I don't want to—to disappear somewhere and never be heard of again! It's their idea that if I'm supposed to be at home it will not only draw off the scent from the job they're trying to do, but at the same time protect me. I was sure that you would understand it."

"For how long?"

"Not more than a few days. Say, definitely, a week. Perhaps less. I'm flying, under another name. It's all arranged. It may not take very long. It's—well, it's a patriotic job to do. Otherwise I wouldn't undertake it."

She said slowly, "I can do that, Arthur, while you are away."

He smiled. "That's my girl. Drink your cocktail, dear. As a matter of fact, there's a rather amusing little slant. It came up today. It's not my idea. But I have to admit it has a certain value."

She touched her lips to her cocktail. Arthur said, "This young lawyer, Dixon. You saw his resemblance to me."

She nodded.

"It's an absurd resemblance, nothing that would deceive anybody who knows me for an instant. But I happened to mention it. It amused me and—they jumped at it." He laughed. "They want him to pose as me. While I'm away. Absurd, isn't it?"

"It's impossible!"

"Don't raise your voice, darling. Well, yes, that's what I said. Waiter . . ." He signaled with a slender hand. "But I must say, after they'd talked awhile it didn't seem so absurd. You see if anybody *is* on the lookout to find out whether I've actually gone—which would suggest to them that this job is actually in the works, this young fellow, Dixon—he just might look enough like me so it would put them off. At the same time, automatically, it would doubly protect me, although I really think the danger is overemphasized."

She leaned across the table, "Do you mean they want him to stay in New York, go to your office? Oh, that's preposterous!"

15

"Not go to the office. Everybody at the office would have to know about it. And not even Rose knows anything about it—and mustn't know. Don't forget that."

He looked out the window. "Or, by the way, Lisa Bayly."

"Lisa!" She said in astonishment. "I wouldn't tell her!"

"No—well, I only thought . . ." He looked at his glass and lifted it thoughtfully to his lips and finished it. "We see so much of her. . . . But the point is they want Dixon to go home with you, so if anybody inquires, if anybody's sent to check on me, there he is, presumably me. At a distance and if somebody didn't really know me, yes, it might work. They say it's a sound protection, not that they care so much about me personally, but they do care . . ." He stopped as the waiter approached with another martini and put it down. It diverted her for a second. She had never seen Arthur drink that much or that quickly. Perhaps there was more danger than he wished her to know, or even to admit to himself.

Then she thought incredulously of the thing he had suggested. "But you *can't* . . . *He* can't. . . ."

"Well, he's yet to be persuaded. I'm sending some things back with him. In fact, I also want him to go with you. Not that you'll be in any danger, none whatever, the worst thing they could do would be to try to get out of you some admission about my whereabouts and you're not to know that. Still I'll feel easier in my mind to know that somebody is with you. I checked on him; he's all right. In his own business and not doing too badly, but he's young of course." He lifted his cocktail. "Do you mind very much letting him stay at the house until I get back?"

"At the house?"

"Why, of course. Where else?"

"But—you can't mean . . ."

"Sarah, it's such a small thing. You can't object to letting him pose as me for a few days. He's a perfectly harmless person. It might bore you a little, having him as a guest, but they say that your co-operation about this will be immensely valuable, as I told you, not only to my safety, but to their undertaking for security reasons."

"Arthur, I can't! It's absurd, it's—I'll be there alone!"

"Don't be childish, Sarah. He's not going to try to make love to you, if that's on your mind."

"I never thought of that!" But there was some obscure, yet very important argument against it, all the same. She said, unevenly, "Pretend he's you! Tell everyone, anyone

16

. . . It couldn't possibly succeed. It would go wrong in a hundred ways."

"Not with you there to prevent exactly that, my dear."

He touched the glittering green bracelet on the table. "Put it on. Don't you like it?"

"There must be some other way. He could stay in the apartment in town . . ."

"In a hotel, with bellboys, waiters, maids, who have known me for years!"

"Well, then—let him stay at the house on the lake. I'll stay in town and . . ."

"Sarah, time is short. Don't be childish and stubborn about this. I have to ask you flatly to do this for me. I believe that you owe me some consideration. If I must remind you of it, there are things that I have done for you. Where would you have been without me?" He smiled and spoke softly as if to give a jocular and rather tender tone to his reminder, but the words remained and his hazy eyes had no smile. "I gave you a job when I knew you needed it. Remember? Since we've been married I've given you, I think, everything a woman could want. I've been willing to support your aunt. I've . . ."

"I am very grateful to you for that."

"Show it then. Listen, Sarah: I have minimized the physical danger to me in the job I'm going to do. I have to say to you that, even if you feel no sense of duty toward me, there's your duty toward your country and mine. Wait, I've not finished." He picked up the little white wrapping paper on the table, and folded it as he talked. "You've bought bonds—with my money if I must say so. You've given to the Red Cross. You've been very proud of some ancestor of yours who signed his name on a scrap of paper nearly two hundred years ago. So far as I know that's the extent of your active patriotism. This is a chance to do something that may be disagreeable, or that you may not want to do. But consider this. It is perfectly true that this affair might end badly for me. Men do—disappear. Read the papers. We do have not one, but, directly and practically, a number of enemies. They may stem from a single source, but they are independent so far as their activity goes. I have no more courage than the next man. I don't want to do this. At the same time I could not possibly refuse. Call it anything you like. No—I've not finished." With one of his habitually neat gestures, he slid the jeweler's box in his pocket, leaving the bracelet upon the table. "You say that you feel grateful for anything I've done for you. I don't want gratitude. But if you do feel any sense of obligation, this is your chance to pay yourself out, if you want to put it like that."

She looked down at her hands. There was danger, more immediate and direct than she had at first understood. That was clear. But mainly she was humbled by the courage which Arthur denied.

Five or six days out of her life was not much to ask. There was no danger, no real reason for reluctance in undertaking the passive role he asked her to play. "All right, I'll do it."

She could tell by his voice that he was smiling again. "That's my girl. It's trivial in a way; I'm not asking you to go forth and do great deeds. It's only very important. Now then, there's not much time. I'll be specific. First, if things go wrong, I've had Dixon draw up a power of attorney for you. That would tide you over any—possibilities and red tape. Second, well—only stick to what I've told you, go along for a week no matter what happens. Say to anyone who inquires that I'm there at the house. Say I'm resting; say I'm supposed not to do any sort of business. Let this young fellow, Dixon, stay there and let him be seen—but at a distance. There are always people around the lake and if anybody is watching the house, let them see him."

After a moment she said, "Costellani! We'll have to tell him."

"Oh, no, that's all right. I forgot to tell you. His daughter's sick. She lives somewhere in southern California. He's gone to see her."

"I didn't know he had a daughter," she said, surprised.

"Neither did I. Maybe he hasn't and it's only an excuse for a long vacation. He left a message at the office and probably didn't want me to question him. It doesn't matter, we can always get another gardener. That was—I think Friday. I told Rose Willman to get a new man from an employment bureau. He can see to the place until or if Costellani comes back. Perhaps you can manage for that length of time without a cook or maids."

Costellani, a wiry little man whose shock of red hair went oddly with his vague but obviously southern European ancestry and face, was the gardener and caretaker. It was the custom at the lake to engage maids for the summer from the village, schoolgirls, or teachers home for the holidays. "All right," she said. "All right."

"The only point I've got to stress is, they say we've got to have about five or six days. So call it a week exactly. I'll let you know if or when it's done, as soon as I can. But no matter what happens—even if it—" his voice became very soft— "even if it happens to me, they want you to understand that you're to go along with this for a week for reasons of government security. Definitely a week, unless I return sooner than that, or unless you have some word from them. Is that clear?"

"Yes. But . . ."

"All right. I'll count on you. I'll tell them." He rose, took her handbag and slipped the shimmering green bracelet inside it.

"Are you leaving now? Tonight?"

"Very soon. I've got to talk to Dixon first. We're meeting, as a matter of fact, secretly. In the park. They thought we ought not to be seen together."

"Suppose he won't do it . . ."

"He struck me as a level-headed young fellow; he was in the Navy for four years. He understands what it's all about. I mean the general situation. I couldn't give him specific details. Well, please take the bracelet."

"Arthur, I hope it goes well." The words were sincere, and sounded trite. He said, "Thank you. I'm afraid I'll have to leave you here. It's later than I thought."

"What shall I do now?"

"Check out at the hotel and send the bag I left there and yours to the airport. Meet me and the lawyer in . . ." He looked at his watch. "Can you make it in half an hour?"

"Yes. Where?"

"Here, I'll write it." He wrote the names of two streets neatly on the paper cocktail napkin. "It's at a corner of the Presidio Park. I'll be watching for you. You'd better have a bite of dinner first. You'll have to go directly from the park to the airport. When you get back to New York go straight to the lake. Don't let Rose talk to Dixon over the phone, she'd know. Keep away anybody who really knows me. That's all."

He paid the waiter and tipped him lavishly.

"Arthur . . ." she began.

He glanced at her with a flicker of annoyance. "What is it? It's late."

She rose. She hadn't known what she intended to say. She had only an impulse to make amends for something, and she wanted from him, perhaps from herself, some gesture of

19

friendliness. He said, "I'm counting on you, Sarah," and led the way toward the elevators.

He knew of course, after those five years, that he could rely on her promise and her loyalty to him. Perhaps what she wanted was some word of affection, of mutual faith. For a second she had an impulse to stop him, take him by the arm, before all those people, under those bright lights, amid the clamor and clatter of the room, demand, "Why did you marry me? You don't love me. Why did you marry me?"

She entered the elevator with him; there were people there, so she said nothing. They reached the lobby. It was packed at that hour with people coming and going. At the door he said, "I'll take a taxi here. See you in half an hour."

He nodded and stepped into the first taxi.

About to cross the street, she paused to wait for the light at the intersection. Arthur's taxi already had swept into the stream of heavy traffic. As the light changed another taxi shot across ahead of her and she had a glimpse of its passenger. It was the man who had been on the plane that morning, and who, with a simper, had tried to pick her up for a dinner companion. Probably, she thought wryly, he was on the trail of some other woman. She crossed the street with the light, back to the Fairmount.

Her bags and the big suitcase Arthur was sending home with her were ready to go; she stopped to tell the bell captain to have them sent to the airport for the nine o'clock plane and went into the dining room where she had a quick and early dinner. It was full dark by the time she emerged from the hotel again and took a taxi to the Presidio Park.

Every city has its own special sounds. In San Francisco there is the squeal of sharply applied brakes at the intersections of the lovely hilly city. Sarah braced herself at each red light. It was a hurtling, surging ride, up and down hills and longer than she, a stranger to the city, had expected. They reached the park, a softly black area, dotted with lights. The driver stopped. "Here you are, lady." He looked back at her curiously.

No one was waiting for her under the street light. She paid the driver and the taxi drifted on more slowly as if seeking another passenger. Sarah stood under the street light, looking around her.

It seemed extraordinarily deserted in spite of the occasional street lights. There were a few empty benches, and behind them the thick shrubbery, the blotted mass of trees, stretched away on all sides. Arthur had said he would be watching for her. She strolled along the walk and after a few yards back again. It also seemed, in contrast perhaps to the busy streets she had just left, extremely quiet. There was only the distant squeal of brakes now and then, or the distant throb of an automobile. None came near the corner where she waited. It was a dark night, overcast, with a faint, chilly mist haloing the lights.

Arthur still did not come along the walk, or from one of those thick clumps of shadows behind the heavy shrubbery. She walked along the path in the other direction, and again back to stand directly beneath the street lamp.

She sat down at last on one of the benches.

She didn't like the park. She didn't like the silence and she didn't like the mist. She didn't like the way the shadows seemed to move a little toward her as the fog wreaths wavered, and then as she looked stood still.

Arthur was always prompt. He made plans down to the last detail, devious plans sometimes, but plans with segments that fitted as neatly as a puzzle. A sense of uneasiness began to pluck at her nerves. Arthur was always prompt. Arthur had talked of danger.

Nothing could have happened during his taxi ride to the park to meet Dixon.

No one, except Dixon and Sarah herself had so much as known of that appointment, unless of course he had told the men who were sending him on his journey.

When Arthur arrived, she must ask him for a name, a specific person or telephone number, some way to reach that particular government agency, in the event of—well, emergency.

But with Arthur, who laid his plans so well, emergency was not really likely to occur. Yet he had talked of danger!

Danger from enemies, who would try to find out whether or not he had gone and, if they knew that, would be enabled to guess accurately where and why. Danger from an enemy who would try to stop him because he was an expert, he was an authority about oil. Danger because his absence would go far to confirm their suspicion that an important plan concerning oil was in the making.

Danger.

Suddenly she was visited by the fantastic recollection of a man in a wrinkled tweed suit with a bright tie (what had he said his name was, Robertson? No, Robinson) running for the plane she had taken, standing outside her door at the hotel, sitting in a taxi which hurled along the street, in the same direction that Arthur had taken! Suppose, in fact, Robinson had followed her, believing correctly that she would lead him to Arthur.

No, she told herself, no. It was a product of uneasy nerves and frightened imagination.

She rose and walked along the path again and then she saw in the distance the figure of a man walking rapidly toward her. He passed under a street light, and came on into shadow. It was Arthur, carrying his dispatch case. She walked quickly toward him, and then she saw it wasn't Arthur. It was Dixon.

He came quickly to meet her. "Mrs. Travers!" he said in a tone of surprise. "I didn't expect you. That is, I was to meet your husband here, half an hour ago. I came and he wasn't here. I waited and then went to a drug store to phone the Fairmount. They said you had checked out. Was he held up? I suppose he sent you to tell me . . ."

So that, then, was why Arthur had given her the bracelet. She was to do her part.

Reaction from the sense of danger that had plucked at her nerves brought a quick wave of anger—anger because Arthur had manipulated the situation, subtly and yet directly, anger with herself because she had not seen it before then. She was to persuade the young lawyer to do what Arthur wanted him to do.

It would have been easy for Dixon to refuse Arthur; it would not be so easy to refuse a woman, and a woman who might be herself in some danger. Already certainly Arthur had suggested to Dixon that he'd wished Sarah to have an escort, in a sense a guard, for the trip home.

So she was to earn the bracelet that she didn't want.

But Arthur had known too that he could rely on her.

She said crisply, still angry, "He wants me to tell you what he wants you to do."

3

In the dim light the lawyer's face looked only perplexed.

She'd say it briefly and quickly. "He wants you to take his place for a week."

"I don't understand."

"It's the resemblance. He thinks you look enough like him to do it. That, is, to pose as Arthur for a week."

"But that—why that's . . ." He stopped, stared at her, and said, "That's impossible."

"He says that the people who want to stop him—or find out whether or not he has actually gone wherever he's going—if they see you they'll think you are Arthur. The idea is to conceal the government's object, and to protect him, at the same time. He wants you to go . . ." She took a breath and said shortly, "He wants you to go to the house, and stay there for a week. Not to go to the office or where people who know him well would see you but to let yourself be seen—by anybody else. He meant, by anybody trying to find out . . ."

He touched her arm. "Wait a minute. Let's not take it so fast. Suppose we sit down on that bench and talk it over."

She crossed with him to the nearest bench and sat down. He put Arthur's dispatch case on the bench between them. She wouldn't try to persuade him, she'd tell him the bare facts, and if he refused, then he'd have refused and that was the end of it.

He said thoughtfully, "Travers said there was some danger. That's why he wanted me to go east with you. He said it would ease his mind a little if I saw to it that you reached home safely. But this . . ." He stopped thought again for a moment and said, "You mean, he wants me to be a—a sort of stand-in for him while he's away?"

"Yes."

"But I—why, I *can't* do that!"

"It would mean a week's absence from your office. I don't think Arthur realized . . ."

He broke in. "Oh, that's all right. He made a point of secrecy about going easy with you when he talked to me.

Nobody knows where I'm going. I told my office girl, there's only one, that I was going on a fishing trip. There's no special case coming up this week. She'd not question it if I didn't get back for a few days. That's why he said to get the plane tickets in his name and yours . . ." He checked himself abruptly and said slowly, "That *is* why! I mean this is why. He phoned to me this afternoon about it. He said to use his name and of course yours and—so this was his reason!"

She found herself arguing, as if irresistibly on his side. "Your family, your . . ."

"That's all right, too," he said thoughtfully. He drew out cigarettes. "My father's in Palm Springs where he lives and my sister's in Europe." She took the cigarette he offered; he lighted it and his own. "But I didn't expect anything like this. I don't see exactly—you mean he wants me to go home with you and stay there till he gets back . . ."

"He wants me to say that he is at home—that is, that you are Arthur, if there is inquiry. He wants me to prevent anyone who knows him well from seeing you. But he wants you to be seen by any strangers, anybody who might inquire."

He shook his head, got up, smoked for a minute, staring at the path, and sat down again. "I don't think it would work."

She said flatly, "Neither do I."

"What about servants? They'd know. I suppose you could trust them . . ."

"There's only one man there now, and he's new. He's never seen Arthur."

"Where is this house?"

"At Lake Saguache. It's about a hundred miles from New York."

He thought over that for a moment. "It sounds rather isolated."

"Well—it is, in a way. That is, it's three miles from the village and there aren't any other houses very close. It's wooded and all the houses around the lake are set off by themselves. But there are always boats on the lake. It's not exactly isolated."

"He didn't say anything about this yesterday when he came to my office."

"It wasn't his idea. That is, it was the resemblance between you. He mentioned it, and he said they jumped at it for security reasons."

"Why did he send you to tell me all this? Has he already gone?"

She answered the latter question. "I don't know. He said he didn't know exactly when he was to leave." Perhaps she had wrongly, in her mind, accused Arthur. Perhaps he had, in fact, got in touch with the men representing the government and been told that he had to leave at once, that the secret departure was arranged and the plane waiting for him. But he had known, nevertheless, that she could carry out his wishes.

"I suppose he's gone, then," Dixon said thoughtfully. "Did he tell you what to do with this?" He put his hand on the dispatch case.

"No. What's in it?"

"Papers, I suppose. He gave the case to me yesterday, brought it to my office. Since he said not to let it out of my sight, I gathered it was important. He said he wanted to add something to them and for me to bring it with me when I came to meet him. Look here, he's not signed the power of attorney for you!"

"I don't think that matters."

"I ought to have made him wait and sign it yesterday. It's only a form, you know, but it has to be signed and notarized. He said he was in a hurry and would sign it today. He must have gone. He didn't impress me," he said rather dryly, "as a man who would leave anything unfinished, not if he could help it." He eyed the dispatch case. "If that thing's got some dope about this trip, figures or information . . ."

"I'll take care of it," she said.

His cigarette glowed redly as he held it at his lips. "It wouldn't be a good idea to let it get in the wrong hands."

"No. I'll see that it doesn't."

Someone was walking along the path. She turned swiftly, with a nervous catch at her throat. A figure loomed up dimly under a light and it was a policeman, his uniform and cap distinct under the light. She sat back again with a little half laugh. Dixon said, "You're frightened."

"No, I—not really. It was waiting here . . ." She glanced back at the massed heavy blackness of shrubbery and shadow behind them, shapes veiled in mist. "I thought of all sorts of things."

The policeman's regular footsteps came nearer; his figure was distinct now. Dixon said, "Good evening, officer."

He stopped. He was young and square, his face barely visible in the shadows. "Good evening, sir. Tule fog coming up."

Dixon said good-naturedly, "We wouldn't know how to live without a fog here in San Francisco."

The policeman laughed. "I guess you're right, sir. Could I trouble you to tell me the time? I dropped my watch just as I was going on duty."

Dixon looked at his watch. The light was so dim, there between the distant street lights, that the little figures made a luminous circle. "Five minutes after eight."

The policeman sighed, "Three hours yet to go," and said with youthful exasperation, "Nothing ever happens on this beat. Thank you, sir," he nodded and trudged on along the path.

Dixon said, "I didn't realize it was so late. There's barely time to make the plane." He was standing, reaching for the dispatch case. Sarah said, "But are you going, too? Are you going to do what Arthur . . ."

"I'll go back to New York with you. I told him I'd do that. Then I—I don't know. I'd like to think about it. Is that all right?"

She hadn't known that an uneasy sense of danger still tugged at her until she felt a heartening rush of relief. "Yes. Yes. Thank you."

"All right then. We'll have to hurry. Our best chance to get a taxi is over at the drug store. This way . . ."

The policeman had now trudged into a shadowy path and disappeared. Some distance along the walk they took a turn and presently another. They emerged onto a lighted, busy street and almost at once Dixon hailed a taxi, cruising leisurely along. "The airport," he told the driver, "and there's not much time."

It was apparently all that was necessary to delight and spur a San Francisco taxi driver. "Hold on," he shouted cheerily over his shoulder, and the cab shot into the street and around a corner with a wild swerve that sent Sarah lurching hard against Dixon. Her hat flew off, her face pressed against his cheek, he caught her in his arms, the dispatch case thudded to the floor.

He held her for a second or two while the taxi righted itself.

"All right?" he said, laughing. "Steady now." She sat back, balanced again. He groped to the floor, found her hat and put it in her lap, found the dispatch case and put it on the

26

seat. "Lean against me, it's going to be like this all the way."

She clutched her hat in her hand. After a moment, as the taxi continued its careening pace she moved, rather stiffly, to sit closer to him, her shoulder braced against his arm.

Annoyingly, for no reason, Arthur's smiling words echoed in her mind: Are you afraid he's going to try to make love to you? She wished Arthur had not said exactly what he had said.

She also wished, with no definable reason for that either, that the man so close beside her was not going to go with her to the house on the lake and stay there for a long week of days and nights.

But then perhaps he wouldn't.

And she had been and still was thankful for the sense of protection he gave her. That, of course, was because Arthur had talked of danger, also because the silence and blackness of the deserted park had half-frightened her, as if from somewhere in those massed and still black shadows someone or something waited, watching her.

She put it down to nerves. But the dispatch case and its contents were real and tangible and obviously a source of possible danger. Dixon would protect that.

It was only Arthur's smiling, edged remark that had induced a wave of self-consciousness on her own part which was as awkward and stupid as it was childish.

However a kind of barrier of silence had arisen between them and neither spoke until they reached the airport. There were only moments to spare. James Dixon saw to the baggage. He had sent his own ahead, he told her briefly. The flight was already called and the plane waiting. By the time they reached it there were no double seats left. Dixon said, "There's one up ahead. Better take that. I'll sit back here." He went down the sloping aisle to the seat ahead. The dispatch case was under his arm. She followed him, giving the other passengers a quick and wary survey. They were busy adjusting seat belts and themselves; nobody so much as glanced at either of them. A priest, round and rosy, sat next the window; the seat beside him was vacant. As she took it he told Dixon apologetically that he was sorry he couldn't let him sit with his wife, but the fact was he was inclined to be airsick and suffered less from it near the front of the plane. Dixon nodded and said to Sarah, "I'll be back there . . ."

He went to another single seat in the rear. She looked back, and he was arranging the dispatch case under his arm, so its least motion would arouse him. But no one was watching it, or them. The other passengers were simply passengers, intent on their own affairs, some of them already adjusting chairs and pillows for sleep.

It was a smooth and easy flight and nothing happened. The chubby little priest put a handkerchief over his face and snored gently. Sarah aroused when they landed at Chicago, but only briefly and she awoke fully an hour or so before they reached New York. When she went back to the little washroom and passed James Dixon he was awake and nodded at her. The dispatch case was across his knees. Cold water on her face was refreshing. She straightened her blouse and combed her hair and put on her hat. When she returned to her seat other passengers were rousing. Dixon said, "Good trip," and she said, yes, and went on to her own seat beside the still gently snoring little priest. It was a sunny day and very clear. Dixon waited for her when they landed and walked down the runway beside her. No one, it seemed to Sarah, gave them a second look.

At the gate, however, a chauffeur in uniform stepped forward. "The car is this way, Mr. Travers," he said speaking to Dixon. "Your office ordered the car to meet you and take you to Lake Saguache."

James Dixon's hand was at Sarah's elbow. It tightened but otherwise he showed no surprise. "All right," he said to the chauffeur. As they followed him through crowds, commotion, baggage trucks, he said, "Not your chauffeur, surely?"

"No. Arthur uses a car-rental service in town; he likes its convenience. I suppose Rose, that is, Arthur's secretary, ordered the car."

"Do you remember that particular driver? Does he drive often for you?"

"N-no. He must have driven for Arthur."

"Obviously not often enough to know him," Dixon said. "Look here, Mrs. Travers, there are one or two things I want to do in New York today. Then, if it suits you, I'll come up to the lake by train. There must be an afternoon train."

"Why, yes. There's the five o'clock from the Grand Central." They reached the car, a long, shining limousine; the chauffeur was holding the door open for them. Dixon said to him, "See to the baggage, will you?"

Sarah searched James Dixon's face. There was no way to know what he had decided to do. He saw the question in her eyes and smiled. "I'm not going to leave you alone—that is, I'll take a look at the situation up there and—we'll talk about it. Right?"

"Y-yes. Thank you . . ."

He touched the dispatch case under his arm. "I'll see to this."

The chauffeur, experienced in the extrication of baggage, was coming back and opening the trunk. Dixon said, "See you tonight then."

"The train comes to the village, we're three miles from there. I'll meet you . . ."

"No, don't. I'll taxi out." Something about her troubled him. He put his hand for a moment on her own as it rested on the door of the car. "Things will be all right. Don't worry . . ." But he stood, watching her and the car—and she thought, other taxis and cars, other people while the chauffeur took his place at the wheel.

He glanced inquiringly at Dixon and she said, "I'm going to the lake alone. Mr.—Mr. Travers," she said, because it was easier, "has an appointment in the city."

Dixon was still standing, watching, as the car moved away. Whatever he saw—or rather did not see—seemed to satisfy him; he waved briskly and the car glided smoothly around curves and onto the crowded boulevard.

She leaned forward and spoke to the driver, "You know the way to Lake Saguache?"

"Oh, yes, Madam. I took Mr. Travers up there—oh, not long ago. He's looking well. The trip must have agreed with him."

A wave of utter incredulity washed over her.

Would it be as easy as that? But the driver couldn't have driven often for Arthur. He couldn't have remembered him clearly; he had many passengers, many drives, every day.

It was not really a long drive, and this time it seemed short. They arrived at the tree-shaded village at the head of the lake about noon, skirted it and took the shore road. The driver knew the way. They came to a narrow road, unpretentious, winding amid pines down to the lake, and turned into it.

As always her spirits lifted, for she loved the sun-dappled woods, the glimpses of the blue lake through them and at last the tall, ivy-covered gateposts which marked the emergence from the narrow, woods road to the more formal driveway, neatly edged and raked, which led in a sweeping curve between lawns like green velvet, great clustering shrubs and, just now, masses of climbing roses, to the house itself.

The caretaker's cottage and the long, white garage lay inside the gate and back toward the left, shielded by shrubbery. The new man should be about somewhere. The car swerved around the roses and she could see the house. It was a long, balconied and pillared house, painted a clean white with dark green shutters and green vines climbing to its red brick chimneys. Beyond it the blue lake sparkled in the sun. Gravel spattered as the car drew up at the front door.

The dogs heard the car first and came hurtling around the corner of the house, her own Kerry Blue, Sinbad, bounding ahead, Arthur's dachshund, Liebchen, old, crotchety, waddling far behind. Sinbad leaped upon her, all great paws and excited yelps, lolloping red tongue and laughing white teeth. Liebchen gave her a more restrained greeting, barely polite and clearly disappointed. A man in work clothes followed them, hurrying, as he saw her. He reached the wide steps as the driver began extracting the baggage. She said, "Good morning. . . . Down, Sinbad! . . . I'm Mrs. Travers."

The new man took off his hat, revealing a moist and sunburned face. "My name is Sam Cleetch. I wasn't expecting you today. I only got here day before yesterday. Monday. The employment agency told me general caretaking. I didn't know—I hope I've done right. I started in mowing."

"That's right. You can take the baggage in." Her key was in her bag. She unlocked the wide door with its huge, old brass knocker. The chauffeur's eyes roved over the grounds and the house. "It's a beautiful place you've got here, Mrs. Travers. Now it's daylight I can get a better look at it. Well, thank you."

She watched the car negotiate the curves of the driveway with elegant smoothness and disappear. Its disappearance gave her an odd sense of loneliness. The house seemed very big, waiting there, the grounds very spacious and very empty of human presence. She turned and followed the new man, Sam, into the hall where he was stacking up baggage.

The wide hall ran through the house to another door on the lake side. It was rather dim and shady in contrast to the brilliant sunshine outside, and it smelled musty.

Costellani always had kept the house well aired and dusted, with the doors and windows open and fresh flowers everywhere when they were expected. A week's dust lay everywhere. The dogs crowded in after her. She was obscurely thankful for their presence. She put her handbag on the table near the door and said to the caretaker, Sam Cleetch, "Take the bags upstairs. I'll show you."

She went ahead of him up the wide stairway. Its polished mahogany banister was dull with dust. Upstairs the air was lifeless, shades were drawn over the windows. Sam came puffing up the stairs behind her. "These go to my room." She pointed out the bags. "Follow me." The dogs had followed. Sinbad bounded lustily ahead of her. Liebchen trotted away toward the closed door to Arthur's room. The house was arranged so the two most attractive rooms lay at opposite ends of the long hall. It was an odd arrangement, for it meant that Arthur's enormous studylike bedroom with desk and bookshelves was at one end of the house, and her own rooms at the other end. They were the largest rooms, and the two best views were at either end of the house.

She entered her own wide room, white with green chintzes and enormous cabbage roses sprawling upon the white-papered walls, a sunny room with white curtains over many windows, and a view of the lake. "Put them down here," she told Sam Cleetch. "Mr. Travers . . ." She hesitated. If Dixon decided to stay and engage upon the masquerade Arthur wished, it would be best to give him Arthur's rooms. She said, "Mr. Travers' bags go in the big room at the other end of the hall."

She wondered briefly if Dixon's bag was initialed. But probably the new caretaker wouldn't notice any marking. He went away and she heard him presently puffing up the stairs and down toward the other end of the hall.

She opened the windows and fresh clear air from the lake blew across the room. Sinbad growled but only mildly as Sam Cleetch clumped along the hall and stood in the bedroom door. "Anything else, Mrs. Travers?"

"No, not now. Have you found everything you need? Are you comfortable in the cottage?"

"Oh, yes, Mrs. Travers."

"Mr. . . ." Again she hesitated and made a decision. "Mr. Travers will be here in time for dinner." Sam Cleetch nodded and went noisily away and out the front door which banged behind him.

The afternoon went swiftly. She showered and changed to a blue cotton dress and unpacked. She went through the house, pulling up shades, opening windows, pausing to give Liebchen, curled up in her accustomed chair in Arthur's room, a comforting pat. Liebchen gave her a sour look and curled up more tightly.

Guided by the sound of the mower she found Sam Cleetch, down below the hedge, and told him to bring in flowers. She went back into the house and began to dust. Sinbad pattered behind her and she was again rather grateful for those thumping paws. She was suddenly hungry. It was long past lunch time. She went to the kitchen. It surprised her a little to find that someone had prepared a meal of sorts, eggs and bacon apparently and coffee, and had left skillet and coffee pot, cups and plates and unwashed silver standing on stove and table.

It was the new man, of course, arriving after Costellani had left, not discovering until later that there was a tiny kitchen in the cottage. She washed the coffee pot and made fresh coffee and sandwiches from the supply cupboard and took them on a tray out through the long French windows of the dining room and onto the veranda which stretched the whole length of the house on the lake side.

The lawn sloped gently down from the veranda to where willows made a thick fringe along the edge of the lake. The boathouse stood some distance off toward the right, its upper deck roofed and screened; beside it a narrow pier began and jutted out above the water. Willows massed around the boathouse and the path leading to it. The day was so still that she could hear the slow lap of the water against the piles of the pier and the boats, a rowboat and a utility launch inside the boathouse, and against the willow-laced shore. A big, new launch, covered now with canvas, was secured to a buoy out in the lake beyond the pier and rocked lazily in the wash of the long flat waves. Lake Saguache was a large lake, irregular in shape, curving in and out and heavily fringed with growth. That day it was blue and smiling and the willows made a silver-green screen for the boathouse and the rocky shores. It seemed a long time since she had sat at the Top o' the Mark and watched the bay. It seemed incredible that it had not yet been twenty-four hours.

She went back into the house and finished dusting. She arranged the flowers which Sam brought in and, in the little flower room with all its assembled vases, she had a short conversation with him. Mr. Travers, she said, might want to have a few days' rest and quiet so she was going to do the cooking and see to the house. Sam kindly volunteered to help. She took the great vases into the living room. The bowls of roses, the tall vases of pink foxglove and blue delphinium, gave fragrance and color to the room. Already it was sunset; beyond the French windows the lake was pink and purple and the wooded shore across it dusky and blue. It was cool, too, so she lighted the fire and it snapped cheerily.

Dinner would have to come from the cupboards. She selected jars and cans and opened them; she put lace mats and china and silver on a bridge table near the fire in the living room. She unlocked the cupboard in the pantry and prepared cocktails. The clock in the hall struck seven, sounding deep and rather ominous through the empty house. The train must have reached Saguache village.

She went upstairs, Sinbad after her. She was fastening the belt of a white summer dress when Sinbad heard the taxi, gave a zestful bark and tore for the stairway. She snatched up a woolen jacket, red as her lipstick, and went downstairs.

The taxi had gone, and James Dixon stood on the step talking to Sinbad, inside the screened door, who, rather surprisingly, was listening, standing squarely on his stovepipe legs. She opened the door. Dixon said, "Is this dog of yours going to take my leg off?"

"No." Sinbad was not kind to strangers as a rule. Now he advanced, although gravely, toward Dixon and sniffed at his ankle. She turned on the light on a table. Then she saw that something was wrong.

It was something about the lawyer's face; it was in his eyes. She caught a quick breath. "What has happened?"

"Is anybody here?"

"Yes. The caretaker."

"Where is he? Can he overhear . . . ?"

"We'll go in the living room. . . ." She led the way. He followed her the length of the long, pleasant room with its flowers, its thin old rugs, the small table set for dinner before the crackling fire. She saw then that he did not have the dispatch case. She said, "The dispatch case . . ."

"No, that's all right. It's something else. I—there isn't any easy way to tell you." He faced her, meeting her eyes as if forcing himself to do so. "You've got to know. Travers was murdered last night."

33

She must have spoken. He replied as if to a question. "In San Francisco. He was found in the park. It must have happened before either of us got there."

A deep silence seemed to hold her and the house and the man who stood before her, suspended somewhere in time, somewhere in space.

Two sounds came gradually through its curtain. A man's footsteps thudded loudly along the hall. Liebchen's feet scrabbled wildly across rugs and polished floor, around the end of the sofa toward Dixon. She skidded then to a sudden stop. And her old lip lifted, snarling.

Sam Cleetch, in the doorway, said, "Good evening, Mr. Travers." Then he saw the dog and came forward. "What's the matter with the little dog?" he asked.

4

As if he had spoken them, words of Arthur's came out of a void of all other sound or knowledge. "No matter what happens. Even if it happens to me. A week."

Sarah moved automatically, as if Arthur's will, too, had projected itself and uttered a command. She stooped to take up Liebchen and Liebchen growled and wriggled under the sofa. Sam Cleetch said, "I was only going to ask . . ." His eyes shifted to the untouched cocktail tray. "Shall I serve dinner in about, say, half an hour?"

Dixon said, "Yes."

She heard and did not hear Sam Cleetch's footsteps, lumbering back along the hall.

Dixon had followed Sam's glance at the cocktail tray; he poured a drink and brought it to her. "Here—drink this. I'm sorry."

"Tell me."

"I didn't know until this afternoon. Isn't there somebody you'd like me to get hold of—a friend, or—or your family lawyer?"

"No. Tell me . . ."

"He was found about nine o'clock. Behind some shrubbery, not far from the corner where he told me to meet

34

him. The policeman—the one who stopped and asked about the time, found him."

She remembered the young, bored policeman, sighing wistfully and saying that nothing ever happened on that beat.

Dixon said, "So far he has not been identified. Whoever killed him took everything from his pockets."

"How do they know? Perhaps it wasn't Arthur."

Dixon's eyes looked sorry for her. "The policeman said that he had talked to him, he'd seen him on a bench with a woman, and asked him what time it was, only an hour or so before he found the body."

"But that was you . . ." she began, and then understood.

"That's how I know it was Travers. The policeman didn't have a good look at me; the light was dim. He thought it was the same man he'd talked to."

After a moment she said, "Nobody told me. They didn't telephone or wire or . . . Nobody . . ."

"He's not been identified as Travers. I'd better tell you . . ." He went to stand before the fire. "I felt—I don't know—uneasy. I thought Travers, even if he'd suddenly got his orders to leave, would have managed to send word to me; I thought he'd have given me more detailed directions as to what he wanted me to do. He'd talked of danger and of course there is danger in a job like that. Today, in New York, first I got rid of the dispatch case; he hadn't said to take it to his office or what to do with it, so I went to a bank and put it in a safe-deposit box. Then I got on the telephone to San Francisco. I thought of newspapers, but there wasn't time—if anything had happened to him—for the papers to reach New York. Besides, unless they had done exactly what they did do, remove all identification papers or cards from him, they'd have got in touch with you. I didn't have anything definite to go on. I couldn't inquire directly of the police. What could I say? Are there any reports concerning an important man in the oil industry, Arthur Travers? They'd say, why? Travers had made a point of secrecy and of course it's a valid, necessary precaution in a deal like this. In the end I got hold of a friend who's a reporter. I made a direct call to him at the paper; he didn't know I was in New York. I put him off with a story about a client of mine; I said that his relatives said he was missing and had got the wind up about it. Bill inquired while

I waited, and came back with this. A man was found, murdered, in the park about nine o'clock last night. The police hadn't identified him beyond the fact that the park policeman on duty at that time had seen him with a woman, sitting on a bench, and talked to him about an hour before he found the same man murdered. So then I knew it was Travers."

"I can't believe it," she said, half whispering, thinking of the misty silence of the park. "Not Arthur!"

There was a pause while the fire crackled. It was dark by then, with the French windows black, and reflecting glimpses of the room, the fire, the flowers and a man standing before the fire, looking down at her. He said finally, with an effect of doggedly getting out all the facts. "I inquired, sticking to my client story, as fully as I could. The police don't know who he is, except for the story of the park policeman. There was only one thing that could be called a clue and that was a box from Gump's found near or under the body."

The box from Gump's.

He saw the look in her face. "Had he a box from Gump's?"

"He gave me a bracelet. He put the box in his pocket."

Dixon's face tightened. "Well, then, they'll trace him by that. I think you'd better telephone now and tell the police."

Again a command from Arthur spoke itself in her ears. "He said to go on with this. He said whatever happened— even if it happened to him. He said for a week."

Dixon turned abruptly away. He went to the French windows and stood with his back to the room. His shoulders blocked out the reflections of firelight, her own white face. He said over his shoulder, "Didn't Travers give you some name, some telephone number to call, if you needed it?"

"No. I would have asked him—I intended to ask him. But then I didn't see him again."

He thought for a moment. Then he came back to her. He sat down on the sofa near her and put his hand gently on hers. "Mrs. Travers, I've got to insist. We can get in touch with the department that sent him very easily and very quietly. Nobody will ever know except people we can trust. Will you let me do that?"

"Arthur said, no matter what happened . . ."

"Yes, I know, but doesn't this alter it?"

He waited for her reply and the only words that came to her were words Arthur had spoken, words which had all the force and impact of truth. Arthur, who had had courage, who had gone into danger knowingly, because he believed in the thing he was asked to do; Arthur, who had given his life as directly and courageously as a soldier in battle.

Dixon said, "I'm a lawyer. Perhaps this is one of the contingencies your husband had in mind when he employed me. I want you to follow my advice. If you don't want me to report to the San Francisco police directly, let me find out the exact government department."

"He said whatever happens . . ."

"It can't affect him, now; it's too late for that. It seems cruel to say that to you, but you've got to see the fact of the situation. It isn't now a question of his safety."

She said suddenly and clearly, "I've got to make it count."

"You mean—his death?"

"He gave his life for whatever it is that they want to do. It's like a battle. He knew this might happen. That's why he said it like that. Even if it happens to me, for security reasons, go on for a week."

He put her hand down as gently as he had taken it. He rose, walked across the room and back again, to stand before her. "All right. This is hard too. But there's another complication. The policeman saw you, too."

There was a significance in what he said and the look in his face and she couldn't just then discover it.

"You don't understand. The police—naturally, they'll try to find the woman who was with him. I can say that I was there; I was the man the policeman talked to. But exactly what will they believe? Did Travers give you anything— well, written? Anything that you could give them as proof . . ."

"They can't think that I murdered him!"

"I don't want them to. But you must tell them the facts."

"Let me think. . . ." She rose; she went to the wing chair where she had sat so many times and poured coffee for Arthur, waiting, smoking, lounging in the deep chair opposite. Arthur couldn't have been murdered, she thought with a sense of unreality. Not Arthur.

Dixon said, "You are thinking that the government will back up your explanation. You want to see it through, make

Travers' life, as you say, count for something. It's only a week. You are thinking, suppose the police do question you; suppose they even suspect you of murder, in spite of the fact that I'm a witness to the story. You think you can stick it out for a week. Undoubtedly you could. It wouldn't be very pleasant. There'd be—things that you could never quite remove, newspapers, ugly, scarring memories. But, you think, in the end, and so soon, it would all be removed. So I've got to say this, too. I realize that Travers was a man of high standing. But in cold fact, to put it bluntly, we have only his word for all this."

The fire crackled and shot out sparks. Sinbad, troubled by their voices, came to nudge her hand.

"It's not easy to make you see it. It's been a great shock, a great . . ." He stared at the fire and said doggedly, "But nevertheless, there it is. Suppose, say, your husband had some business deal on, something that required his absence for a week, something he didn't want, say, a rival to know about, something he didn't want anybody to know about until it was accomplished. Suppose it was important to him businesswise, to make it appear that he was here, resting as he said, at home. And suppose it was so very important that he wished to insure your compliance and your help. So —suppose he arrived at a scheme which would appeal strongly to your patriotism."

"You think he did that!"

"I only say, suppose. In ten minutes—well, an hour or two at the most—we could confirm the whole thing."

"I believe him."

"So do I," Dixon said. "But you must look at the possibilities. Because if by any chance it was not true, any of it . . ." He got up with a quick movement and came to face her directly so she had to look up into his eyes. "It's better for you to be in the clear about his murder."

"You can't mean—they'd suspect me!" she cried incredulously again.

"If by any possible chance Travers' story was not true, it'd be a very fishy thing to tell the police. So fishy that it alone would put you in a very odd position. Of course there may be evidence, there undoubtedly will be some evidence, leading to the murderer. Your husband, like most men who have gone to the top, may have made a few enemies. Did he have an enemy . . . ?"

"Nobody who would murder him! Except the people who wanted to prevent this trip . . ."

"As soon as they identify him, they'll make inquiries. They may discover the murderer—perhaps immediately. But I want you to protect yourself."

"But they *couldn't* believe I murdered him! I had no reason, no motive . . ."

"He was a very rich man. I'm only trying to look at it from their angle. You were seen in the park, not long after your husband was murdered. They think now, that you were there, just before your husband was murdered because they saw me with you. They don't know that the girl the policeman saw was you, but he can eventually identify you when they discover it was Travers. You and the box from Gump's, which they will trace, are their clues. Providing of course nobody identifies him before that. It may take them a little while to run down purchases of bracelets from Gump's. They'll question everybody who made such a purchase, beginning probably with the more recent purchases. Probably they'll interview people in the San Francisco area first. But eventually they'll get to Travers. And to you."

"I can't believe . . ."

"Perhaps before then they'll have nailed whoever murdered him. Or the other side of the thing, if Travers' story was fact, the government people will take a hand in it. That's looking at the hopeful side of it. The crux of the thing is whether or not Travers' story was true. I don't mean that I doubt it, I only mean that I want you to have a solid fact. It's a big stake. If you were my client, and in a sense you are, I'd advise you to have things cleared up at once. It's so simple, so easy. Will you let me do it?"

He was kind, determined and sensible. It was the sensible course, obviously.

It was also exactly what Arthur had said not to do. "I don't know," she cried unsteadily. "I don't know."

"Well, then, let yourself be advised by me. If—if it's as likely to endanger whatever it is they are trying to do, as he evidently made you believe, I'll take the blame . . ."

"But I do believe it! I still believe it." She had felt humbled by Arthur's courage in going, knowingly, into danger. And there *had* been danger. He had been killed under orders, like a soldier. The weight of her own humility was heavier. It made a decisive balance.

She turned from Dixon, and went to the window and stared blankly at her own face, white and strained, reflected in the black, shining glass. Whatever Arthur had been to her or hadn't been, her obligation was deep. In a curious way her own honestly admitted lack of grief added to her obligation.

Dixon said, at last, "I've hurried you. Perhaps there's more time than I expected. Think about it."

Suddenly an argument entered her mind. She faced him. "*They'll* know it! The government—whoever sent him. They'll know it."

He nodded, watching her. She cried, "You thought of that."

He put down his cocktail glass. "It occurred to me that perhaps they had already told you. Advised you. Then when I saw you I knew that they hadn't."

"Is that why you don't believe that Arthur . . ."

"Wait. I believed it when he told me as much as he told me. It squared all right. Yes, I believed him. I still believe it. But I have to say again, I want you to spare yourself anxiety and the possibility of a very unpleasant experience by confirming it. I can't see what possible harm it could do."

"There must have been some reason," she said slowly. "Something we don't know about."

He stared at the fire for a moment. Then he said abruptly, "All right. But think about it. Give yourself some time."

Sam Cleetch was coming through the dining room, carrying a tray laden with soup plates. Neither of them moved while he put the plates on the little table, surveyed it and said, "I do hope things are all right. I can do plain cooking, if you'd like me to, while Mr. Travers is resting."

Sarah said, "Thank you." He clumped away. Dixon said, "Mr. Travers?"

"I didn't know, I thought it better to say that you—I mean Mr. Travers was coming tonight."

"Naturally. That's all right." He went to get a small chair which he brought up to the table. He held her chair for her and she sat down. He went to get another chair for himself. She said, leaning across the small table with its crystal and silver catching rosy gleams from the fire, "But if Arthur—there's no need for you to stay now. There's no need for a substitute. That is, I don't know what you had decided . . ."

He sat down. "I hadn't decided. Drink your soup while it's hot."

"You could have phoned to me, told me, and then gone back to San Francisco. I am very grateful . . ."

He said rather dryly, "I'm doing only what I was employed to do."

"What are you going to do now?"

He didn't answer for a moment. Then he said quietly, "I'll not do anything without your consent. I was acting as your husband's lawyer. It's not my place to go against your decision. It *is* my place to advise to the best of my ability to advise. And I could be very wrong." He looked at her. "Please try to eat. It's better for you. I'll tell you exactly how I feel about it. When you told me your husband's suggestion that I take his place here, try to impersonate him if anybody tried to check too closely on his whereabouts, I didn't take to it. Frankly I thought it was the impulsive kind of suggestion that somebody might have thrown out —jumped at, as you said—but that honestly wouldn't be of any particular value. Maybe I was wrong. I really didn't think that the danger he spoke of was likely to be as—as real and imminent as obviously it was. So I was wrong about that . . ." He stopped.

Sam Cleetch was lumbering through the dining room again with a laden tray.

They waited while he removed the soup plates and put down dinner plates already served. "Is it all right to serve the plates before I bring them out, Mrs. Travers?" he asked, his face flushed and moist from cooking. "I'm not much on serving."

She said something, anything. He looked pleased and went away again. When his clinking progress was cut off by the pantry door, beyond the dining room, Dixon went on, "I didn't think, either, that whatever this thing he was sent to do, was as important as it obviously must be. People don't murder, as a rule, without an extremely urgent and important reason. If that is a government affair, then . . . Well, I'm an American, so are you. So was Travers—assuming, as we do, that he was telling the truth."

"I am sure of it."

"Yes, I understand that. So if it's true, and that important, I have as direct an obligation as you to try to—do whatever I can. Anybody would feel like that."

"But you said, you hadn't decided."

"That was before I knew about Travers."

"Do you mean—stay here and pose as Arthur? But there's no need for that now! They—the people who were behind his—his murder—they'll know. They've succeeded. They stopped him . . ."

"If Travers was telling the truth, as we believe he was, he already outlined a procedure in case this thing happened. He foresaw this contingency. That's why he retained me."

"I don't understand. You said I ought to clear it up, give up the plan that Arthur . . ."

"No, I didn't say quite that. I told you what I thought you ought to do, for your own safety and peace of mind. It's perfectly possible that the government men will ask you—and me too for that matter—to go on for a week, as Travers planned. They may have had some intention that we don't know anything about. There might even be a value in confusing the enemy. I don't know. But we can easily find out. If you'll let me."

She said, confused and troubled, not knowing what course to take besides the course Arthur had laid out for her, "I don't know what to do—I don't know."

"Eat your dinner. Get some sleep. In the morning you can decide."

Sam came with coffee.

"On this table, Mrs. Travers?" He put the coffee tray on the small table by the wing chair. They watched while he cleared away dinner. As he made a last trip to fold up the table and carry that away too, he said to Dixon, "Do you want me to lock up, Mr. Travers, or do you . . . ?"

Dixon lighted a cigarette rather carefully before he said, "I'll see to it. Thanks."

Sam went away carrying the table. She thought, at least one person would say, to anyone who asked, Mr. Travers is at home, he was at home last night. I served dinner for him and Mrs. Travers.

"How was he murdered?" she asked suddenly.

"I hoped you wouldn't ask that. It had to be a quiet way, something nobody would hear."

"How . . . ?"

"He was stabbed. It must have been very quick. Please don't think about it."

She rose and walked again to the window, her hands

locked tightly together. There was not in her heart the despair of grief that she would have had five years before when she had loved and married him, but she wouldn't have wanted him to die or to die like that.

Dixon said, behind her, "I wish I could help you. I'm sorry. Isn't there somebody? Some friend? Somebody . . . ?"

"No," she said. "No. That is, there's Aunt Julia. She's at Swampscott." She turned to look at him. "I owe Arthur so much!" she cried. "Aunt Julia—she—oh, she's everything to me—father and mother and . . . He was always so generous; he never begrudged the money. Last winter, she had that long illness. It cost so much. He sent her south, then to Swampscott for the summer. Everything money could do for her. I owe him so much!"

"It makes it harder."

"Mr. Dixon, if I do exactly as he told me to do—if I don't agree to get in touch with the government men, or to do anything except what he told me to do—what will you do?"

He waited for a moment, looking at her. He was in that moment very unlike Arthur. His eyes were darkly blue and very direct. His broader, more generous face had a resolute firmness in chin and mouth, yet there was something rather gentle and troubled in his expression. Then he turned away from her, walked slowly to the fire and faced her again, one elbow on the mantel. "I don't like murder," he said. "If you decide to stick it out along the lines Travers planned, I'll stick it out with you."

Sinbad suddenly lifted his head, growled and started up. He listened, ears alert, and then charged for the window behind Sarah, pushed his nose against it and growled deep in his throat.

5

Dixon sprang across toward her and opened the long French window and the screen. Sinbad charged across the porch and away into darkness. Dixon ran after him.

Sarah followed out onto the porch. Sinbad's savage barks were going in the direction of the boathouse and pier. She could hear Dixon running along the graveled path. The light from the living room behind her streamed out through the long windows and lay in diffused patches on the porch. The light had turned blustery, with a wind that tossed the shrubbery and willows, making thick, moving shadows. The trees murmured and sighed and waves were stirring on the lake, rocking the motorboat out at the buoy and crashing in upon the shoreline. The night was alive with tumult and sound.

Liebchen whined from the living room and Sarah opened the screened door. Liebchen trotted down the shallow steps, seemed half a mind to follow Sinbad and Dixon and then wandered out of sight among the swaying shadows of the shrubbery. Sinbad's barks were less frequent. She heard Dixon whistling for him.

They came into sight, emerging slowly from the darkness. Dixon had Sinbad by the collar and Sinbad twisted to utter a threatening growl back toward the willows and the path. Dixon stepped up on the porch.

"What was it?"

"I don't know. Sinbad hunted around through the willows down there by the boathouse. If anybody was there he'd have got him."

Liebchen came waddling up the steps again, paused to stare suspiciously into the darkness and then at Dixon. The wind off the lake was cold, sweeping Sarah's skirt around her, ruffling her hair, moist and chill on her face. Dixon opened the door and Liebchen shot under the sofa again. Sinbad followed them back into the living room reluctantly, pausing again to look out onto the porch and growl. Sarah said, her voice uneven, "There are never prowlers or—or tramps. We don't even lock the house at night. Do you think . . . ?"

Arthur had expected someone to check on his movements, watch his house, make sure whether or not he was there. Dixon guessed her thoughts.

"I don't think anybody was there. Sinbad would have found him. Probably it was—oh, the wind. Some noise the dog didn't like."

"If anybody is watching the house . . ." But they wouldn't watch the house now, because already they had succeeded.

Dixon said, "It might be a good idea to lock up. It's an isolated place. If anybody was sent up here to check on Travers, he might not know yet that Travers . . ." He stopped and said, "No point in inviting unpleasant company," and went to bolt the two other French windows.

She followed him. Together they made a circuit of the house. Sam had gone to the cottage; the kitchen was shining and clean and empty.

They locked the kitchen door and the wide front door which gave upon the drive; they locked the porch door at the lake end of the hall. Dixon looked at window bolts. "All right," he said, "get some sleep, I'll stay down here awhile before I turn in."

Her handbag still stood on the table where she had dropped it; she reached absently for it. "I had your suitcase put in Arthur's room—that's at the end of the hall, toward the right." The house seemed again very large and very empty with wind rattling the shutters and pushing at the glittering black windows. She added inadequately, "Thank you . . ."

His eyes were troubled and kind. "I wish I could have made it easier. What about the aunt you spoke of? Why not get her to come?"

"Aunt Julia?" A wave of longing for Julia caught her. "I'll phone to her. Yes . . ."

"Better wire. You can't say much. Better not give her a chance to question until she gets here. Tell me what to say. I'll send it."

The telephone was in a small enclosure below the stairs. She dropped the handbag on the table again and followed him. "Miss Julia Halsey," she told him, and the address, and a guarded message. "Can you come to Saguache tomorrow afternoon train? Love, Sarah."

He put down the telephone. "That'll do it. It's better to have her here, too, in the house with you."

A moment in the hurtling taxicab in San Francisco, returned unexpectedly to her. "I didn't think of that. I—I didn't think of you either, your family, your wife. I can't let this be an embarrassment to you."

A flicker of a grin crossed his face. "I'm not embarrassed. I'm not married, either. Good night, Mrs. Travers." He turned back along the hall toward the living room, digging into his pockets for cigarettes as he went.

Sinbad hesitated and then followed her, thumping up the steps behind her. Liebchen came too, snapped at Sinbad irritably and crawled under the chaise longue to sleep. Sinbad sprawled down with a thump and a sigh beside the door.

The wind increased in violence as the night wore on, sighing and gusty by turns, so the rustle in the woods was like an army of stealthy footsteps advancing, retreating and advancing again upon the house.

It was very late when Dixon came upstairs; she didn't hear his steps, but Sinbad got up, snuffled at the door and lay down again. Much later, weary of pacing the floor, staring out at the black, turbulent night, she turned off her bed lamp and still could not sleep.

Eventually she came to a decision which was, however, not a decision, so much as an expedient, and that was to open the dispatch case which Dixon had put in safe deposit. Arthur had stressed its importance. Therefore there must be papers of some kind, notes or memoranda, which might have a bearing upon Arthur's trip. If there were such papers, they would provide the confirmation Dixon wanted.

But if not, then her promise to Arthur still held. There was a solemnity about a promise to a man who gave his life, literally, for his country and her own. Five days out of her own life was not much to give.

Toward dawn the wind went down and she fell into an uneasy sleep.

Morning was sunny and clear. Sinbad, scratching at the door, awakened her. She let him out and he thudded down the stairs. Liebchen roused crossly and followed him. When she went downstairs later Sam Cleetch was sweeping the wide porch of the leaves that the wind had scattered over it during the night. Mr. Travers, he told her, had already had breakfast and had gone, he thought, for a walk along the lake.

The lake was blue and sparkling. Twigs and broken, small branches littered the green lawns which sloped down toward the willows and the lake. Sam said, "I'll get your coffee now, Mrs. Travers."

It was very strange, she thought, how the routine of life in a man's house went on; lawns had to be raked, hedges trimmed, porches swept, though Arthur would never stroll across that lawn again, or sit in the deep chair which was his favorite, watching the lake and the boats.

The telephone in the hall behind her rang and she went quickly to answer it, her heart pounding. Was this the message that her fancy had conjured up during the night? A remote, impersonal voice, telling her of Arthur's death—telling her what to do?

46

It was Rose Willman.

Her voice was so controlled and precise that it summoned up an instantaneous vision of Rose, with her black hair framing her small white face and vehement dark eyes. She recognized Sarah's voice and said, "Can I speak to the chief, please?"

She always called Arthur "the chief"; it was not so much an affectation as it was a straddling of a small, feminine issue. She didn't want to call him Mr. Travers; their association had been long and close. Perhaps Arthur had not encouraged the use of his Christian name. "The chief" was the answer. There was another little problem in the way she addressed Sarah; during Sarah's three months in Arthur's office, Rose had called her Halsey. Not Sarah, nor Miss Halsey, but crisply, Halsey. But that, in its way, was an affectation. Sarah's marriage to Arthur had presented a problem to which, for five long years, Rose had still not found an answer. She was reluctant, and Sarah knew it, to call her "Mrs. Travers." Besides, it would not come naturally between them. She had not, perhaps she could not, yield to friendliness and say, simply, "Sarah." There was consequently a rather stilted third-person technique which she employed.

Rose would grieve for Arthur, sincerely and deeply. She must see Rose; she must try to make it up to her for what might have been.

Rose repeated her question sharply. "Is the chief there? I'd like to speak to him."

What had Arthur said about Rose? Rose didn't know about his mission; she was not to know. Sarah said, automatically, as if Arthur had spoken to her, reminding her, "He—no, he's not in the house. Is there any message?"

There was a long pause. Had Rose detected the uneven note in her voice?

But when Rose finally spoke, she was crisp and decisive but, which was unusual with Rose, she sounded worried. "Yes. I thought I ought to tell him. A man has been inquiring for him, nobody whose name I know. In fact he didn't want to give me his name; he said it is Richard Wells . . ." she paused. "You'd better write that down."

"I'll remember it."

"Tell the chief that somehow I didn't feel that that was his real name. At any rate, he had inquired at the airport, apparently and found that the chief arrived yesterday morning. He must have inquired, too, at the apartment, so then he telephoned to me and insisted asking me where the chief is, and if he's at the lake. I wouldn't tell him of course. But he might turn up there. He was very insistent and rather unpleasant. I thought the chief ought to know."

Sarah's heart was beating hard again, drumming the pulses in her ears. "How was he unpleasant?"

But for once Rose was not decisive. "I don't know. I got the impression that he was someone the chief wouldn't want to see, that's all. Please tell him."

"Did he have—any sort of accent?"

"Accent! No. What do you mean?"

Sarah had thought an enemy, an emissary from a foreign country. But obviously while such an enemy would be the instrument of a foreign country, he need not have been sent from that country; there were enemies, too many of them, as Dixon had said, within the gates. "I'll tell him."

It satisfied Rose. "Be sure you get the name right. And don't forget to tell him," she said crisply and rang off.

The telephone rang again as Sarah started away from it. This time it was a telegram from Julia saying briefly but promptly that she would arrive that afternoon. Aunt Julia had never failed her. Sarah went back to the porch, heartened by the telegram.

Who was Richard Wells? What was his real name? Had he come, that curiously persistent stranger, in the night, to see with his own eyes whether or not Arthur was at the lake? Sinbad did not as a rule charge with savage barks at nothing—a noise, wind in the trees.

For the first time it occurred to her that Dixon might be in danger if he remained at the house. His likeness to Arthur, his presence in Arthur's home, made him a target. Clearly Richard Wells—who could have called himself by any name —had checked the passenger list on the plane, and found Arthur's name. Mr. and Mrs. Arthur Travers. He had inquired. All at once she was sure that he had come to the lake, had prowled around the house under cover of the wind and darkness, had peered in through the glittering black windows and had seen Dixon—so like Arthur, in Arthur's home, actually with Arthur's wife. So that hidden, relentless enemy might assume its instrument in San Francisco had made a mistake, had let Arthur Travers escape. So then they would try to stop him, this time with certainty. Dixon would be their target.

She couldn't let him remain in that house. She couldn't let him pose as Arthur, not for five days, not for another moment.

The day seemed less sunny. The woods seemed too closely to encircle the house, with their complicated, shielding patterns of light and shadow. The lake provided too easy and silent an approach to the house; a rowboat could drift along behind the lacy curtain of willows close to the shore, unobserved.

Sam came out from the hall door, a tray with coffee and orange juice in his hands. He put it down on the old-fashioned wicker table near her and went away again.

The day was very still. She could hear the slow wash of the lake upon the shoreline and the little, distant slap and rock of the motorboat secured to the buoy. Across the sparkling blue of the lake, toward the opposite shore, a sailboat was maneuvering, trying to catch a breeze. Somewhere toward the village a motorboat chugged leisurely along.

She was so deep in thought that she did not see that Dixon, with Sinbad following him, had emerged from the path around the wooded point in the opposite direction from the pier and the boathouse, and were approaching the house. Dixon's footsteps on the gravel aroused her; for an instant his likeness to Arthur, strolling there with his black head and strongly arched eyebrows distinct in the sunlight, gave her a kind of shock. So she had seen Arthur stroll along the path many times. And again, on second look, it was the unlikeness which was surprising. His walk was different, his movements, his whole appearance, in a hundred small indefinable ways which, yet, were instantly recognizable. But no secret enemy could recognize those differences.

He looked at her and made a kind of gesture of greeting and smiled, and the small gesture, the smile were not like Arthur's. He was wearing a light lounge coat and slacks. Sinbad trotted happily beside him, saw her and bounded across the lawn and upon the porch. Dixon followed him. "Did you sleep?"

She nodded and thought that she had not deceived him.

"Have you decided?"

"Yes."

"You're going to go on with it. I thought so."

She thought of Sam, pottering about the house, dusting, within earshot of the many opened windows. "Let's walk down toward the boathouse. I want to—to explain."

He fell into step beside her. Sinbad, delighted, ranged ahead. "You don't need to explain," Dixon said. "I understood last night."

"No, there's something else. Rose Willman phoned—she's Arthur's secretary. She doesn't know about this. But she told me a man—he called himself Richard Wells—has been trying to find Arthur." Their footsteps crunched on the gravel. Sinbad disappeared into some willows. Dixon listened while she told him the brief story.

"You think Wells was here last night?"

"I think he might have been. I can't let you stay. Don't you see? If they see you here, they'll decide that the man who murdered Arthur in San Francisco made a mistake. They'll . . ."

"Nobody's going to murder me."

"You'd be a target. You can't stay."

"Well, I've been a target before now." But he was frowning and thoughtful, too.

"There's another thing. The dispatch case. If there's anything in it, any notes or memorandum about whatever it is that they wanted Arthur to do, that would—" she used his own word—"that would confirm it, wouldn't it?"

They talked on slowly several steps before he said, "Do you have any doubts yourself?"

"No. I thought of it because of what you said."

"That was a lawyer's advice, for your own safety and peace of mind."

"I know. I suppose the case is locked. We can get it open and . . ."

"We might thus be in possession of some rather dangerous —certainly some very secret information. Presumably whatever it is that the government is trying to do isn't going to be given up because of Travers' death."

"It would remain secret. We can put the case back into safe deposit."

After another pause he said, "In fact, of course, legally, you have no right to open it as things stand. The power of attorney wasn't signed. Nothing can be touched until his death is established and his will probated. That of course was why he wanted you to have a power of attorney. He knew that this might happen."

"That was like him," she said slowly. "He always planned for every contingency, down to the last detail."

He was silent for a moment again. Finally he said, "In

the circumstances I think you'd be justified in opening the dispatch case. We'll go into town today if you like. There may be nothing in it, of course, except letters or business records which Travers wished to send home by me. Suppose there's nothing else?"

"It's only for five days."

"And you propose to stay here alone, while such fellows as this Richard Wells might be hanging around the place . . ."

"Aunt Julia will be here. I had a telegram. She's coming this afternoon. I'll not be alone."

"Two women! I don't think you quite realize . . ." he broke off. The path narrowed as it neared the boathouse, and wound through willows which pressed close on either side. He stopped to let her enter the narrow path with its dappled shade, and silver curtains of willows. He said abruptly, "You must have loved him very much."

I didn't love him, she thought bleakly; I didn't love him—and that's why I've got to do this. She didn't say it. He held back a low branch of feathery willows. She entered the narrow path.

"Do you mind talking about him?" His voice behind her sounded rather careful and formal. "I mean—oh, I know that he's an important figure in the oil industry. How did he get into that business?"

"He was a lawyer. He managed to save enough money to get an oil lease."

"Where was that?"

"In Baton Rouge. He was lucky. He was always lucky. He went on from there."

She was walking ahead of him with willows brushing her hands. It was true; Arthur had always believed in his luck. She said suddenly, "He was always lucky. I can't—I *can't* believe that he's dead. Not like that. He was—I can't explain it—invincible, victorious. Always."

"Stay here!" Dixon said sharply.

She saw then that Sinbad ahead of her, half-hidden by the turn in the path which led upon the pier, was standing very still, growling strangely. Dixon drew her back and went ahead of her, running. He passed Sinbad and disappeared beyond a thick clump of willows.

When she reached the curve Dixon was leaning over toward the rocky shoreline, shaded by willows. Sinbad was backing away, oddly, growling.

51

The boathouse made a block of light and shadow, dappled by willows screening it. The pier went out like a tunnel through shadow into bright sunlight over the water.

Someone, something lay at the water's edge.

It was a man, half in the water, half out of it, on one side, an arm and hand moved sluggishly. A wave washed gently against the rocks, gurgling among the willows, slapping against the boats in the slip beyond, slapping against the pier. The hand looked leaden, moving slowly as if it had not the power to clasp the willows. The dappled shadows seemed to move and circle around her. It was very still and very hot. Dixon said, "Who is he?"

"It's—it's the gardener. Costellani."

The body lay nearly submerged in the shallow water; it, moved a little in the rock of the water, giving it a grisly semblance of life. It was half turned but there was no mistaking the matted wet red hair. She turned blindly away; she went to sit on the wooden steps of the boathouse. Everything wavered now, the moving light and shadows on the water were dizzying; the steps themselves seemed infirm and uneven. Sinbad came and stood at her knees as if he made himself a barrier against an unknown and perplexing foe. Dixon's broad shoulders concealed her view. Sunlight made a pattern across his coat. It seemed a long time before he rose. The planks of the entrance to the pier rattled as he came to her. "You'd better go to the house."

"He was going away. He was going to see his daughter . . ."

"Please come . . ."

"How long . . . ?"

"I don't know. Some days, I should think."

"Was he—drowned?" Even as she asked it she knew that Costellani, who swam as easily with that wiry body as he walked or raked or pushed the mower, had not drowned. Dixon said, "He was stabbed."

It was very hot and still. She whispered, "Like Arthur . . ."

His hand touched her wrist. "I want you to go to the house."

"What are you going to do?"

"I don't know. I'll have to notify the police."

It didn't seem right to leave Costellani there. It didn't seem right to do nothing for him. How many times had she seen his stooped shoulders and shock of red hair moving about among the flowers, about the lawn and hedges. . . .

She steadied herself by Dixon's hand. The willows brushed against her as if they were warning, ghostlike fingers. They emerged from the path and the sun beat down with dazzling brilliance. They crossed the bright green lawn. Sinbad, puzzled and worried, was close beside her. The hall seemed dark after the dizzying brightness of the sun.

Dixon went to the telephone. She listened and did not listen, but she heard it distinctly when he said, ". . . the Travers place. It's murder." The telephone clicked dully when he put it down. "The police are coming. Do any of them know Travers?"

"Know *Arthur?*"

"Does the constable know him? Do any of the police know him?"

"No. I don't think so. No."

"No little traffic accidents?"

"I don't think so. Arthur never drives."

"He's not friendly with them? Doesn't stop to pass the time of day with them?"

"No. . . . You said murder."

"The body had been in the water for some time. There was an end of rope around one ankle; probably it was weighted. I think the wind last night wore the weight through the rope and brought the body ashore."

"But . . . Costellani!"

"What do you know about him? How long has he worked for you?"

"Since Arthur bought the place. Nearly five years ago."

"When was he supposed to have gone away?"

"I don't know exactly. Sometime last week. He said his daughter was sick."

"Do you have her name? Her address?"

"No. It must be among his things in the cottage."

"Did Travers say anything about him? I mean, did Costellani know anything of Travers' plans?"

"No. He couldn't have. He said he was going to see his daughter. That was Friday. Arthur thought it might have been an excuse for a vacation. Arthur didn't talk to him; he left a message at the office. Rose got the new man, Sam, to see to the place till Costellani came back."

He thought for a moment. "All right," he said. "The police will be here in a few minutes. I'm Travers, remember."

Only then she perceived the intent of his questions about Arthur and the village police. "No! No, you can't . . . Not with the police!"

He turned away from her. He went to the wide front door and stood for a long moment looking out across the graveled driveway, brilliant in the sun, the green hedges and heavy clusters of roses. His black head, his broad shoulders blocked sharply against the brightness beyond. He said at last, "He said a week. That's only five days more."

"This is different."

There was another long silence. Away off in the kitchen Sam dropped a pan.

Dixon said, in a different, gentler voice, "Yes, it's different. Seeing it is different. But in fact it's the same thing."

"Do you mean Costellani—some way—somehow was a part of this . . . ?"

"Is Travers known much in the village? Is he here often?"

"No. But you can't do this."

"I told you last night. I don't like murder. And I don't like . . ." He turned abruptly, came to her and demanded in a queer, almost an angry way, "Do you think I'd leave you to try to work this thing out alone? I'm going down to the pier. Send them there, when they come. Tell them I'm Travers."

He walked along the hall, his footsteps hard and quick. The door banged behind him. She had a glimpse of his tall figure crossing the veranda down the steps and out of sight, toward the path to the pier.

Sinbad thudded after him as far as the door and stood there, a stiff black figure, watching.

6

He ought to have gone, then and there. He could have been miles away before the police arrived—on his way to New York and then home to San Francisco, and removed from entanglement in murder. It would have been the prudent and expedient course. Arthur would have taken it.

It was an uninvited thought and Arthur's courageous death denied it.

Costellani stabbed, and Arthur had been stabbed! It seemed to link the two murders. Stabbing as a means to murder was swift and silent; it also implied haste, a certain improvisation, as if the need in both cases had arisen unexpectedly. It required, too, a certain desperation, a strength of will and nerve. A gun would have been easier.

Yet those secret enemies were known to be adept and ready. The means to accomplish their purpose had no significance; a knife or a gun—a thrust from a moving train, a lethal beating, anything that sufficed to remove an obstacle from a ruthless course of destruction.

How could Costellani have provided an obstacle?

She was sure, then, that he had. There was nothing else to account for his murder. Somehow he had stood in their way.

Had they got wind of the mission Arthur was to undertake? Had they consequently come to the house before Arthur had gone to San Francisco?

Arthur had gone to San Francisco Saturday night. Before that he had telephoned to Rose, telling her that Costellani was to be away for a month, and asking her to find a substitute, Sam Cleetch, for the time of Costellani's absence. Clearly somebody, one of those wily, hidden enemies, had telephoned to Arthur or sent him a message signed by Costellani, in order to cover their precipitate murder. So, then, was it possible that in the night, perhaps, the murderer had mistaken Costellani for Arthur?

A likelier reason occurred to her. The murderer, the emissary, had not been well briefed; he hadn't known Arthur by sight. So he had blundered and had stabbed Costellani simply because he was a man on the place, in Arthur's home.

She thought of Costellani, with his red hair and dark, stolid face moving quietly and constantly about the place, tending his flowers and lawns, and all but invisible because he was a thoroughly accustomed part of it. She realized with a kind of shock that she knew almost nothing about him. He had been efficient; he had had almost no friends. She had not known, even, that he had a daughter. She knew that he spent almost nothing of his salary, or at least, if he did, there were no signs of it; he had several times asked for a raise in salary which Arthur, grumbling a little, had given him. There was a passive, silent force about Costellani. She had always felt oddly that he knew more of them and their affairs than he had given any evidence of knowing; she had felt oddly again that there was not a cupboard, not a drawer, not so much as a magazine in the house whose contents the silent little man was not fully aware of, yet there were never any evidences of that passive absorption; nothing was ever out of place, and certainly he was honest.

And somehow he had made himself an obstacle; somehow he had blundered into affairs which were deadly, violent, out of his orbit—and fatal.

Therefore they had to tell the police the possible cause for his murder. They could not suppress evidence, not even for five days.

But of course they could. Murder investigations sometimes dragged out for weeks and months. Five days was not a long time.

Arthur could not have foreseen this.

She swung again to the other side of her inner argument: Costellani was dead, there was nothing that could be done for him. Arthur had said that, whatever happened even if it happened to him, a week, a vitally important week, was needed.

Arthur had given his life for that crucial week.

Dixon, sensible, a lawyer and once a Navy man, was determined to go contrary to what must be his own instincts, and provide that week.

A spattering of gravel, a squeal of brakes broke through Sarah's deep and troubled debate. The police arrived and she directed them to the boathouse; Mr. Travers was there, she told them, and they had found the body of the gardener, Costellani.

They went, running, across the lawn around the end of the house, toward the pier and the boathouse.

She knew the constable vaguely. His name was Harris; he was heavy, middle-aged, with a sallow face which sagged over hawky features, and dark, heavy-lidded eyes. She knew the young policeman who came with him, who was, as a rule, on traffic duty near the post office in the village. Later, she supposed, there would be others, the state troopers, county officials. She was reasonably certain that Arthur wouldn't have known any of them, or more importantly, just then, they wouldn't have known Arthur: he rarely went to the village and never talked to, or had any interest in its year-round residents. Sinbad barked wildly, and clawed at

56

the screen door, and Sam, attracted by the sound of the car came into the hall. She told him briefly what had happened.

Sam's red face turned a slow, ashy purple. "Murdered! That's why his room—I looked at it; I saw his things everywhere, so I took the other bedroom in the cottage. But—I thought then it's queer there's so much here. I mean—it looked as if he hadn't packed anything to take with him. Even in the bathroom—comb and toothbrush and everything." He sucked in his breath and stared at her with small, bright eyes.

He was going to say that he'd like to leave. She couldn't have blamed him. He said instead, "I'll just go down to the boathouse. See what's going on . . ." and wheeled, his white apron flapping. Sinbad wanted to get out the door, too. She called him and Sam thrust him back; the door slammed and Sam's thick, hurrying figure disappeared.

She went into the little study at the left of the front door. Liebchen curled tightly in a chair looked at her sourly. They said that dogs always knew. But Liebchen didn't know about Arthur—it wasn't true that they always knew. She wasn't grieving; she was cross and ageing and, as was her custom unless Sarah watched, had eaten too much; her sleek sides bulged. Sinbad came and sprawled down in the doorway with a frustrated rumble in his throat.

Sarah was standing at the window staring at nothing when the telephone in the hall rang again; again she ran to answer it. However it was again a familiar voice (not a distant, strange voice, saying, "We regret to inform you," saying, "We are sending Mr. So-and-so to see you"). It was Lisa Bayly. "Sarah? I take it you've got back from your trip. Rose Willman—I telephoned the office—Rose Willman said you'd got home. I thought—it's such a perfect day, I thought I'd like to drive up to see you."

Lisa who, Arthur had said, was not to know anything of his journey or its significance!

"Oh, no," Sarah said sharply and took a breath. She said quickly, "I'm sorry, Lisa, it's not—not really convenient just now."

There was a rather long pause. Then Lisa said, a little less smoothly, "Oh, well, of course—if the house is full of company . . ."

"It isn't that. Arthur—perhaps Rose told you—he's supposed to . . ."

57

Lisa said, "Oh, yes. The Willman said he wasn't to be disturbed." Her smooth voice had a slight edge. "But that doesn't exclude me, does it?"

For a second Sarah thought of telling her that police were at the place, that Costellani had been murdered, that it wasn't a time for her to come. That, however, was more likely to bring Lisa—at once rallying, she would say, to their support.

Lisa said, "By the way, is Arthur there? Can I speak to him?"

"He . . ." Sarah faltered. "No," she said flatly.

There was another pause. Finally Lisa gave a silky, light laugh. "Well, my dear, I only wanted to tell him about a picture he was interested in. It's in a gallery on Fifty-seventh Street—oh, well, it's not important." Outside another car shot into the driveway and stopped. There were men's voices, more police, and someone at the pier must have heard their arrival and come to meet and take them to the pier, for their voices dwindled in the distance. Sinbad listened at the front door and then barked furiously and then galloped to the door upon porch and lake. And Lisa said suddenly, "Is anything wrong? You sound a little—odd."

"No. That is—no."

Lisa waited a second and then laughed, softly and Sarah knew angrily. "All right. Good-bye. And—tell Arthur I phoned." She hung up after the faintest smallest pause, so quietly that Sarah could barely hear the distant, faint click of the telephone in Lisa's white, jeweled hand.

She put down her own telephone. She hadn't managed the conversation well, she had indeed aroused a quick suspicion in Lisa's agile, shrewd mind. She had never really liked Lisa Bayly, and she wondered how it had happened that Lisa had drifted, gracefully yet persistently, into a kind of intimacy. She came often to stay at the house on the lake—to lounge, sunbathing on the pier in bathing suits that set off the lovely curves of her figure, or to take the motorboat with Arthur for long leisurely trips around the lake and, later, to sit across from Sarah at the table, with Arthur between them, her clear light gray eyes sparkling in the candlelight, her smooth blonde hair shining, her red lips always smiling. Sarah couldn't remember, even, how or where they had met—she had only a kind of general recollection, nothing specific, that Lisa was a friend of some business acquaintance of Arthur's. Certainly sometimes she had dinner with

Arthur when he was in the city and Sarah was at the house on the lake; he had mentioned it, casually, now and then.

However, her conversation with Lisa roused her to the immediacy of another problem. Arthur Travers was well known. Arthur Travers' gardener, Arthur Travers' home! Reporters, photographers! After a moment's thought she telephoned New York and to Rose Willman.

"Rose," she said, "I'm phoning for—for Arthur. There's been—a terrible thing has happened here. Costellani—that's the gardener . . ."

"Yes, I know."

"We—he was found this morning. He was murdered."

"Murdered!" Rose said sharply. "But he was going away. He—when was he killed? Why do you think it was murder?"

Sarah told her shortly. "The police are here now. I called you because there might be reporters and . . ."

"Of course. I'd better give them a statement. . . . I don't think it's much of a story, really. Tell the chief I'll do everything possible to keep them away. . . . Probably Costellani had some quarrel with someone and was trying to get away! That's it, of course. You never knew what he was doing, while you were away from the house. He could have got involved in any kind of racket. I never thought—I hope you don't mind my saying so—that you quite kept him up to the mark. However, I'm sure I can see to things. Is the chief with the police now?"

"Y-yes." There wasn't anything else to say. How easy it was, Sarah thought suddenly, to say, merely yes, and it was a lie.

"By the way . . ." Rose's voice was icy. "Miss Bayly phoned to inquire whether or not you were at the lake. I believe she intended motoring up to see you. I told her the chief was under doctor's orders to rest. I hope you told her she couldn't come."

"She's not coming," Sarah said.

"He needs rest. He's been working very hard. . . . Of course you wouldn't know that but . . ." She checked herself and added, neatly and precisely, "Tell the chief not to think about the newspaper angle. I think I can manage."

Rose, Sarah thought, who didn't know that the center of her tense and concentrated life had dissolved. She wondered briefly, as she had wondered before then, whether Arthur had ever returned even a small measure of Rose's selfless,

59

passionate devotion. Probably not; probably he had taken Rose's devotion for granted.

What were they doing down at the pier?

Had they questioned James Dixon? Had they accepted him as Arthur? Or—sometime, when Arthur was driving through the village, had the young policeman seen Arthur close, remembered him too well?

Another police car, a state troopers' car, stood behind Harris's car in the driveway. She went to the door toward the lake and stood beside Sinbad who pushed at it and whined. Already several boats, attracted by the commotion down at the pier, were idling offshore, the occupants watching avidly. One of them, a rowboat, had drifted fairly close in toward the willows and a fisherman in dungarees and sunglasses, his wide hat pulled low over his face, was letting his rod drift laxly while he watched the pier. His sunglasses winked toward the house; all at once, as if he had seen her standing at the door, he took up the oars and pulled away, with rapid thrusts of thick, strong shoulders, toward the wooded point, opposite the pier, where the boat disappeared. She could see nothing of the men at the pier, because the willows screened the path and the boathouse.

It seemed and was a long time before they came to the house, Dixon and the constable, walking thoughtfully across the grass. The state troopers and the young policeman from the village—and of course Sam, curious and excited—were still at the pier. She saw from Dixon's face, in the quick look he gave her that, so far, no one had questioned his status in the house. The constable took off his hat, revealing a bald head fringed with black hair. Dixon said, "He'd like to use the telephone, Sarah . . ." and led the constable toward the front of the hall and the little telephone room.

He came back to her as the constable spoke to the operator. He said mutely, with his lips, "It's all right," and added audibly, "They're sending for the doctor—the county medical examiner. His name is Wilson, Dr. Wilson." His eyes questioned. She said, "I know him. I went to him the time I sprained my wrist. I don't think he knows—you at all. He's never been to the house."

He nodded. The constable was talking loudly, giving directions. "Okay, Doctor . . . No, he's been in the water for several days, I think. . . . Okay. I'll wait here till you come." The constable emerged from the little telephone room, wiping his bald head with a handkerchief.

He looked at Sarah kindly. "This was a shock for you, Mrs. Travers. I'm sorry. I remember seeing you at the Christmas benefit last winter. You bought a cake my wife baked." He glanced at Dixon. "Can't say as I remember seeing you, Mr. Travers, as long as you've lived here. Except driving through town once or twice, maybe." There was not a flicker of question or perplexity in his face. "You've been here more than your husband, Mrs. Travers. Your husband says Costellani was supposed to have gone to see his daughter last week."

"Yes."

"My guess is that somebody tried to break into the place. Mr. Travers says there wasn't any burglary or anything of the kind . . ."

Sarah shook her head. "No, nothing . . ."

"But maybe he caught somebody trying to break in. Tried to stop him. We don't have many prowlers around the village, but still . . . You don't happen to know whether or not he'd had, say, some quarrel with anybody?"

"I don't think so. I don't know, of course, but . . ."

"If he was leaving," the constable said, "he might have had some travel money. Cash. Maybe it was a thief and Costellani tried to defend himself. The thief got scared when he saw he'd killed him and thought he'd get rid of the body. There's some old pieces of concrete blocks behind the boathouse. Might have weighted the body with one of them." He sighed. "We don't often have any trouble around here like this. But it could happen, all right. Isolated spot. How long has he worked for you?"

"Nearly five years. Since we bought the place."

"How did you get him? Where did he come from?"

"We advertised; he answered. I checked his references at the time. I don't remember the names, but everything seemed all right. He was a good gardener and caretaker, honest and reliable."

"Have any trouble with him? I mean—oh, drinking or—friends coming to see him—or might be some sort of racket he'd got into, too."

"He didn't drink, and I don't think people ever came to see him, although I suppose he knew some of the people in the neighborhood. He didn't seem to mind being alone while we were away."

"Your new man, Sam, said nobody was about the place when he got here Monday. You say Costellani sent a message saying he was leaving on Friday. Looks as if he was killed Friday, then, or Saturday. Well—I'll take a look around his room. Might be something there."

"It's in the cottage, out near the garage. I'll show you," Dixon said.

Again it seemed and was a long time while Sarah waited. Waited and lighted cigarettes and put them down half-smoked, waited and walked restlessly around the room, up and down the wide hall, waited. She heard the doctor's car when he arrived, but apparently he was hailed by the constable at the garage, for he stopped the car without coming to the house. She heard the men crossing the graveled drive at the front of the house, walking around it again apparently down to the pier.

Julia's train was due at the village at half-past four. Sarah went upstairs, to the room next her own with windows over the lake, which Julia used on her rather rare visits. Arthur had given lavishly to supply Julia's needs, but he did not encourage her visits. Sarah went about the room, opening the windows, dusting, getting fresh linen. She went to her own room, then, showered and changed from her wrinkled blue chambray dress to a fresh gray linen. She put on green sandals and remembered the jade bracelet Arthur had given her, still in her handbag, standing on the table in the hall. Suddenly the permanency of material things struck her with a sense of surprise. The jade bracelet, incapable of motion and life, still existed and would exist. Arthur, who had chosen it, whose hand had opened the handbag and slid the bracelet into it, was dead. Sinbad barked wildly somewhere downstairs; another car drew up at the front door. She went into the hall and heard Sam's voice from the hall below. ". . . at the pier. Yes, they want you to go down there."

She spoke to Sam from the top of the stairs. "Who was it, Sam?"

He looked up. "They're taking pictures. Then they're going to take him away. I'm fixing you some lunch, Mrs. Travers. It's nearly four o'clock."

She went back to her own room. Sinbad was barking again, this time at the door on the porch. Eventually she knew it when at last they went away, for Sinbad kept a troubled, barking watch. She heard the cars leave, one by one; she heard the front door bang when Dixon returned at last to the house. She went down then to meet him. Sam was in the hall. He said, "I'll get something for Mr. Travers to eat, too. I've just brought him a whisky and soda."

Dixon, a glass in his hand, came to the door of the study. "Well, they've gone."

But they hadn't gone. A car swerved rapidly around the drive and stopped with a quick thrust of brakes at the steps. It was a convertible. The top was down. Lisa Bayly was driving.

Sarah had a quick glance of her smooth blonde hair, her slim leg thrust out backward as she got out. "It's Lisa—that is, somebody who knows Arthur."

Dixon moved back quickly into the study and closed the door. Lisa's high heels tapped up the steps to the front door. She saw Sarah, opened the screened door and came in. Her red lips were smiling, her pale eyes as hard as stones. She said at once, without a greeting, without a breath, "I decided to come and have things out with you, Sarah. There is no reason why we can't settle it in a perfectly civilized way."

I've got to get rid of her, Sarah thought, and then she thought blankly, Settle what?

Lisa said, "Don't pretend you don't know. That's why you didn't want me to come. Arthur told you. He said he'd tell you."

"Tell me what?"

Lisa's eyes were a hard, opaque gray. "You'll only make it harder by taking that attitude. Besides it couldn't have been a surprise to you. You must have seen that I—that Arthur . . ." Still smiling, she said, "We are adults, Sarah. We are civilized people. I've waited a long time, but . . ." She paused, took a breath, and said rapidly, "Arthur wants to marry me and I want to marry him. He promised to tell you." She looked past Sarah, along the wide hall. "Where is Arthur? He's here, isn't he? He'll tell you that it's true."

7

Sarah said in a voice that did not belong to her, "He isn't here."

Lisa must have driven hard and fast from New York.

63

She didn't show it; not a hair of her smooth blonde head was ruffled, and not a fold of her thin beige suit was out of place. She must have been angry, too, making up her mind to take that step (knowing perhaps that Arthur wouldn't have liked it), determining what she would say and how she would say it, rehearsing it in her mind all the way from New York. She didn't show that, either. Whatever her emotions were, they were silkenly and smoothly under control. She knew exactly what she intended to do.

Sarah's first moment of blank astonishment gave way immediately to a kind of matter-of-fact comprehension. It was as if a missing piece of a jigsaw puzzle had been found, a piece which had up to then been represented merely by a blank space. Once she saw the piece, its pattern clearly fit the puzzle.

What was there, now, to say? She was increasingly aware of the gravity of the situation.

Lisa had grown tired of waiting. "Don't you believe me?"

"I believe you. I don't know what to say."

Lisa leaned forward, an eager light coming into her pale gray eyes. A large moonstone set with diamonds flashed on the hand with which she gripped the arm of the chair. From some dim memory Sarah remembered Arthur saying, "Lisa's eyes are like moonstones." Arthur must have given her the ring. Lisa said rapidly, "You must have seen it. We were very careful. I mean"—she caught herself—"of course we didn't want to hurt your feelings. But at the same time—there is my life and Arthur's. I can't wait forever. Arthur told me, he promised me before he went to San Francisco, last week, that he'd have it out with you. He—" A flicker of uneasiness came into her face; she glanced rather warily this time along the hall, toward the porch and living room —"he wouldn't have wanted me to do this. But I didn't see any other way. I had a note from him, from San Francisco. . . ."

So he hadn't been able to leave, in the end, without sending some message to Lisa. It would clear the way, then, to the truth she must tell Lisa. "Do you have it here? Will you let me see it?"

Lisa hesitated, her pale eyes studying Sarah and her motive. Finally she opened her handbag and took out an envelope. "Here it is."

The postmark was San Francisco. It had been mailed

Tuesday, the day Sarah arrived in San Francisco. Sarah read the letter.

My dear Lisa,

> *Only a quick note; Sarah arrives today; by the time you receive this I'll have had a talk with her. But these things take more time than a woman realizes. When I return I'm going to the lake for a couple of weeks. I think it best (indeed I must insist on your compliance) for us not to see each other at all until I have worked things out with her. I'm sure you'll understand the necessity for this. If by any chance I'm held up here with business, don't talk to Sarah. I mean this—I'll let you know when the skies have cleared.*

It was signed simply *A.*

Sarah read it again, slowly this time.

It was so like Arthur that he might have been standing beside her, speaking the words it contained. It was devious. He did not want Lisa to know anything of his real intention and journey, but he gave an explanation for his absence, and he wanted her to stay away from the house on the lake.

She replaced the letter in the envelope and gave it to Lisa.

Lisa said, "You said that Arthur isn't here? Is that the truth?"

"It's the truth." Arthur, across a continent, Costellani at the edge of the lake, linked together in death by the manner of it and the ruthless purpose behind murder. She'd tell Lisa of Costellani's death and the police investigation. She'd tell her that at least. She said, "Lisa, I've got to tell you . . ." and Lisa interrupted her. "Well then! There's really no need for me to see him. Not—just now. Since you and I understand each other." She put the letter in her handbag and closed it with a decisive snap. She said smiling, "Perhaps I sounded cruel, coming to you like this. But you see, I knew —I've known for a long time that you aren't in love with him. Perhaps you were in love when you married him; you must have been very young and dazzled. But perhaps you only thought yourself in love. And I do realize, any woman would realize that it will be very hard for you to give up—" her gray eyes traveled around the spacious hall; she said lightly "—all this. He has so much—well, so much money. Let's not deceive ourselves."

Sarah said slowly, "I wanted to save my marriage, Lisa. I didn't know about you."

"Oh, naturally!" Lisa said slightly smiling, "But Arthur

65

has been very generous. Furs, jewels—everything. Generous to you and to—" her smooth melodious voice sharpened a little—"and to your aunt. And of course you've done things for Arthur. I used to wonder why he married you. But then I began to understand. There's something about you—that schoolgirl face of yours." She hesitated; a faint perplexity came into her face. "I began to see that you gave him the background he wanted at that time. These business dinners, men and their wives whom Arthur had to convince of his own—call it honesty, integrity, something. You—you backed him up. Oh, not directly, I suppose. Probably you didn't know anything of whatever deal was in the air. But they'd feel, perhaps without thinking really, that—that anything Arthur proposed was square and above board. A man with a wife like you. But now . . ."

"Lisa, I've got to tell you . . ."

"Oh, yes, I'm talking too much. But I've had time to think. And this—" she said suddenly—"is between us. Arthur needn't know. There it is!" She laughed a little but with a kind of uneasy, perplexed air. "You see? I know that you won't tell him what I've said. Well—we've settled it between us, haven't we? Arthur will make a handsome settlement. You can count on that . . ."

A yellow taxi came slowly along the drive and stopped. Lisa said, "*Who's that?*"

It was Julia. She was getting out slowly, assisted by the taxi driver. Sarah's heart went out with a rush toward the stately figure in its neat black suit and Queen Mary hat, about whom the taxi driver was depositing various bags and boxes. She started toward the door and Lisa caught her wrist. The smile was gone from her red lips; her eyes were bright with anger. "So you did know! You've been lying to me! You've sent for her to help you. I can fight too!"

Sarah pulled her wrist away. Lisa caught her breath. In an instant she concealed her anger. She was smooth, polite, poised. She said, pleasantly, "I'll be back," and went out as Sarah opened the door. She met Julia on the steps. "Good afternoon, Miss Halsey," Lisa said coolly and got into her car. Julia turned a blank face from Lisa to Sarah. "What's she doing here?" she said, but rhetorically, with disapproval.

Lisa's little car started up and swept smoothly after the departing taxi.

"I didn't meet you! I forgot—I didn't realize it was so late."

"Nonsense," Julia embraced her warmly. "What are taxis for? I knew something had delayed you. I didn't know it was that woman." The scent of violet sachet came from the snowy white lace at her throat. Her rocky old face shone, now, with pleasure. Her eyes, however, faded but shrewd, held a question—why did you send for me? Sinbad, inside the study, was barking wildly in welcome. The door to the study opened and Dixon came out and Sinbad bounded ahead of him.

It was getting toward sunset; the light in the hall was dim. Julia said, "How are you, Arthur . . . ?" and stopped. She peered at him for a moment. Then she turned to Sarah. "Who is this young man?"

He had been in the study. Sarah had thought only of Lisa. He must have heard the entire conversation. She remembered swiftly that Dixon had said, speaking of Arthur, you must have loved him very much. Well, at any rate he now knew the truth; she'd sail under false colors no longer, accepting sympathy for the kind of grief she had not felt. "This is Mr. Dixon . . ." she began, and Dixon spoke to Julia. "My name is Dixon. I'd like to tell you why Sarah asked you to come." He went to Julia's bags. "Shall I take these upstairs? Which room?"

Sarah told him. "The blue room—at the top of the stairs."

Julia said slowly, "He looks like Arthur!"

"Yes. That's part of it. I'll tell you."

Julia gave her a long, shrewd look, took off her hat and put it on the table; she removed her spotless gloves and patted her neatly waved gray hair into shape. "I think, first, that I'd like a cup of tea. . . . Run along, dear, I'll talk to this young man while you make it for me."

"Oh, Aunt Julia, I'm so glad you've come!"

"Well, now," Julia said crisply, "no need to cry about it. Nothing can be that bad! . . . No fancy blend, remember; plain kitchen tea." She leaned over to pat Sinbad who was demanding a greeting. Sarah went back through the dining room and pantry to the kitchen at the far end of the house.

Sam Cleetch was not there. It took a long time for the kettle to boil. Her hands were unsteady as she arranged the tea tray. She had blundered with Lisa. She had been stupid and inept. It would have been better, kinder, to blurt out the fact of Arthur's death at once. Kinder to Lisa, who loved him, and whom Arthur had loved.

And then she thought in sharp reaction, am I really so

high-minded, so magnanimous? Isn't the fact rather that this relieves me of any self-reproach because my marriage was a failure and I have no grief for Arthur?

The kettle boiled and she made the tea. "If you do feel a sense of obligation this is your chance to pay yourself out —if you want to put it that way." Arthur had said that.

But he hadn't claimed it for himself; he was acting in a very direct sense under military orders, a military mission.

She carried the tea tray back through the long dining room, rosy now from the glow of the setting sun through the long windows. Dixon and Julia were at the end of the living room and had been talking. Julia was sitting upright but very white. Dixon came to meet Sarah and take the tea tray from her hands and put it down on the table beside Julia. Julia said unsteadily, "He's told me about Arthur. He's told me everything. I'm very proud of you, my dear." As it was her nature to do, she sheered away from too openly expressed emotion. She glanced at Dixon. "And may I say I think you have behaved very creditably, young man."

Dixon's face tightened. "I've done what Travers employed me to do," he said shortly. With a kind of gentle deference in his manner he poured Julia's tea and put the cup in her hand. "I have to say that I think the gardener, Costellani, changes things. I don't suppose you'll do it, but I think you and Sarah ought to leave here. Go to town—stay there until it's over."

Julia said, "You think they murdered Costellani, too?"

"I think it likely."

Sarah said, "No. I'm going to stay here."

Julia sipped her tea thoughtfully, "*Is* anybody watching the house?"

"I don't know," he said slowly. "There was a rowboat hanging around this morning. There were several boats of course, curious people. But this fellow . . ."

"I saw him!" Sarah said. "He saw me. He rowed away beyond the point. But he needn't have been one of them."

Julia put down her cup. "If I understand you, their effort was to stop Arthur because his opinion would have operated for our country and against them." She gave Sarah a troubled glance but went on. "They did stop Arthur, by a terrible wicked means. But why should anyone continue to watch the place? They must know . . ."

Dixon said, "It is possible they think there was a mistake. Certainly they didn't call off their thugs. A man who said his name was Wells checked up about our trip here—Travers had told me to have the tickets reserved in his name. He phoned Travers' office and found that, ostensibly, Travers was at home. He may not be one of them, of course. But it suggests surveillance."

"Have you seen him? Was he the man in the rowboat?"

"I don't know. Tomorrow Sarah and I will look at the papers in the dispatch case Travers sent home with me. There may be something there. I'd like . . ." He went to the table before the sofa and took a cigarette from the box. It seemed to Sarah that he lighted it rather slowly and deliberately, giving himself time to frame words. "You see everything depends upon Travers' word for this. Sarah believes him without question. I believe him too. But I'm a lawyer."

"I see," Julia said. "Yes. Yes, I see." The last rays of the sun struck through the open window near her, and sharply upon her bleak, troubled old face. She was tired, Sarah thought with compunction; the strength of her spirit was such that it outran her physical frailty. Sarah said, "All this —I ought not to have sent for you!"

Julia looked up with a flash in her faded eyes. "Who else would you send for?" But her gaze went past Sarah out toward the lake, already taking on the purple and grays of night. "Gives you an odd feeling! Somebody out there somewhere . . ." She rose rather unsteadily, holding the arms of her chair. "I'll rest now, my dear. Only I want to say—I've lived through two wars. I've bought bonds, I've knitted and rolled bandages for the Red Cross and I've not done another thing." She stood facing Dixon and suddenly, warmly, smiled. "What is your name?"

"Dixon," he said again. "James Dixon."

"What do your friends call you?"

An answering little smile touched his face. "Jake."

"Jake? Well then, Jake—if I may say it too—there's not very much an old woman can do for the country she loves and has lived in many years, but what there is—let me do it."

She turned before he could reply and started toward the stairs. He took a quick step after her. "How about the stairs? Let me help . . ."

"No, no. I take them easily, a few at a time . . ." Her gray head high and indomitable, she moved into the hall and out of sight. They heard her presently, climbing the stairs, slowly. Sarah said, at his questioning glance, "No, she hates to be helped. . . . Did they find anything in the cottage?"

"Nothing. Oh, there were all his things, clothes, a bankbook, insurance receipts, a few letters, not many."

"From his daughter? Did they find her address?"

"Not so far. They took away everything they found. Something might turn up. There's nothing so far that suggests a motive. It's possible that his murder has nothing to do with Travers, so let them investigate. We'll tell them the whole story as soon as we can."

"But you think they killed him . . . ?"

"I think he got in somebody's way. I think he may have put up a fight." Dixon went to the long window. "It's getting dark. I'll take a look around the grounds. Come on, Sinbad." Sinbad bounded after him. He stood for a second, blocked strongly against the faint rosy glow of the sky. Then he stepped off the porch, beyond the thick shrubbery and out of sight.

As he did so Liebchen set up a shrill, excited yelping. Her feet scrabbled down the stairs and across to the door overlooking the driveway. She clawed at the screen, and yelped excitely and clawed.

As if a film had rolled back and stopped at some faraway, very distant scene Sarah thought, That's Arthur coming home.

8

She caught back her own thought with a kind of horror of the tenacious trickery of habit and custom. She went into the hall and Liebchen clawed and whined to get out. She opened the front door and the little dog shot out down the steps and across the drive where she stopped, turned her wrinkled, puzzled face toward the woods, toward the garage, dashed off toward the garage and stopped again. After a second or two she whined and then waddled slowly toward the kitchen end of the house. Old Liebchen, tricked as Sarah had been tricked by some habitual sound, steps along the driveway, or the click of some door! Sam, probably going from the cottage to the kitchen.

Sarah stood for a moment, however, listening. Twilight

70

had already fallen within the woods, which seemed to encroach more closely upon the lawn and driveway. Across the lawn, through the vine-hung gates, she had a glimpse of the narrow road winding through the woods. Sam had left a light burning in his room in the cottage; it shone feebly now, combating the lingering glow in the sky. In the distance, down toward the pier, Dixon whistled to Sinbad.

Liebchen was old and crotchety, not much interested in comings and goings about the house; if anybody had been on the grounds seeking to approach the house Sinbad would have known it. Sarah went upstairs and Julia called to her from her room. She was on the chaise longue stretched out beside a window over the lake, wrapped in her neat printed silk dressing gown. Her face had weary gray shadows. But she was only tired, she told Sarah firmly, watching her with troubled eyes; she'd have her dinner there if it wasn't too much trouble. "I've been thinking about Arthur. We—never quite got on, Arthur and I. I couldn't honestly say anything else. Yet he has been so generous to me. I had no claim upon him. All last winter—doctors, nurses, oxygen tents—there wasn't anything that cost too much."

"Arthur never minded spending money."

"I was thinking, too, of that year after your father's death. Professors of English in little colleges don't have much to save; it wasn't his fault. Besides, I think the heart went out of him when your mother died, so young, such a child herself."

"You made everything up to both of us."

Julia's wrinkled hands moved restlessly. "We didn't have a cent. You did everything you could, typed, read English themes, tutored little brats . . ."

"I brought all their algebra problems to you! Remember?" Sarah hoped Julia would smile.

Julia shook her head. "And still the bills for coal and groceries stacked up. Then you took that secretarial course and then—after you met Arthur everything changed for us. He gave you a job, he . . ." Her kind, faded eyes were searching. "I was never easy in my mind about your marriage. I was afraid it was because of me. Old age and no money—yet you seemed to be in love with him."

Sarah took a light blanket from the foot of the bed; the night air was cool coming from the open window. "I was in love with him." There was a pause while she adjusted the blanket over Julia's feet.

Julia never required i's to be dotted and t's crossed. There was pain and regret in her rocky old face. "We both owe him very much, Sarah."

Sarah leaned over and kissed Julia's soft, wrinkled cheek. "Don't think about it. I'll see to your dinner."

As she went downstairs again she was glad she had resisted an impulse to tell Julia about Lisa. No matter how much Julia had seen of her marriage, no matter how much she guessed or—now—knew, she would be afraid that it had hurt Sarah. I'll be back, Lisa had said. But perhaps she wouldn't; certainly she wouldn't take things into her own hands again, like that. She'd wait.

She went to the kitchen and prepared a tray for Julia; Liebchen lay under a chair, nose on her paws, and watched greedily. Sam in his flapping white apron went about awkward preparations for dinner. "I'm not much of a cook, Mrs. Travers, but I do want to help you. Such a terrible thing!"

Sam ought to be warned. She said carefully, "Sam, if you *should* see anybody around the place . . ."

His eyes flickered rather uneasily toward the windows. "I don't blame you for feeling nervous, Mrs. Travers. But Costellani was alone here. Nobody's likely to try to break in or rob the place now. . . . That's a very nice lady, your aunt, Mrs. Travers. I took her up some flowers."

"Thank you, Sam."

"I've set the table in the dining room for you and Mr. Travers. But maybe you'd better fix the cocktails. I don't know what Mr. Travers likes before dinner. . . . Here, let me take that tray."

He went away carrying Julia's tray. She didn't know, either, what Dixon liked before dinner. It struck her as odd that she didn't know that small preference, when somehow she knew so much about him. She went to the pantry and got out a decanter of whisky, soda and ice. As she took them into the living room she heard Dixon and Sinbad coming in the front door. Dixon went upstairs, and Sinbad bounded down the hall to find her. It was almost night by then; the pale, flat lake held the last glow of the sky. There were not any fishing boats, but it was too late for them; the fish had stopped feeding long ago. The line of willows and the shrubbery pressing close around the long porch were blots of blackness. It was a quiet night with no wind. She left the French windows open and turned on lights so the long room leaped into color. Instantly by contrast the screens blackened; insects buzzed lightly against them.

It was a long time before Dixon came down; she heard him running down the stairs and his hard quick footsteps along the hall. Arthur always walked precisely and very lightly, so lightly that often she hadn't been aware of his approach until he spoke to her. Dixon came quickly into the room toward her, his black hair moist from a shower, and crisp. He looked less white and tired, and when he saw the whisky, said, "That's a welcome sight," and poured a drink for her and for himself.

"Mr. Dixon," she began.

He interrupted rather crossly. "Nobody calls me Mr. Dixon. It makes me think you're addressing my father. Jake's my name."

"Jake, then—I've been thinking. You can't go on with this."

He settled down on the sofa, drank thoughtfully and said, "We had all that this morning."

"But the police—murder—you said it was dangerous."

He ruffled Sinbad's ears and didn't answer. She said, "Besides—suppose the man in the rowboat—suppose this Richard Wells—suppose they think that you are Arthur . . ."

"That's what they're supposed to think," he said shortly.

"But if they do think that they made a mistake in San Francisco because now they think that you are Arthur . . ."

He put down his glass and rose and came to her. He put his hand over her own. "Stop it. That's settled."

The pressure of his hand was hard and warm. His eyes were dark and determined. A moth whispered lightly across the black screen beside them. Somewhere away off on the darkening lake a motorboat chugged leisurely along. Its sound had died away before he said, firmly, "It's my decision, not yours. Besides—" he went back to sit on the sofa and stretch out long legs—"besides if I should be a target, I'm a forewarned and alerted target, if you want to put it like that. Has Travers got a gun?"

"Yes." She rose. "I never thought of it. It's in his room. In the table by the bed."

"Wait, it's not there now. I looked for it. Is there any other place where he might have put it?"

"I don't know. . . . In the hall. In the study . . ."

They looked, Sinbad thudding at their heels. It was not in the drawers of the chest in the hall; it was not in the coat closet; it was not anywhere in the little study.

"He may have taken it to the apartment in town," she said at last. "I can't remember seeing it for—oh, months."

"Maybe he took it with him on his trip."

She considered. "He may have."

"I looked through that big suitcase upstairs. Did he have any other baggage with him?"

"Yes. A small bag . . ."

"Obviously they took his wallet, everything in his pockets; probably they've got that too. . . . Don't look like that! It's all right. As a matter of fact the value of a gun is rather over-rated." He took her arm and turned her back toward the living room. "The only time when anybody needs a gun is when he's going to shoot with it, and as a rule it's better not to shoot. . . . What is it, Sam?"

Sam stood in the dining-room doorway. "Dinner, sir."

He had lighted candles; the night was so still that the flames stood without wavering. The night was growing cooler, as always on the lake, but not a breath of moving air came through the row of open French windows along the porch side of the room. By chance or more likely because it was the logical place for the master of the house to sit, Sam had laid a place for Jake at Arthur's place, opposite her, with Arthur's armchair drawn up to it.

This time Sam served, awkwardly, lumbering around the table, kindly trying to help. Because of his presence they made a little conversation. If anyone had stood out there in the darkness peering in through the French windows it would have made a domestic—and too convincing—picture. Later, when they returned to the distant end of the long living room and Sam brought coffee, Dixon lapsed into a thoughtful, frowning silence. He put down a cigarette at last with an air of finality and said she'd better turn in; they'd get an early start to town in the morning.

"I'll phone the constable and tell him before we leave. In case there's anything." He hesitated, looked at her and said abruptly, "Look here. I couldn't help hearing when that woman—Lisa?—was here. It's not my business. I'm not going to pry . . ."

"I knew you must have heard. . . . It was all true."

He looked down at his cigarette, stubbing it out slowly. "You hadn't known of it?"

"No. That is—I ought to have known. It explained—yes, I ought to have known. It doesn't matter except I blundered with Lisa."

"I thought," he said presently in a remote and impersonal voice, "that you were very—" he paused, "—you were very

74

kind to her. Most women in such a position . . ." he stopped.

He had admired what he took to be her courage. She said with an impulse toward honesty, no more false colors, "I wasn't kind. I think in fact I was grateful to her. It made Arthur seem—different somehow—more—different! But mainly it relieved me of—self-reproach."

"Self-reproach?" Sinbad put his black head on Jake's knee; he tugged his whiskers lightly.

"Because I had made a failure of marriage. It wasn't Arthur's fault. It wasn't exactly mine, either. I suppose these things happen. That's all. . . . I've got to tell Lisa about Arthur."

Jake scratched Sinbad's ears. "Not yet. I didn't mean to draw you into talking about it. I'm sorry."

"No. I wanted you to know. You were sorry for me, you thought . . ."

He glanced at her and away. "I think," he said unexpectedly, "that you are a very honest and brave woman." He gave Sinbad a pat and rose. "What I wanted to ask you about was this letter she had from Travers. Had he told her anything about his trip?"

"No." She hadn't read the letter aloud; he hadn't therefore known what was in it. She repeated it as nearly as she could remember.

His face took on a rather enigmatic look as he listened. "He doesn't sound too enthusiastic about Lisa," he said shortly. "Maybe that was his way. At any rate obviously he didn't want her to know about his trip."

"He told me not to tell her."

He studied her for a moment. "*Will* she be back?"

"I don't know. I don't think she'd come to me like that again. I think she'd wait until Arthur . . ." But Arthur wouldn't return; Lisa would telephone, she'd try to reach him.

Jake said, sharing her thought, "We'll face that little problem when we come to it. . . . I'll lock up, if you want me to."

As they had done the previous night, they made a tour of the house. Sam had gone to the cottage. The dogs, let out the porch door, showed no disposition to linger or explore. As they closed the long line of French windows and bolted them, the shining glass gave back reflections of Jake's black head and light lounge coat, of Sarah's face with its red lip-

75

stick, her short, closely shaped hair making a halo touched with reddish lights, her arm stretched out toward a bolt. This time Jake followed her up the stairs and paused with her at the open door of Julia's room. Julia was in bed, propped up with pillows, pretending to read.

It was just then that the telephone rang, pealing sharply and somehow ominously through the house. The nearest extension was in Sarah's room. She went to answer it and Jake followed. It was the constable. "Mrs. Travers? I'm sorry to call you so late. Can I speak to Mr. Travers?"

She gave the telephone to Jake. She listened while he replied to the distant rumble of the constable's voice. "Yes . . . No, that's all right . . . The San Francisco police? What did they want? . . . Oh, I see . . ." He said at last, "Why, yes, that's right. Yes, from Gump's. . . . No, I haven't any idea. Unless—I suppose it might have been lost and somebody picked it up." He held the telephone so the constable could hear him and looked at Sarah over it. "The constable says a box was found—that is, there was murder in San Francisco and they found an empty box from Gump's near the—murdered man. The police are checking recent purchases. His eyes warned her. "Your bracelet wasn't stolen, of course. Do you remember what you did with the box?"

Sarah could almost see Arthur's fine long fingers folding the wrapping paper neatly, sliding it and the box into his pocket so as to oblige her to take the bracelet. She knew what Jake wanted her to say, however, and immediately he said it himself into the telephone. "She doesn't remember, Constable. Probably she left it in the hotel—yes, the Fairmount. What? . . ." There was another long pause. Then Jake said, "The Presidio Park? Mrs. Travers was in San Francisco only a few hours. Took the night plane back. She wasn't near the park—Right. Of course you had to inquire. Is there anything about Costellani? . . . All right. . . . All right." He put down the telephone and addressed it as if he spoke to the constable. "I'm sorry, Constable. In four more days you can kick me if you want to."

"The San Francisco police telephoned to him?"

He nodded. "They got under way faster than I expected."

"They asked if I had been in the park where he was found?"

He nodded again. There was, however, a kind of reservation when he answered. "I thought it as well not to give them

76

any ideas. The young Irish cop might have described you too accurately."

Julia called from her room. "What was it, Sarah?"

She listened while Jake told her. "That may serve to identify Arthur," Julia said then, slowly. "The name might suggest it to them."

"It might," Jake said.

"This young policeman saw Sarah?"

"Yes. But not really distinctly."

Julia's face looked bleak and old. "But even if they found out that you were there, Sarah, they can't—" she took a breath and said—"suspect you of murder. The government, the men who sent Arthur, they'll know who killed him."

Jake's eyes held again a kind of reserve; he said good night, told Julia the house was locked up and everything quiet, and went down the hall to Arthur's room at the end of it.

The house was locked, windows were bolted.

Nevertheless during the night someone entered the house.

There were in fact, two visitors. One visitor entered the house secretly, in spite of locks and bolts, and so secretly that it did not rouse either of the dogs.

The other visitor—certainly, as it developed, a different, a second visitor—came with a curious mixture of stealth and boldness. Sarah heard his approach.

It was a dark night, with low-lying clouds and very still. There was no wind that night to rustle in the shrubbery and toss waves among the willows, against the shore. The woods stood as if not a leaf moved within their thick curtain of blackness. The only sound was the soft whisper of water against the shore and pier, its light slap against the motorboat out at the buoy. So when, very late, Sarah thought she heard a sound from the lake, she sat up abruptly to listen.

It came again and was the steady, unmistakable sound of oarlocks.

She got up and went to the window. The night was so dark that the lake made a barely discernible patch which was faintly less black than the heavy fringe of willows bordering it.

The click of oarlocks was very near, as if the boat were barely beyond the willows. Almost at once there was a soft grating and a little confusion of sounds, like a footstep on the wood, a kind of rock and motion of the boat, a little

77

swish of willows, and then, after a second or two, footsteps came softly up the gravel path to the steps. The porch was directly below her. She could see nothing move in the thick blackness. But she heard footsteps cross the porch. She heard a soft knock at the hall door.

It was clear and definite, yet soft, too; it was repeated as if whoever stood there and knocked believed himself expected.

9

Sarah pressed her face against the screen across the window and could see nothing within the thick band of deep shadow below her.

Clearly again, yet softly too, the knock was repeated.

Why didn't Sinbad bark and rouse the house? She'd call Jake. She groped through the darkness, snatched her dressing gown and went out into the hall. It was then that she discovered that there were two visitors at the house that night. There was no light anywhere and someone was moving very cautiously through the wide hall below. In the utter silence of the darkened house she heard an incautious footstep somewhere in the black well below.

She thought that it was Jake, and that he had heard the stealthy knocking at the porch door of the hall and had gone quietly down to investigate.

Holding the banister she fumbled for steps in the darkness; she was halfway down the stairs when she thought that Jake had reached the door toward the lake and had opened it. She heard the heavy click of the latch and the rasp of a hinge.

The railing guided her down the remaining steps and around the newel post. The night air sweeping in through the open door ahead of her was chill on her face. When she reached the door itself there was only impenetrable blackness outside. Nothing moved along the porch; there was no faint crunch of a footstep on the gravel path. A long, slow wave washed in upon the shoreline and whispered among the willows.

Jake must be on the porch. She could see the deeper black line of shrubbery; the pillars were dimly lighter. She went out onto the porch cautiously, holding the door so it wouldn't click. There was a sudden motion, like the shuffle of a footstep, toward the end of the porch. She turned so quickly that her sleeve caught on a chair and whirled her around and down, across the chair. As she fell a revolver shot rocked the house, reverberated over the lake.

It seemed very near and was stunning in its impact of sound. The rough wicker of the footrest raked her cheek. A bright area of light lay suddenly on the grass and the figure of a man was running across it toward the lake. Julia, upstairs, screamed. Sinbad somewhere in the distance was barking.

Julia's light had gone on. The two windows directly above Sarah were brightly lighted, streaming across the porch and onto the grass. The running figure disappeared beyond the rectangle of light. And someone else was running very lightly away from the porch and the light, but not toward the lake, running toward the kitchen end of the house.

She knew that. Then the night fell back into silence except for Sinbad still somewhere off in the distance. A light from the hall streamed out across the porch. The long porch, the wicker chairs, the white pillars sprang into being and no one was there; no one moved on the porch. Julia's slippers were tapping along the hall, and at the same time Sarah heard the steady dip of oars off in the blackness that was the lake.

She was on her knees, struggling to get to her feet. Sinbad hurtled out of the darkness and across to her. She cried, "After him, Sinbad, after him . . ." and he charged distractedly out across the steps, across the path of light and vanished toward the lake.

It was, of course, too late. Light spread out eerily upon shrubbery and grass and then lost itself abruptly against the curtain of blackness into which Sinbad had vanished.

"Sarah—Sarah . . ." Julia cried, and Jake crashed through shrubbery at the end of the porch and ran toward her. It was Jake who disentangled her and the sleeve of her dressing gown, still caught and twisted by the chair. He had had a boat, she heard herself telling them over and over. It was too late, he'd got away, he'd had a boat.

They were in the brightly lighted hall. Jake said something to Julia and was running across the porch again, out beyond the patch of light toward the lake. Sinbad was barking furiously and angrily, frustrated. By now the boat was far out in the inky blackness of the lake.

But there'd been footsteps, running too, so lightly, so softly toward the kitchen end of the house. She tried to tell Julia and Julia's face was a rocky, white mask; she didn't listen, she wouldn't listen. She went through the dining room, turning on lights there too, and into the pantry. Sarah could hear Sinbad, and Jake whistling for him. Julia came swishing back through the dining room her long blue dressing gown billowing out around her. She had a glass in her hand. "Drink it." She held it at Sarah's lips. "Drink it." Her hands shook so the little glass trembled against Sarah's mouth; she took it and Jake's tall figure, in white shirt and dark slacks came running back along the graveled path. He had Sinbad by the collar.

The door slammed behind him as he came into the hall and released Sinbad, who flung himself at the screened door, clawing and barking.

"Is she all right?" Jake cried and Julia said, "Yes . . . Yes, I think so," and sat down as if she collapsed on the bench near the door.

"There were two men," Sarah cried. "One had a boat—he got away. Somebody else ran around the house that way . . ."

Jake's face was as white as his shirt. He too came to her, touching her, his hands on her shoulders. "You're sure it didn't hit you?"

"No. No! I fell, I stumbled—he got away. There were two men . . ."

But by then Jake knew that there had been two visitors at the house for one of them had come by automobile. It was parked in the woods road, some distance back along it. It was the car, not the sound of that furtive yet steady knock at the lake side of the hall, that had roused Jake.

"I was on the couch in the study. I decided to sleep down here so I'd be more likely to know if somebody was prowling around the house. Sinbad heard the car and whined. Then I heard it, some distance from the house, in the road through the woods. I got Sinbad by the collar. Just as we got out on the front steps the engine was turned off. I kept hold of Sinbad and went out across the lawn and then through the woods instead of following the driveway; I thought I'd have a better chance to find out who it was if he didn't hear me coming. It took some time to find the car; it was off the road behind some firs. The car was empty when I got there. Then I heard the shot . . ."

"But you were in the hall," Sarah began. "I heard you—you opened the door, and went out . . ."

He hadn't; he had already, some minutes before, gone to hunt for an automobile and a man driving it. Therefore one of those stealthy visitors had in fact entered the house, while the other stood on the porch and knocked so lightly, yet as if he were expected, at the door beside them.

"How did he get in?" Jake said blankly. "I closed the front door behind me. The night latch was on; it locked. I was sure of that. I intended to go around to the porch and call to Sarah to let me in again."

He looked then, searching the house, going from one window to another, trying the doors. The two women followed, turning on lights which blazed up brightly everywhere. It was a strange search, like a segment from a nightmare. The windows were bolted. The night latch on the front door had locked it. The door off the kitchen entry was locked. But, there, they found a forgotten window. It was in the little flower room off the kitchen entry. No one had remembered it. It was open and the screen was unhooked. Liebchen was there.

She whimpered when they opened the door of the flower room with its sink and tables and shelves for vases. A drinking dish for the dogs stood near the sink. There were no marks on the window sill; Jake examined it. But undoubtedly someone could have made entrance there.

He could have closed Liebchen in the room.

And Liebchen was not like Sinbad. She was shy of strangers; she rarely flew to an attack and never with Sinbad's fervor.

It added to the puzzle when Sam Cleetch came, running, to the kitchen door and rattled it loudly and shouted. Jake unlocked the door. Sam was in an undershirt and insecurely anchored khaki pants which he clutched at the waist with one hand. In the other hand he carried a shovel which he brandished as he darted in out of the night. "I heard a shot. What's happened? Where is he? I heard a shot . . ." Jake took the shovel, which threshed dangerously near them, and explained.

Sam thought he had himself shut Liebchen in the flower room. "The little dog was in the kitchen while I was washing up. She trotted into the flower room and I heard her drinking. Then I—forgot her. I finished up the kitchen and I remember shutting the door of the little room. I didn't think of her."

"Are you sure she was there then?" Jake asked.

Sam didn't know. "She went in for a drink a few minutes before. If I'd seen her I wouldn't have shut her in. But I forgot her . . ." He looked at Sarah. "That was a lucky miss, Mrs. Travers." His glistening red face turned to Jake. "Shouldn't we call the police?"

Jake said slowly, "I think they've got away by now. No way to trace them. They are not likely to come back tonight. We'll see about it tomorrow."

Sam was not satisfied. "It was the burglars—the fellows that got Costellani." He eyed Jake and then Sarah. "Maybe they think you have some jewelry, Mrs. Travers." He hesitated. "Mind if I sleep in the house? I don't like staying alone down there in the cottage, I'll tell you honestly. And if they do come back, I'd be here if Mr. Travers needs any help."

There was a room at the top of the back stairs, Sarah told him; it was the cook's room; he was welcome to use it if he wanted to. She told him where to find bedding. Sam trailed after them, however, to the front of the house again. All of them watched while Jake explored and found a splintered, jagged hole very high in the casing of the door.

They watched while he stood on a wicker chair and dug out the bullet with a kitchen knife Sam brought him.

They looked at the bullet in the palm of Jake's hand. Sam uttered a whistling sigh. Julia's old face was gray and bleak. She said in a queer, numb voice, staring at the bullet, "Why would anybody try to kill Sarah?"

Jake's hand closed over the bullet. "I don't think he meant to shoot at Sarah. It was dark. He couldn't have seen it was a woman. Besides . . ." he eyed the splintered hole in the door casing, "Besides it's very high. As if he didn't want to kill anybody."

"But then why . . . ?" Julia began.

"Might have been rattled—shot too high. But maybe . . ." Jake measured the height of the bullet mark. "Maybe it was only a threat."

A threat? Intended only to convince Arthur of the deadly tenacity of their purpose? Only to frighten him?

"They came together," Sarah said slowly. "They are working together—they couldn't have seen me. They must have believed—"

Jake nodded, "—believed they had Arthur Travers." He glanced at Sam. "Please make some hot tea for Miss Halsey, Sam."

Sam lumbered away. Julia said to Jake, "He thought she was Arthur. That is . . . You . . ."

Jake of course. Posing as Arthur. A target.

The night was very still again. The house blazed with lights. They were outlined too clearly, too sharply, there on the porch amid those lights. The distant shapes of shrubbery seemed to watch and listen; the night itself had invisible, waiting eyes.

Jake slid the bullet into his pocket. Julia said, with a kind of shiver, "Let's go into the house."

Jake locked and bolted the door behind them. The French windows glittered, reflecting the lights. Julia led the way back to the study, which seemed smaller, more protected. Julia pulled the red curtains over the windows above the driveway, and sat down then, wearily, on one of the deep chairs. Yellow linen cushions from the drawing room were crushed down on the red leather sofa where Jake had been sleeping.

"One in a boat and one in a car," he said. "Which one knocked? Which one got into the house?" Sinbad whined nervously and then settled down with a thump. Jake said, "And which one had a revolver?"

"What about the car?" Sarah asked.

"It was an old car, prewar—I think a Pontiac. Either dark blue or black. License was muddy, probably on purpose. I was scraping off the mud and lighting matches to try to get the number when I heard the shot. . . . It may have been a rented car."

Julia said slowly, "Enemy agents. Are you going to call the police?"

Jake took out the bullet, examined it, turning it over and over in his hand and then put it in his pocket again. "I don't think I should report it now to the police. It would be easy for government men to watch the house and—pick up these men. There must be a reason why they don't want to do it now. I'll give them the bullet later. Report what I know of the car. It's not much evidence but it may help. Later . . ."

Sam brought the tea. It added a final touch of nightmare to the scene, Julia pouring and drinking tea in the cheery little study—with the open door giving a view of the hall where someone had walked so lightly, so cautiously.

The shock of a revolver shot rocking the night, a bullet embedding itself in wood high above her head seemed to Sarah a thing observed, unrelated to her. Yet at the same time she could feel the rake of her cheek across the wicker footrest, the instinctive terror which held her crouching low against the chair.

Julia put down her cup with a faint small chime of china. Jake said, "You'd better go upstairs, both of you. I'll stay down here." He drew Sarah to her feet and toward the stairway. Julia said, "Come, Sarah. We can't do anything now."

It was of course true; in four days more they would report it to the police, tell them the whole story. Unless before that a voice over the telephone gave them other instructions.

What could the police have done? What would they do if Jake reported, then, the story of the night?

They'd inquire about a man who had taken a rowboat out into the night—what man, from what hidden point along that long, curving shoreline, from what secret willow-fringed cove? Or a man who had driven a car along a highway at night. A bullet—from what gun? They would say, as Sam had said, burglars.

Their inquiry would be thorough, because they were inquiring into Costellani's murder. Probably, without the whole story, it would yield nothing.

Mainly, the whole object of Arthur's plan had been to distract enemy agents, to make them believe (until the job was done) that it had not been undertaken.

Jake was right; they couldn't have called the police.

Jake, downstairs, was wakeful too. Once Sarah heard him speak in a low voice to Sinbad; the faint fragrance of cigarette smoke drifted upward from below. The night was quiet and still black and overcast when at last, wearily she went to sleep.

In the morning, later than they had intended, she and Jake went to New York.

Julia insisted on their going. Nothing could happen while they were away, in the full light of day, with Sam coming and going about the house. Besides nobody would attempt to enter the house, and she was in no danger. It was again a bright sunny morning; the night had cleared, sun beat down on the lake, the light striking upward in bright reflections. Jake went down early to look at the willows where the rowboat had been beached. There were no marks anywhere, no footprints, nothing. He and Sinbad took a long swing around the place. There was no evidence of either of the visitors of the night, no tire marks where the car had stood behind a clump of firs along the woods road. Nothing.

Nothing except a small piece of lead.

They took Sarah's small convertible, and Sarah drove.

Before they left Jake telephoned to the constable and told him he had to go to town and would be back in the afternoon. The constable apparently did not demur. There was no new evidence about Costellani; they had not discovered his daughter's address, or indeed any evidence of her existence among Costellani's letters. They were beginning to believe that there was no daughter and that Costellani had invented one as an excuse to leave, yet, if so, he must have intended to return.

"Anything about the man in San Francisco?" Jake asked. Sarah, ready to go, picked up her brown alligator handbag, still on the table where she had left it, it seemed to her, a long time ago. It wasn't the right bag for her thin, navy blue silk suit but it didn't matter. She listened while the constable talked for some time before Jake put down the telephone. "They haven't identified him," he said. "The constable reported that you didn't know what had happened to the box. The police are going on the theory that robbery was the motive; the murderer might have stolen a bracelet and either thrown away the box or lost it in the park. But no bracelet has been reported to them as stolen."

Sinbad would have gone with them and was restrained by Julia. There was, when they left, no rowboat lingering offshore and the road through the woods was deserted. When they turned into the highway they were not followed. Sarah watched the mirror and she thought Jake watched it too.

It seemed a short trip. Jake sat in a remote, thoughtful silence most of the way. There was not much traffic. They reached the bank and the safe-deposit vault about noon and Jake signed the card.

But when, in the little cubbyhole to which they were shown, Jake unlocked and opened the dispatch case, there was nothing in it. Not a scrap of paper, not a letter, not a memorandum—nothing.

Sarah had been prepared to find perhaps, only letters, contracts, business memoranda. Its barren emptiness was surprising.

10

The bright light above the bare table shone down bleakly upon it and the empty divisions of the dispatch case. Jake closed the case. "All right, let's go. . . . Might as well take this along."

"He said you were not to let it out of your sight! That's why he wanted you to come to New York!"

Jake touched her hand, warning her of the thin walls of the tiny cubicle. "How about lunch?"

She waited at the desk while Jake closed out the safety-deposit box he had rented. The car was parked at the Rockefeller Plaza garage and they walked up Fifth Avenue to the Café Louis XIV. Jake glanced around the table to which they were shown: "See anybody you know?"

"No . . ."

Jake ordered quickly. The empty dispatch case with its initials, A.T., stood on the floor beside him. She said, "Could anyone have got hold of it and taken the papers out?"

"Not a chance. The only time it was out of my hands, almost literally, was when I left it on the table in your living room at the Fairmount. Nobody came into the room then. I took Travers at his word. He emphasized its importance."

"Why?" she said. "Why . . ."

The waiter put down jellied consommé. Jake said, "Well —he may have emphasized it because of the papers he said he was going to add to it. Just to make a strong impression in my mind. Or he may have been thinking mainly of you. That is, he wanted me to accompany you and he didn't want to make too much of possible danger. The dispatch case was an excuse, a specific chore he could direct me to undertake. That's one explanation."

It was an explanation which, knowing Arthur, she was inclined to accept. Arthur often accomplished his purposes by methods which were devious and indirect. "I think he might

86

have done that—I mean, for that reason. It's—like him. Besides what other explanation is there?"

Jake glanced at the waiter who whisked away the soup cups and put down cold lobster and poured iced coffee. When the waiter had gone Jake said abruptly, "Do you mind telling me something about Travers? I mean—well, this woman Lisa. Had you ever talked to him about her?"

"Lisa! No. Never. I didn't know anything about it until yesterday."

"Well, then . . ." he hesitated. "Was there anything else you—differed about? Money or property or anything? That is—I knew you were not in love with him when I overheard your talk with Lisa," he said in a remote and impersonal way, barely outlining facts. "Was there any way in which, say, you opposed him?"

She replied directly. "No. If he had wanted to marry Lisa and had told me so I would have agreed. As to property, there is nothing I own. Nothing I would have opposed him about. Why?"

He put down an unlighted cigarette. "I don't know. Nothing, perhaps. Had you known Travers for a long time? I mean before your marriage?"

"No." The bare facts of a story that had lasted five years could be compressed into a few sentences. "I lived in a little college town, so little you never heard of it. My father taught English. Aunt Julia saw to us. He died and of course there wasn't any money; I—oh, did odd chores for a year. But it wasn't enough money to keep us going so I took a secretarial course. Then I met Arthur. It was at a friend's house—Isobel Blanchard. Her husband knew Arthur."

She paused for a moment, carried back to the week-end at Isobel's. Isobel had married into a gay and glamorous world, and that week-end had given Sarah her first and dazzling glimpse of that world.

"Go on," Jake said.

"There's not much to tell. She told him that I was looking for a job. Several weeks later he wrote to me and said there was a place in his office. I took it, of course. It wasn't much of a job, but I wasn't much of a typist, either. Then—well, that's all. We were married in the fall."

That was all, but it brought back pictures, sharp as if drawn on the white tablecloth. Herself in a white tennis frock, borrowed from Isobel, playing tennis with Arthur, the sun dazzling her eyes. As perhaps that week-end had dazzled her eyes, too. Long drives in the country during the late summer, with the leaves beginning to turn and an early trace of wood smoke in the air. Week-ends again at Isobel's house on Long Island. Julia, rather silent, her eyes questioning; Sarah's wedding in the cottage near old college buildings, with the woodbine red over the walls. And, then, five years.

Jake was watching her; she knew it and looked up to meet his eyes, and he knew, he understood what she had not told.

He looked away. The communication was cut off. Again, as during a moment or two in a swaying taxicab, across the continent, on their hurried way to the airport, silence came between them.

The waiter, hovering near came to the table, poured more iced coffee. His foot touched the dispatch case and with a murmur he picked it up, flicked it with his napkin and set it on the vacant chair across from them. Jake said then, "I thought the case seemed light. But then—a few papers don't weigh much."

"We have some nice melon, sir," the waiter said. "Or perhaps the lady would like a sweet."

They ordered melon and Jake glanced at his watch. Sarah thought of Julia, alone in the house on the lake. "We ought to be starting home."

"Yes," Jake said. "Look here, what I'm going to say sounds brutal—but—is there any chance that Travers was trying to frame you?"

"Frame *me!*"

"I mean, say, give him an out to marry Lisa. Suppose he came back, found you with me, in his house, posing as Travers. He could have devised the whole thing, you see. And he'd have had you in a very difficult spot. . . . Oh, I know how it sounds. And if he had such a scheme certainly it went wrong. He . . ."

"He was killed," she said, staring at the white cloth.

"Yes. Yes—forget what I said. Yet—the crux of the thing is Travers himself. I know his standing in business; I didn't know him. You knew him. These men last night—in fact everything squares with the explanation he gave you and with the thing he asked you to do. But there might be—" his voice hardened—"other explanations. And our stake, in a very definite sense, is Travers'—call it integrity, honesty—whatever you want to. To me, that's an unknown quantity. It's the X, the ultimate X." He glanced at the dispatch case which had confirmed nothing, which had yielded no information of any kind. "If you still believe him . . ."

"He gave his life . . ."

Jake rose. "All right. So you're going to go on with it."

"Yes."

"Then I'll go along with you." He picked up the empty dispatch case. The waiter brought the check. Out on the street the strong warm sunshine of summer New York fell upon them. They crossed the street. Sarah stood inside the vast parking garage, waiting while Jake went to claim the car. She watched as he turned around the corner of the long row of the cashiers' counter. In a few days more he would walk, like that, out of her life.

How would he remember her? An episode out of the busy dramas that engage a lawyer's life? A client, whose interests were for those few days his interests?

That was Friday. She had seen him for the first time on Tuesday. It was strange but very wrong to feel that he knew her so well, as if he had known her—and she had known him —for a long time, all of her life.

A few more days, and that would end.

A woman, laden with parcels, put the parcels in a small gray car, got in herself and drove away. A family of tourists checked baggage anxiously and discussed the route they were about to take and drove away. There was the scent of gasoline and carbon monoxide and damp pavement. Jake came back with a bundle of newspapers under his arm, her car shot out from a cavernous tunnel and stopped and the uniformed attendant got out. This time Jake drove and she went through the newspapers, one at a time.

Rose had done her work well—either that or, as Rose had said, Costellani's murder had little news value. There were only two items concerning his murder and they were short and inconspicuous, in the back columns. The date lines were Saguache Village and the facts were brief. Alfred Costellani, a gardener on the estate of Arthur Travers, oil tycoon, had been found murdered. Attempted burglary was the probable cause. Mr. and Mrs. Travers had been in San Francisco, and the gardener was alone on the place when the murder must have occurred.

She read the brief items aloud to Jake.

"There's one value," he said presently, guiding the little car through the late afternoon traffic. "It'll convince *them* that Travers is at the lake."

It would also serve to convince them that Jake was Arthur Travers. The target.

Jake said, "This is Friday. Tuesday will make it exactly a week. If we've heard nothing by then, I'll get in touch with Washington and report the whole thing. I wish I had more to tell, something specific to identify these men. A bullet but no gun. The description of a car which applies to any number of cars. The possible name of a man—Wells, which may not be his name, and he may not be an enemy agent." They stopped for a toll gate. As they got under way again he said, "Sarah, is there anything, anybody, no matter how unimportant it seems to you, that could possibly give them a lead? Is there anything at all that maybe Travers told you some time, or—I suppose there isn't. You'd have remembered. But surely if enemy agents knew that this thing was in the wind, they'd have been keeping an eye on Travers."

A small, absurd incident came to her memory, a man in a wrinkled brown suit and a bright tie. Robinson, who had asked her—or pretended to ask her to have dinner with him.

She told him briefly. There wasn't anything in it—she had dismissed it—yet Robinson *had* taken the same plane that she had taken from New York. She had seen him in a taxi, going in the same direction Arthur's taxi had taken. She had thought of him while she waited in the chill mist of the silent park.

"Robinson," Jake said. "Robinson. Are you sure that was his name?"

"That's what he said. But . . ."

"But it may not have been his name. And he may have had nothing to do with this. Still, it's a line to check on."

"Do you think *he* . . . ?"

"I don't know," he said. "Somebody was at the house last night. Somebody fired that shot. Somebody killed Travers."

The miles of parkway unrolled before them and they were approaching the village before he spoke again. "Three more days," he said shortly then. "We can hold out till then. Is this the turn?"

She nodded and the little car swerved from the highway into the long road that wound through the woods and into a tunnel of shade, toward the house which someone had entered the night before. Toward the lake where a rowboat, its oarlocks clicking swiftly, had disappeared into darkness. She said unsteadily, "Suppose they come back? The men last night . . ."

"We know what to look out for. That's the main thing. I'll leave you at the house. I'd like to take your car. Whoever these men are, they've got to have some sort of base somewhere. They can't camp out under the trees. I'd like to find out about the car that was parked here, too."

"What are you going to do?"

"Inquire at the hotel in the village and make a tour of the little motor courts around the lake, see if the garage in the village rented a car." He turned through the gates and into the driveway. "We've got a bullet. We have two names which may not be the right ones, and may or may not be enemy agents. Such evidence as there is, I'd like to be able to give them when we . . ."

Lisa's shining little car was drawn up before the steps. Sarah cried, "It's Lisa!"

Jake stopped the car. "Get out here. I'll back around so she'll not see me . . ."

The front door opened. Lisa came out and stood there on the steps waiting for them.

At the same time three men came walking from the garage toward them.

The whole scene was suddenly like a stage setting. It was as if she and Jake were an audience. The car had stopped just inside the gate; there were hedges, roses, the sweep of green lawn and the glittering circle of the driveway. Lisa saw the three men approaching them, taking a course across the driveway and grass. She looked at them and then back at the car. She knew the car. Of course, she had been waiting for it.

Jake said, "There's the constable and a state trooper. I don't know who the other man is. I'll meet them. Go to the house and get Lisa inside. Get her away if you have a chance. I'll see to them."

He drove forward a few feet and stopped the car again in the shadow of the heavy thicket of lilacs. It screened him and the car from Lisa.

Sarah got out. Lisa was watching the constable and the men with him, a young lieutenant in state trooper's uniform and an elderly man in a rather wilted seersucker suit. It was Jake they wanted to see. The constable nodded across the lawn toward Sarah. She reached the steps and Lisa still stared

91

at the three men. The sun gleamed on the leather holster strapped to the young state trooper's sturdy waist. Sarah could hear the slow tread of their feet; Sinbad, somewhere inside the house, barked and was silent. The roses, warmed by the sun, were overpoweringly sweet and fragrant. The car door, behind the green screen of lilacs, closed. Jake had got out of the car to meet the constable and the other men.

Lisa had a rolled-up newspaper in her hand. Sarah said, "Please come into the house, Lisa," and opened the door.

Julia was at the telephone. Sarah heard her voice. "No, he isn't here—yes, yes. Miss Willman at his office would know. You might get in touch with her . . ."

Lisa turned to face Sarah. She wore a pale gray shantung dress; her eyes were as pale and had as little light in them. "Who are those men?"

"The village constable and a state trooper. Costellani, that's the gardener . . ."

"I know. It's in the papers." Lisa held out the newspapers in her hand. The moonstone on her finger caught a dull, stormy light. "When was he killed?"

"Some time last week. Friday or Saturday, they think."

"You didn't tell me yesterday. Why didn't you tell me?"

"Why should I?" Sarah said.

A curious half-pleased, half-defiant gleam came into Lisa's eyes. She said however smoothly, "Naturally I am interested. . . . I'll wait and see Arthur."

Julia was in the doorway. "Sarah, Rose Willman is on the telephone. She wants to talk to Arthur. Lisa came five minutes ago." Her eyes met Sarah's in sharp anxiety. How can we get rid of her? It was as if she had spoken the words. Lisa, watching the men across the grass, her eyes now narrowed, said suddenly, "They're coming to the house." She turned and went into the hall ahead of Sarah.

Julia said, "Why not wait in the study, Lisa, until the police have gone? Arthur . . ." Her voice wavered; she said the name again more steadily, "Arthur would prefer it, I'm sure. The police ask so many questions."

Lisa said, coldly and politely, "Thank you," and went into the little study. Julia said, "Do you want to talk to Rose?"

Julia would stand what guard she could over Lisa. With the feeling that every opposing force that could arise had converged upon them at the same time, Sarah went to the telephone. "It's Sarah, Rose. Arthur is—talking to the police."

Rose's voice was unusually clear, so it seemed near. "Tell him this Wells phoned to the office again. He was very unpleasant. In fact . . ."

"*What did he say? Where is he?*"

"Wait a minute." There was the rattle of a coin in the telephone. Rose said then, "Tell the chief to look out for him. I'll phone again and talk to him myself."

"Wait—Rose!" The telephone clicked. "*Rose . . .*" Sarah jiggled the receiver and an operator, the village operator, said, "Number, please." Julia in the doorway to the study beckoned urgently; Sarah went quickly into the study and Lisa was standing at a window.

It overlooked the terrace and the driveway and the stretch of lawn. Over Lisa's shoulder she saw them full in the sunlight; Jake with his black head lifted, his broader face, his different walk, so unlike Arthur, was talking to the constable.

Lisa saw him, too. She caught her breath, gave Sarah a blank look and turned again to stare at Jake. "Who is that man? Where is Arthur?"

Sarah closed the study door and stood with her back against it. The front door opened. There were footsteps and voices in the hall. The constable said clearly, "The county attorney has already seen the place where you found Costellani and we've taken another look at the cottage. He wants to question you about him, Mr. Travers."

Jake had seen the closed door and guessed. He said, "All right . . . come into the living room, will you? This way . . ."

Lisa's lovely face was stony. "Mr. Travers! Who . . . ?" Comprehension came into her eyes. "He looks like Arthur! You're pretending that man is Arthur! You've told the police—they think he's Arthur! Why?" She caught Sarah's arm; her fingernails dug into Sarah's wrist. "*Why? Where is Arthur?*" With a strong, lithe movement she thrust Sarah back and flung open the door.

11

Julia stood in the hall momentarily blocking Lisa's way. And there was only one thing to do. Sarah cried, "Lisa, I'll tell you . . . I tried to tell you yesterday."

Something in her voice caught Lisa's attention and held it. For an instant she stood perfectly still, her hard light eyes seeking into Sarah's. Then she said, "All right. . . . What is it?"

They went back into the little study. Julia closed the door after them. It shut off the little study with its red chairs and red curtains, its rows of books along the walls, as if it was removed a long way from the rest of the house, from Julia and Jake, from the constable and the state trooper with his uniform and gleaming leather holster.

Sarah said, in a flat weary voice, drained of feeling, "Arthur was murdered."

There was a deep flash in Lisa's eyes, like the shutter of a camera opening and closing. "I don't believe you!"

"I ought to have told you yesterday . . ."

"Yesterday? But he was here then! What are you trying to say?"

"I'll tell you the whole thing. It was in San Francisco . . ."

In its essential facts it was a brief story. There was no change in Lisa's face, yet as she finished Sarah knew that behind that hard yet beautiful mask Lisa was thinking furiously. "And so," Sarah said, "Jake—the man you saw, the lawyer Arthur retained—is going to stay here for three more days. Until it's done. Until they let us know that it's finished."

"It," Lisa said then. "What exactly is it?"

"Arthur couldn't tell me. Something about oil—it could be—oh, anything. The possibility of a new oil field. A conference with other men, representatives of friendly countries. It could be—there are so many possibilities, it doesn't matter what it is. It's important."

The fixed, blank look of Lisa's eyes didn't waver, but

she seemed to consider it deliberately. Finally she said, "Arthur didn't tell me about it."

"No. He couldn't—they said not to tell anybody."

"But you say he told you."

"He had to. That's why he wrote to you as he did. He said they had to have a week."

"What about this man . . . ?" She still carried the rolled-up newspaper. "Costellani? What about him?"

"Jake thinks—I think that he may have been murdered by mistake, perhaps at night. That, or he found somebody who was sent to watch the place—one of the men who came here last night."

"Who were they?"

"We don't know. Enemy agents . . ."

"The same men who murdered Arthur?"

"We don't know. But we believe that they have seen Jake and believe him to be Arthur."

Something in her voice caught Lisa's swift attention; there was a flicker of light in her gray eyes. She thought for a moment, and then she said, "Have you no idea whatever about these—as you call them enemy agents? Who are they?"

"There is a man who calls himself Richard Wells; he has telephoned to Rose, and inquired about Arthur. He checked the passenger list. Jake had taken the tickets in Arthur's name, as Arthur had asked him to do so."

"Richard Wells," Lisa said thoughtfully and shook her head.

"There's another, a man in San Francisco. He was on the plane I took out there, and he was at the hotel, outside Arthur's rooms—he was there in the corridor when I came out and asked me to have dinner with him. But it may have been exactly what it seemed—somebody who had seen me traveling alone, tried to make a pickup for dinner. There's nothing really to connect him with this."

"What was his name?"

"He said it was Robinson."

"Robinson? Arthur saw him last week. Here."

"Here! Robinson! Lisa, how do you know? Did Arthur tell you?"

"He said Robinson," Lisa said slowly. She paused, then gave a kind of shrug. "There's no reason why you shouldn't know. We motored up here last week. That was Thursday night. Arthur—told you he had a business dinner."

Sarah thought back to the preceding week; there were so many business dinners. Thursday? Lisa said rapidly, "Arthur had one of those cars he uses in town, a car and chauffeur . . ."

The chauffeur, Sarah thought, who had greeted Jake as Mr. Travers, and who had commented on the beauty of the house—now that he could see it in daylight. Lisa was going on swiftly, "We came up here and had a little supper. We cooked it ourselves. And then—Arthur had come up here, he said, to meet a man. He sent me for a drive around the country in the car. The man was supposed to come to the house."

"Did you see him?"

"No. I told you I went for a drive."

"What did Arthur tell you about him?"

"Nothing. He said he was going to meet him; that was all."

"How did Arthur seem? I mean, was he apprehensive or nervous or . . . ?"

Lisa said slowly, "I didn't think anything about it except I understood that he was some business friend of Arthur's, somebody perhaps who knew you or—at any rate Arthur didn't want him to see me. I understood, naturally. When I came back . . ." Suddenly she stopped. For the first time her eyes left Sarah's. She got up, went to the window and stood there, her back turned to Sarah. Her smooth, light hair, her lovely figure outlined against the light.

So it was Lisa and Arthur who had had supper, cooking it themselves in the kitchen, leaving the little clutter of dishes and silver which Costellani had not cleared away. And the man Robinson, with the swarthy face and little eyes and flapping bright tie *had* followed Sarah. She had led him to Arthur.

Had Robinson murdered him? Robinson who had visited the house on the lake—on what pretext?

But Arthur then had escaped him. It was Costellani who had been murdered.

"Was Costellani here then? Did you see him?"

Lisa didn't reply. She said over her shoulder, "This man —this lawyer, you call him Jake." She turned slowly and looked at Sarah. "You like him, don't you?"

The question was unexpected; Sarah had had no warning. Lisa came a step nearer. "I think you more than like him. There was something in your voice, something in the way

96

you said Jake—Jake this, Jake that. Why is he doing this? If what you've told me is true he is deliberately exposing himself to danger. Why? You're in love with him."

What had Lisa said? What had she plucked out of the air?

She couldn't answer, or ask any questions in her own heart; not then, for there was danger in Lisa's face and in her words. Sarah said steadily, "I saw him for the first time in my life Tuesday. He is doing what Arthur employed him to do."

Lisa laughed. "So that's the way it stands. I wondered yesterday, when I told you about Arthur and me. I wondered why you didn't care. Now I understand." She came back to the chair and sat down. "It is this man, this lawyer . . . When you said Miss Halsey was coming I thought that you had decided to fight not for Arthur but for his money. I didn't know that you intended to have his money—and your handsome young man, too."

That at least had an answer. "That is not true."

Lisa's face was no longer lovely. It seemed to have shrunken and narrowed. She put back her head with a touch of arrogance. She said, rather carefully, rather cautiously, "What did Arthur tell this young man to do? When he retained him, when he employed him, before—he suggested this preposterous masquerade?"

"We believe that Arthur thought something like this might happen. He sent a dispatch case back with Jake. We opened it today and there was nothing in it; we believe he made that a pretext merely to make sure that Jake would come east with me. . . . Oh, yes; he had Jake draw up a power of attorney . . ."

"For you?" Lisa said sharply.

"Yes. Arthur knew there was danger . . ."

"Do you really expect me to believe all this? What a fool you must take me for! I see now—I understand it all. Obviously you want me to keep still. You say for three days." She paused, looked at Sarah with a calculating gleam away back in her eyes and said, "Arthur was a very rich man. You will be—you are now since he's dead, a very rich woman. I," Lisa said softly, "have nothing."

There was a long, strange silence. Something significant had been said in the quiet little room. Sarah said slowly, "I don't understand you."

"I think you understand perfectly. Arthur is dead. What's done is done. You have told me a long and extraordinary story to account for his death. The facts in it are these. Arthur was murdered. You are here in his house, with another man—a man who resembles Arthur in a superficial but in a rather convincing way. You are in love with this man. . . . Oh, don't try to tell me you are not; I know. Conveniently—oh, very conveniently, this man, this lawyer, has drawn up a power of attorney for you. Those are the facts."

"Lisa . . ."

"Wait. I'm not going to accuse you—or this lawyer. I'm not going to accuse you of anything . . ."

"You can't. There's nothing—Arthur . . ."

Lisa's face was beautiful and smooth again. She touched her hair and the moonstone on her hand gleamed dully. She stroked her chic, smart skirt down over her knees. She said softly, very smoothly, "But I think that Arthur would have wished to provide for me."

That was the significance; that was what had been said, yet not said, in the quiet little room where there was only Sarah to hear. She said slowly, "You are trying to blackmail me."

"Not at all. I'm only putting the facts before you."

Sarah rose. "You've forgotten. The government department, the men who sent him, they know the facts."

Lisa said softly, "Do they?"

Jake had said, only a few hours ago, "Our stake is Arthur's integrity. It's the crux of it." He had said, too, "It's the unknown quantity, the ultimate X." But Arthur's death was a tragic proof of the truth.

Lisa said, "You are being rather stubborn, aren't you, Sarah? There's enough money. Enough for you and this young man. Enough for . . ." She smiled a little and lifted fine, penciled eyebrows.

Suddenly Sarah had had enough of Lisa, willing to trade her silence for Arthur's money. She couldn't talk to her, she couldn't listen, she couldn't breathe the same air. "I believed you when you said you were in love with Arthur. I have told you everything. Now please go."

Anger came slowly into Lisa's face, anger and finally belief. She rose at last. "You're a very foolish woman," she said, and opened the door.

The constable, the county attorney and the young trooper were in the hall. They were leaving. Jake was with them. The constable was speaking. "Thank you, Mr. Travers. We've set the inquest for Monday . . ." He broke off; all of them looked, surprised, at Lisa and Lisa said clearly, "This man is not Arthur Travers."

Jake gave Sarah a quick look and came to stand beside her. No one else moved or spoke and Lisa said very slowly, very smoothly, "My name is Lisa Bayly. I know Arthur Travers very well. This man is not Arthur. His name is Dixon; he lives in San Francisco. He came back from San Francisco with her—with Arthur's wife. Arthur—" she caught a quick breath—"a man was murdered in San Francisco. She—his wife admitted it to me. That man was Arthur Travers."

The constable took a heavy step toward Jake and then he stopped, staring at him. The old county attorney's faded blue eyes were staring, too, at Jake. The young state trooper however looked at Lisa admiringly. She sensed the admiration; she went to him and put her hand on his uniformed arm, her lovely face was grave and pleading. "This is a terrible thing to say. But Arthur's wife and this man are in love with each other. Arthur was murdered. He was a very rich man. He was older than Sarah. This man, this lawyer had drawn up a power of attorney for Sarah. He is posing as Arthur. Those are the facts."

The constable opened his mouth, started to speak, closed it again. The county attorney got out a handkerchief and wiped his bald head. The young trooper put his hand on his revolver. Jake looked down at Sarah. "They'd have to know soon. It doesn't matter . . ."

There was a kind of scramble and patter of a dog's feet upon the stairs; Liebchen came waddling down, stopped to take a look at the strangers in her domain, fixed her eyes upon Jake and lifted her old lip in an angry, suspicious snarl. It was as neat a piece of accusation as Arthur himself might have devised. And it was more convincing than all of Lisa's angry words. Sarah said to Jake, "All right. Tell them . . ."

Lisa cried shrilly, "You see! That's Arthur's dog. She knows . . ."

The constable came heavily toward Jake. His sallow, sagging face, his heavy-lidded eyes were ugly and menacing. "What are you trying to do? You said you were Travers . . ."

The trooper cried, "Look out for him. If he's murdered Travers . . ." His gun was now in his hand.

"I didn't murder Travers," Jake said. "But it's true. I'm Dixon. It's rather a long story."

"We've got time to hear it," the constable said.

Jake stood at Sarah's side, so close she felt the steady pressure of his arm. "All right. Here it is . . ." She listened while he told it, in concise phrases. Travers had come to his office to retain his legal services; he was to go east with Mrs. Travers, taking a dispatch case. Travers himself was leaving, he was to take a trip.

"Where?" the constable asked, his eyes dark with suspicion.

"I don't know. It is a government affair; he was asked to give his expert opinion about something that for security reasons was to be kept a secret." The look of suspicion in the constable's face deepened. Jake went on. He was approaching the difficult part of the story, the incredible part of it, Sarah thought suddenly, facing that combined wall of suspicion. But incredible or not, it had happened. "I was to have another interview with him. I didn't. Apparently he'd had orders to leave at once. He sent a message by his wife; he asked me to pose as Travers, here, for a week."

Lisa gave a short laugh. Jake went on, "This, too, was for security reasons. It was suggested by the government agency that sent Travers. There were two reasons for it. First, Travers is identified with oil. He is an important and well-known figure, and if an enemy country had wind of this project, his absence alone would suggest that such a project was not only contemplated but under way. Second, Travers himself was in some danger; it was believed that by posing as Travers I might also protect Travers himself by drawing off any possible attack on the part of enemy agents. Obviously Travers was in danger, but only if they believed he was about to undertake this mission. Their aim was to stop him. They succeeded in that."

"The man in San Francisco," the constable said. "You mean —you admit that was Travers?"

"I believe it was Travers, yes. I'll tell you why . . ." He paused and then said, flatly, "I was to meet Travers in the park—where the murdered man was found. He wasn't there. While I was waiting a park policeman came along and asked me about the time. He saw me, but not distinctly, because it was dark by then and we were some distance from the street lights. When he found the body he reported that it was the same man he had spoken to an hour or so before he found it. Travers and I—there is a resemblance; he thought I was Travers . . ."

"How did you know that?" the constable said quickly. "I didn't tell you. The San Francisco police didn't tell me."

"I asked. I telephoned to a friend there who told me. The point is, all this can be very simply and quickly confirmed. In an hour or two at the most you can get in touch with the people in Washington . . ."

The constable said slowly, looking at Sarah, "So it was your husband. He had the box, the jeweler's box."

The trooper said suddenly, "Wait a minute. Didn't they say the park policeman saw him just before he was murdered, with a woman!"

So they knew that, too. Jake's careful omission was detected.

"You!" the constable said. "You were there, too!"

Lisa caught her breath.

Sarah said, "Yes, I was there. Let me tell you . . ."

"Please do," the constable said, with angry sarcasm.

That wasn't a long story, either. She told it, as it had happened. She knew that Jake didn't want her to tell it, and there was nothing else to do. She finished, her voice faltered and stopped, and she didn't know what they believed or didn't believe.

There was a suspicious, thoughtful silence as if they were testing her words, asking themselves whether or not her hand had held a knife. And killed a man.

The constable's eyes shifted to Jake. "You told me she didn't go to the park. You told me . . ."

"I wanted to keep her out of it," Jake said. "It happened exactly as she told you. You'd have known all of it in three more days. Tuesday. Travers asked for a week exactly. By that time whatever they are trying to do will be finished. Now then, there are two men here, somewhere in the vicinity. They were at the house last night. One of them had a revolver and shot at Mrs. Travers—certainly thinking in the dark that she was Travers. She had come out of the house. Here's the bullet." He took the bullet, wrapped in paper, from his pocket. He gave it to the constable. "One of them came in a car. I can give you its description, but I didn't get the license number. There are also two names which may or may not be names of enemy agents. One is Richard Wells; he has been inquiring into Travers' whereabouts."

Sarah interrupted, "He phoned again today. Rose Willman, that's Arthur's secretary, called a few minutes ago. She said to—to look out for him."

"Where is he?" Jake asked quickly.

"That's all she said. She'll phone again." She turned to the constable. "But there is such a man. She'll tell you. And there's another man, Robinson. Arthur knew him! He met Robinson here last week! Lisa told me . . ."

That, too, was news to Jake. He turned quickly to look at Lisa and Lisa said, "I don't know what you're talking about."

Sarah cried, "You said he was here; Arthur came here to meet him! You said . . ."

Lisa shook her head gravely. "I said nothing of the kind."

"You told me that! You can't deny it. You . . ."

"I do deny it. I know nothing of such a man. You are lying again . . ."

The county attorney intervened with a clap of his wrinkled hands. "Now, now—what about this Robinson, Mrs. Travers? Is there any real evidence of such a man?"

Anger made her voice uneven, and, she felt, unconvincing. "He was on the plane I took to San Francisco. He was at the hotel. I think I—I led him to Arthur. I can describe him, I can tell you. He was swarthy and dark; he wore a brown suit . . ." There was no belief in any of the three faces, but she went on. He had stood outside, in the corridor. When she saw him, he'd invited her to have dinner with him; she'd seen him later, in a taxi going in the same direction that Arthur's taxi had taken. He could have murdered Arthur.

She stopped, there was no yielding, no chink in that wall of disbelief.

Lisa said with a grave, shocked air, "Why are they accusing someone else? Why are they trying to make you believe that someone else, some man called Robinson, killed Arthur? I'll tell you why. They murdered Arthur."

The county attorney said in a thin, dry voice, "That is a very serious accusation, young woman."

Lisa cried, "It is a terrible thing! Arthur would have given her a divorce. He'd have let her marry this—this lover of hers. But they wanted his money."

Jake said to the constable, "That is not true. I saw Mrs. Travers for the first time in my life on Tuesday in San Francisco."

Lisa held the young trooper's arm, she looked beseechingly up into his tanned, admiring face. "He drew up a power of attorney for her. Arthur is dead. They could have used this important week he talks about to get money, turn securities into cash. And then escape. Yes, yes, I realize how serious and terrible it is. But what other explanation is there? They have told you a preposterous story. I don't believe it and I don't think . . ." She glanced swiftly around from the constable to the attorney. Her wide gray eyes lingered on the young state trooper. "I don't think that you can possibly believe it."

The admiration deepened in the young trooper's face; his hand tightened on his gun. He said to the constable, "She's right. I'm for arresting them now, both of them. There'll be evidence and we'll get it. But arrest them now."

12

The constable glanced at the county attorney. The county attorney wiped his face with his handkerchief. "We'd better do this so it's all in order. The first thing to do is telephone Washington. Find out whether there's a chance of its being true."

The constable turned the bullet in his broad palm. He said to Jake, "You didn't fire a gun yourself, did you, just to back up this story?"

"No. The shot was very high. I'll show you. It was more like a threat than an attempt at murder."

The trooper was eager, "What about this gardener, this Costellani, that was knifed? Maybe they had to get rid of him. He knew Travers; he wouldn't have been taken in."

"Costellani was murdered before Mrs. Travers and I came to the lake. There's corroborative evidence. Sam Cleetch, the man who came to take his place, says Costellani was not here when he arrived. He came on Monday. We arrived here Wednesday."

The constable said slowly, "You might see if there's a gun in the house, Lieutenant."

Jake said, "Travers had a gun, but it's not here. I looked for it."

The constable turned over the bullet in his hand. Then his dark eyes went to Sarah. "What kind of gun? What calibre . . . ?"

"I—don't know."

Jake said slowly, "He'd have to have a permit. There's a record."

The constable's sagging, suspicious face turned toward the trooper. "If Dixon fired this bullet, the gun's somewhere in the house."

"Or in the lake," the young trooper said obstinately. He was both eager for action and reluctant to retire from the scene. Perhaps he was a little reluctant, too, to leave Lisa; he hovered, torn between action and curiosity. The constable said, "Suppose we go over this again, Travers—I mean, what did you say your name is?"

"James Dixon."

"All right, Dixon. I'd like to get some things straight about this story of yours." He saw the open study door and led the way into the little room. Jake gave Sarah a quick look in which again there was a kind of current of communication. He might have said in so many words, Stick with it, I'm with you whatever it is. The trooper hesitated and then as Lisa followed them into the study, he went, first, upstairs. Sinbad somewhere up there, obviously shut in some room, heard him and gave forth resounding threats which stopped abruptly. Julia probably was in the same room, and had quieted him.

The constable settled himself wearily in the deep red armchair, where Lisa had sat and told what she knew of Robinson—and then denied it. Her reason for denial was clear enough. She had told Sarah of Robinson before it had occurred to her to accuse Sarah and Jake of murder; when she saw the possibility of a demand for money in exchange for her silence, she saw, too, that Robinson might be a suspect and thus threaten the strength of her position. How much of her accusation was sincere, Sarah could not know. It was difficult to believe that any of it was sincere. It was rather a swift and angrily impulsive revenge.

Jake stood beside Sarah; he said quietly, "We'd have told the police the whole thing in three more days. It's better really for it to come out now. Travers didn't foresee Costellani's murder. And the man last night . . ." He looked at the constable. "We need some help. I hope you're going to see to it that we get it."

The constable's heavy-lidded eyes shifted to the attorney who was staring at the rug. The constable said, "Well . . . Let's get this straight. Did you see either of these men you

104

claim were here at the house last night and took a shot at Mrs. Travers?"

"No. One came by car. The other brought a rowboat in to the shore and got away in it." He told them in detail what had happened. There was a little silence when he'd finished. The constable shifted uneasily in the red chair. Finally he said, "What about this power of attorney?"

"It's of no value. It isn't signed. Travers told me to have it ready for his signature, but then, as I told you, I didn't see him again. So it's not signed and it means nothing."

Lisa said in a low, smooth voice, "Arthur's signature could have been imitated."

Unexpectedly Jake grinned. "Forgery is not my line. Constable, you can settle this thing in ten minutes . . ."

"Tell me the whole thing again."

Jake went to the fireplace and leaned his elbow on the mantel. "All right. On Monday afternoon Travers came to my office . . ."

"Wait a minute. When did he go to San Francisco?"

Sarah replied, "Friday night. On the night plane."

"You said that Miss—Miss Bayly said that Travers had come to the lake to meet this man you called Robinson. When was that?"

"She told me it was Thursday last week, before Arthur left."

Lisa said a little too swiftly, "That is not true, either. I didn't say that."

A small but now important incident came to Sarah's mind. The chauffeur of the rented car in which Lisa as well as Arthur had come from New York to the house. She said, "She came here with Arthur. He used a rental car service in New York. The chauffeur would remember both of them; I don't know which driver, but it is the same driver who met me at the plane and brought me up here Wednesday morning, this Wednesday. They'll have the record . . ."

Lisa saw that she had made a mistake. She said smoothly, "I'm sorry, I was thinking of this man, this Robinson. I never told her that. I never heard of him. But yes, I came up to the lake with Mr. Travers. I believe it *was* Thursday of last week. There was no one here. I know nothing about anybody called Robinson."

Jake said, "Costellani was here then, wasn't he?"

Lisa had not replied when Sarah asked her the same question. She said now, after only a second's hesitation, "I don't remember seeing him. Really I don't know."

"You knew him by sight, of course," Jake said.

"Naturally," Lisa said. She added pleasantly, but with guarded cold gray eyes meeting Jake's, "I've been here often as Sarah's guest."

"She wasn't here that Thursday night?" Jake asked, pleasantly, too. And Sarah saw the direction of his questions. He knew the situation between Arthur and Lisa; he knew all of Lisa's claims. But he was leading her to acknowledge something of it herself, and thus to disclose a motive for her direct accusation. It was a better and a more subtle method than to say directly to the police, this woman hates Sarah because she wanted her husband.

Lisa however saw it, too. Her wide eyes narrowed a little. "She wasn't here then, no. And Arthur Travers was a friend. But if you are trying to suggest . . ."

"I'm not trying to suggest anything," Jake changed his position neatly. "I'm asking you directly. Isn't it true that you wished to marry Travers?"

Lisa hesitated for only a second or two, facing Jake then she turned to Sarah. "So that is why you had to murder him. You quarreled with him about me!" She moved toward the old attorney, her blonde head lifted, her voice shaken and sad. "It's true that Arthur—loved me. He wanted Sarah to divorce him. She refused, but Arthur wouldn't give me up. So she . . ." She put both white hands over her face as if in horror. "That was her motive. She wanted this man, this lawyer—but they wanted Arthur's money, too." She seemed to sob. "How could you! Sarah, how could you . . ."

Sarah's own voice sounded too cold, too angry. She knew it and could not change it. "That is not true. Look at me, Lisa. You're not crying! Look at me. Arthur didn't talk to me, ever, about you. We didn't quarrel."

Lisa took her hands from rather bright and tearless eyes. But she said, sadly, "She quarreled with Arthur about me! His love for me cost him his life." She went to the constable and put her hand beseechingly on his arm. "Believe me. Oh, believe me."

"Well," the constable said uncomfortably, "well—exactly what did happen the night you were here with Travers, Miss Bayly?"

His manner was noncommittal. The old county attorney lifted faded blue eyes to survey Lisa.

Lisa recovered promptly enough to reply with some care. "Why, nothing in particular, Constable. We motored up here. We arrived, I think, about six. Perhaps later. We . . ." she invented as smoothly as she spoke, "There was something Mr. Travers wanted from the desk here. I don't know what. I assumed it was some memorandum or letter. He thought that I might enjoy a drive around the lake, he said—he said there were some things he wanted to see to about the house. The chauffeur took me for a drive. When we came back Mr. Travers was ready to leave and we motored back to New York. If I saw the gardener anywhere I don't remember it."

"Did Travers tell you anything of a government errand?"

"He said he was going to San Francisco. However, he said nothing at all of any government request." Her tone implied that no such request had existed.

"Did you see him again before he went to San Francisco?"

"No."

"She had a letter from him," Jake said. "She brought it here. Mrs. Travers read it . . ."

"I had no such letter. They are trying to make you believe . . ."

The county attorney's thin voice cut through Lisa's. "Let's get on with this, Constable. I'd suggest that Dixon go over the entire story again. Let us get some of the facts straight, then telephone to Washington . . ."

Jake said, "When was the letter dated? When was it postmarked?"

"There was no letter!" Lisa flashed.

Sarah said, "I saw it. It was dated Monday. The postmark was San Francisco. I can tell you what he said . . ."

"That is not true!" Lisa's hands were doubled into fists.

Jake said, "She had it in her handbag . . ."

Lisa's eyes gleamed. With a sweeping gesture she took the bag, hanging over her arm, opened it and went to the constable, to the attorney. "You see, there's no letter there!"

"There was a letter," Sarah said. "I'll tell you what he said." She repeated it, as nearly as she could remember it. And met again a kind of wall of skepticism.

The old attorney said dryly, "All right, Dixon. Now, then, let's have this story again."

Jake began, "Monday morning Travers came to my office . . ."

It was the same story. There were no facts to add to it.

"I've told you everything either of us know about it," he finished. "But I think you ought to identify Travers."

The constable said in heavy sarcasm, "Did you think we wouldn't?"

"That's not quite what I mean. You see the man may not in fact be Travers."

There was a sharp silence except for a sudden little beat, like the roll of tiny drums in Sarah's ears. Arthur—alive?

The constable said, "But that policeman, the park policeman! You said he saw you, he saw the murdered man, he said it was the same man because you look like him."

"The light was dim. He could have made a mistake. He was young. He must have been excited when he found the murdered man. He could have been simply mistaken. It's perfectly possible that Travers is now wherever he was sent, accomplishing whatever he was sent to do. Now then—we've told you everything we know. Mrs. Travers has tried to do what Travers asked her to do. There has been some danger. We have a right to demand your co-operation and your assistance."

Lisa cried, "This is a fantastic story. There's not a word of truth in it. . . ."

The attorney rose. "Just a minute, young woman. What's your name and address?"

"My . . ." Lisa paused. In a smooth, polite tone she told him and the constable wrote it with a stub of a pencil pulled from his pocket, in a worn little notebook. The attorney said thoughtfully, "These are troubled times. Stranger things than this have happened."

"Do you believe Dixon?" Lisa cried. "Do you believe her?"

The attorney turned to the constable, "I think we'll inquire into this. It could be true."

Lisa's face was white with anger. "But aren't you going to arrest them? They'll get away, they'll . . ."

The constable said shortly. "They'll not get far." He stopped. A tumult burst like an explosion above them. Wild barks, shouts, screams from Julia, a man's voice, "Stop him —get him—get this dog off . . ." The state trooper broke into wild swearing; Julia above it all could be heard, "*Sinbad —Sinbad . . .*"

There was a deadly and rather significant silence on Sinbad's part. There were thuds and bumps on the stairs. Jake leaped into the hall, and Sarah ran after him. The trooper thumped and sprawled down the stairs with Sinbad thumping after him, hanging onto his leg.

When a Kerry Blue once decides to fight the rest is automatic; he cannot stop.

The constable, Jake and Sarah pulled at Sinbad, while the trooper fought and swore and Sinbad snuffled hideously through his nose and held on. It was Jake at last who got him by the collar and choked and choked until at last Sinbad had to take a gasping breath and the trooper jerked away. Jake dragged Sinbad, threatening violent death and destruction, into the study and closed the door. Sinbad flung himself upon the door.

The trooper got to his feet and examined his leg. The attorney had a very faint smile on his face. He said dryly, "I think you'll live. He got your boot."

The lieutenant was wearing shining leather boots. He straightened up angry, red in the face and puffing, and glanced rather nervously at the door to the study which held under Sinbad's furious charges. "That's a dangerous dog!"

"All right," the constable said. "Did you find a gun?"

"No," the trooper snapped, rubbing his leg. Sinbad's tooth marks showed in the glittering leather. Sarah said, "Are you sure he didn't . . . ? Can I get a doctor to look at it . . . ?"

The trooper gave her a furious glance. "It's lucky I had these boots on. But that dog's dangerous. You have no right to keep . . ."

"I'll help you look for the gun," the constable said. "We'll start here."

"In there!" the trooper demanded, looking at the study. "No, thanks!"

Jake said, "All right, I'll hold him."

It was in the end the old attorney who followed Jake into the study and searched while Jake forcibly restrained Sinbad. The constable and the trooper searched the lower floor of the house.

Julia came halfway down the stairs and stopped, her hand on the bannister, "I'm sorry. Sinbad was in my room. I took him so he wouldn't—but the trooper opened the door suddenly . . ."

"It's all right. His teeth didn't get through."

Julia said slowly, "You've told them?"

"Yes, everything."

Lisa said, "So you are in this too, Miss Halsey. I might

have known it." She turned to Sarah. "I've seen him somewhere before, the lawyer, the man you call Jake." Whatever her motives had been, and her lies had been frank enough, there was a real perplexity about her then. She said slowly as if to herself, "It was when he ran to get the dog. There was something . . ." Without finishing she went out the door. For an instant her chic, lovely figure with its smooth blonde head was outlined against the lengthening shadows over lawn and driveway. Then a car door slammed. Her shining small car swept smoothly past the entrance and out of sight around the circle of the driveway.

Julia came on down the stairs.

It took a long time for the men to search for so small an object as a gun. Jake sat with Sarah in the living room while they searched through drawers and under cushions and behind curtains and through the shelves of books; they searched the pantry and the kitchen and the county attorney came to join Sarah and Julia while the constable and the trooper went upstairs again. "I'm too old for that sort of thing," he said. "Leave it to younger men."

But he questioned Sarah. There were not many questions. His attitude was neither threatening nor credulous; he was polite and gave her time to reply. Had her husband gone on such government missions before? Not that she knew of. Had he told her anything that would lead her to guess at his destination? Nothing. Had she seen either of the men the previous night clearly enough to recognize him if she saw him again? No. Well, he remembered; it had been a dark and overcast night. She had never seen this young man, this lawyer, Dixon, before her husband retained his services? No. Had her husband to her knowledge had any enemy, anyone he had quarreled with? No. And he had given her no specific name, no particular government agency or department? No. She had intended to ask for a name or a telephone number, but then she hadn't seen him again. But he had said definitely a week? Then the supposition was that in that time he would either return or someone representing the agency that had sent him would tell her what had happened? Yes, she had assumed it. All of his questions seemed based upon the premise that the story she and Jake had told them was the true one.

"Why did your husband go to San Francisco?"

"I don't know. I suppose to meet the men, the people who sent him."

"No business conference of any kind?"

"I don't know," she hesitated. "Rose would know. I mean Rose Willman, in his office. She is his secretary."

He asked for Rose's name and the office telephone number and made a note of them in a shabby little red book. He slid the book back into a sagging pocket and then drew it out again. "There must be somebody in San Francisco who could identify Travers. He must have acquaintances there. Who?"

An endless parade of faces and names, half-remembered, across dinner tables, at cocktail parties where she had been Arthur's hostess floated across her memory and there was no one face, no one name that associated itself with San Francisco. She said again, "Rose might know of someone."

"I see." He put the shabby little book in his pocket again and leaned forward, his wrinkled old hands on his bony knees. He said directly, "Mrs. Travers, do you believe that the murdered man in San Francisco is your husband?"

"I—yes. The policeman said . . ."

"I know. But is there any other reason?"

"My husband had named the park as a meeting place. I saw him leave in a taxi and Robinson . . ."

"Yes. But is there anything else, anything conclusive?"

"There was the box. He had given me a bracelet . . ."

"The box from Gump's. The constable told me—yes. Mrs. Travers, will you let me see the bracelet?"

"Certainly." She rose. The bracelet was still in the brown handbag. Where was the handbag? She had carried it into New York with her, and she had put it down somewhere—in the hall, in the study. The attorney unfolded himself stiffly and followed her.

The handbag was on a chair in the hall, beside the door. When she opened it however the bracelet was not there.

13

She searched for it incredulously, digging down into the corners of the big, brown alligator bag, turning it upside down at last over the table, so compact and lipstick and handkerchief, her little engagement book, mirror, small gold-rimmed comb, even a tiny flacon of perfume fell upon the table. There was her billfold; there was her change purse. There was in fact everything but the glittering cool and lovely heap of green.

The bracelet alone had disappeared. There was not much money in her billfold, but so far as she could remember what money there was had not been touched. Sam, summoned at length and tactfully and indeed, kindly, questioned by the old attorney, was obviously innocent and unaware of the bracelet's existence. She had left the handbag on the table, a table in her own home, and no question of the safety of the bracelet had occurred to her.

She replied to their questions. The bracelet had been in the handbag, and during the plane trip to New York it had never been, really, out of her hands. She had taken it with her in to New York that day, but again there had been no conceivable way in which anyone could have stolen the bracelet.

It was the attorney who suggested that one of the furtive visitors at the house during the previous night might have taken it. The trooper snatched it up. "They said this was an enemy agent! Maybe there was somebody all right, but this shows he was only a burglar. Are you going to let them get away with this story of enemy agents?"

Sinbad, behind the study door, heard the threat in his voice and replied savagely in kind. The constable's sallow face had sagged into suspicious but also, Sarah thought, perplexed lines. Jake's eyes were inscrutable, perplexed too, but there was something reserved, something withheld about him. He said however to the constable, "Find this Richard Wells. Find Robinson. Phone the F.B.I. Tell them the whole story. Give them the bullet." He glanced at the young trooper. "I think, except for that, this thing should be kept strictly between us."

The constable said, "That's my business, Dixon."

They had found no gun.

Neither, it developed, had they found a knife.

Sarah had not known until then that they had looked also for a knife which could possibly have been used—by whose hand?—to stab Costellani. She listened with a kind of horror and incredulity while they talked of it; there were kitchen knives, certainly, there were tools in the cottage. "But there's the lake," the trooper said again. "My guess is it's at the bottom of it."

Sam rubbed his hand nervously on his apron.

Finally the constable and the attorney left. The young trooper followed them. The constable said to Jake, "You'll stay here. No need to tell you we could pick you up, like that—" he snapped his fingers—"if you or Mrs. Travers try to get away."

It was late by then; the shadows were long across the lawn when the two men clambered into the constable's car and the trooper shot away with an angry burst of speed in his own car.

Sam said, "I'm sorry about this, Mrs. Travers." He knew by then something of the inquiry. He glanced hesitantly at Jake. "If there's anything I can do, Mr.—Mr. Dixon . . ."

"All right, thanks."

"I'll just get on with dinner then," Sam said and lumbered away.

They drifted back into the living room. The sun was very low by then, streaking through the French windows. The lake was very still, with a few fishermen in rowboats drifting out beyond the willows, but none of them seemed to take an interest in the house. As they talked the boats gradually disappeared; the tiny ripples spread outward as the fish leaped for their evening feeding, flattened out so the lake was a blank sheet of light.

They talked and said only what had already been said. It was all right, Jake told Sarah: she'd had to tell Lisa the truth and it was better for the police to know—they'd have had to know in any circumstances, in only a few days.

But he questioned her minutely about her conversation with Lisa; a remote, thoughtful look came into his eyes as she told of it.

"She tried to blackmail you!" Julia's rocky old face was stern and white with anger.

Jake said slowly, "Why do you suppose she wanted to see Travers today? I expected her to wait for him to make the next move."

There was no answer to that. Sarah remembered Lisa's parting comment. "Lisa said she had seen you somewhere, Jake."

Jake shook his head. "I've never seen her before. I haven't been in New York since last year."

There was no answer, either, to the disappearance of the bracelet. The only intruder had been the man who tiptoed softly through the house the previous night to meet the man

113

who had approached on the lake side of the house, the two of them like the flanking forces of a hidden army surrounding the house. It didn't seem likely that anybody would pause to explore a woman's handbag on a table in the hall. Besides, the hall had been dark; if he had had a flashlight neither Sarah nor Jake had seen it.

"I suppose," Julia said, "that anything they see lying about they'd consider just a—an extra; they don't seem to have much respect for private property." She paused. "Besides, why would he enter the house? It might have been to—to trap you, Jake. The other man was to knock on the door, rouse you; the man inside may have intended to wait in the house and surprise you when you came to the door."

"Ambush?" Jake said. "Maybe . . ."

"But he might have seen the handbag on the table. It's near the window. I think he may simply have decided to—to . . ."

"Make a haul," Jake said.

A little private looting. It was as reasonable an explanation as any.

Again it was a very quiet, still night; again the candles in the dining room stood straight, without a waver, while Sam plodded earnestly around the table. Again they locked up doors, and bolted windows, this time not forgetting the window of the small flower room off the kitchen entry. If anybody, that night, tried to enter the house he would be disappointed; this time they made sure of that. Sinbad investigated dark corners hungrily, as if hoping for a more satisfying chunk of the trooper's leg, as he padded after them. Liebchen, after her one untimely emergence in the role of an accusing witness, had eaten a large meal and retired again to the study.

It was however that night that Jake had his singular interview with a man who called himself Richard Wells. And whoever Richard Wells was, he was not Robinson under another name.

Jake took command; he did not expect the pattern of the previous night to be repeated, he told them, but nevertheless he intended to stay downstairs, on the lookout. Sarah and Julia were to go to bed and try to sleep. He'd keep Sinbad with him; Sinbad would give an alarm if alarm were necessary, which, Jake repeated firmly, he did not expect.

Julia, tired and worn, with ashy shadows around her mouth, obeyed. Eventually, because Jake refused to let her

114

share his lookout, Sarah followed Julia. The night was dark and overcast with a threat of rain in its oppressive stillness. Again from below there was a drifting fragrance of cigarette smoke, or the patter of Sinbad's feet prowling zealously from door to door.

She did not, however, hear Richard Wells's approach; she did hear again, a light yet clear knock at the door below her windows. She ran to the window. Sinbad was growling and snuffling below as if somebody had a tight grip on his collar. Through his frustrated, surging snarls she heard the low murmur of men's voices.

Then the door opened and closed; the murmur of the voices diminished.

Could Jake have let whoever stood there into the house— a man who thought Jake was Arthur? A man who had a gun? She wrapped herself in her dressing gown and ran into the hall; it was lighted. The white steps with their mahogany bannister went down into the lighted hall below. She reached the third or fourth step and heard Jake say, clearly, "What do you want?"

Sinbad gave a choking furious gasp. Liebchen, attracted by voices, waddled to the study door, peered along the hall toward the opposite door and turned tail and went back to crawl under a chair. It struck Sarah as strange, somehow, that the hall below with its rugs and flowers, its lamps and the light chintz cushions on the chairs looked exactly as it always looked, perfectly ordinary, perfectly in order. She could not see either of the men. She heard another voice however, clearly, too—a strange voice, heavy and ugly and somehow rather rusty: "Don't give me that, Travers. You know what I want. Get that dog out of here."

"He'll not go for you," Jake said calmly, "until I let him. Why did you come here?"

There was a little pause. Then the other voice said, rather thoughtfully, "You've changed, Travers. Your fat life is good for you."

"Never mind my fat life. What do you want?"

"You know what I want! I came to tell you that I mean business. Everything Robinson said goes. He warned you."

"I'm willing to talk to you. Let's get this straight . . ."

The heavy, threatening voice seemed to jeer. "Lawyer talk. I've had enough of that. Listen, Travers, there's just one thing you can do and you know it. You think I haven't got a leg to stand on. You think law—your law—will protect you.

115

There's one thing that will end it. A bullet through your heart."

Sarah ran down the steps.

Jake was holding Sinbad who wriggled and rumbled ominously, eyes lambent, every hair menacing. The man facing Jake had a gun in his hand.

He was a tall man with very powerful-looking shoulders, but his flesh seemed to sag thinly over his big frame; his face was thin, too, over a hawky nose and receding chin and gray hair. He wore dungarees and a white shirt open at the base of a corded neck. He was the man who had pulled away from shore, with powerful thrusts of those humped shoulders. She hadn't seen his face clearly—he'd worn sun glasses and a hat—but the shoulders were unmistakable. He shot one bitter glance at her and jerked back toward Jake. "So you're trying to hide behind women. That secretary of yours. Your wife. You think I won't make war on women."

"Please go back upstairs, Sarah." Jake said it very quietly, not looking at her, not taking his eyes for the fraction of an instant from the man facing him.

She didn't move. The big man with the huge shoulders and sunken pallid face said, "Your wife is going to stand by you, Travers. It's more than you deserve."

He wasn't going to shoot. He still held the gun, yet it was somehow a gesture, a threat, but only a threat. She didn't dare look away from his face, yet she was conscious of the bluish-black gun, held in his hand. She thought it had lowered a little. And he was going to say something. If he'd been going to shoot he wouldn't wait to talk, would he? He said, "Does your wife know what you're trying to do? Tell her. She's young and pretty. Ask her if she wants to be a widow."

Jake said, "I want to talk to you. . . ."

The gun gave a small move upward. "There's no need to talk. I'm not going to meet you somewhere else away from your house; there's no use trying to get me to do that. You tried to get away from me. You went to San Francisco and —but it's no use, Travers. You can't get away from me."

Sinbad gave a lunge forward and Jake pulled him back. "Who is Robinson?"

The big man laughed shortly and contemptuously. "He's a buddy of mine. We're in this together."

"Did he kill Costellani?"

116

There was a slight perplexity in the big man's manner. "Costellani?"

"The gardener here. Last week."

There was another slight effect of hesitation. Then the big man said, "I don't know anything about it."

"Did you kill him?"

His eyes flashed. "No! You're not going to get me for a murder rap. You're not going to get me for anything."

"Why did Robinson come here last week to see—me?"

Unexpectedly the big man's shoulders seemed to shake with a kind of repressed laugh. "Because he's a peaceable man. He's afraid of guns. He doesn't like shooting. He wouldn't kill anybody! He thought he could talk to you, make you see it our way. He—" the ugly short laugh stopped—"he knew I'd kill you."

But still the gun didn't move. Still it was a threat.

"Was it Robinson here with you last night?"

"Robinson! Nobody was with me. I came alone. I'm not afraid of you."

"Did you have that gun with you?"

The big man's grin was like a snarl. "I could have killed you then. I heard you come out on the porch. But I aimed high . . ."

"Why?"

"To show you I mean business. Next time . . ."

"Were you in the house last night?"

A gleam of something like hatred shot into the big man's eyes. "I wouldn't be a welcome guest, would I, Travers?"

Jake said coolly, "A bracelet disappeared, a jade bracelet set with . . ."

"I won't settle for a trinket!"

"Are you Richard Wells?"

The gun jerked upward then. Its round black muzzle pointed straight at Jake. Sarah heard her own voice in a whisper that was like a scream. *"Don't! Don't!"*

The big man's eyes flickered toward her; they were blazing with hate. "So you don't want me to shoot him! All right, tell him what he's got to do. If you don't do what I tell you, you won't forget Richard Wells in a hurry. You'll never forget . . ."

Jake jumped for the gun. Wells dragged it away from Jake and Sinbad, let loose, charged upon him. Wells struck savagely at the dog with the gun, missed him and suddenly

117

squirmed out the screened door and slammed it against Sinbad. His pallid face was ghostlike against the blackness beyond. "We've warned you! Next time it'll be too late."

He leaped back and out of the light, across the porch. Sinbad lunged, clawing at the screen. Jake flung toward the door and Sarah caught his arm. "He's got a gun! *Jake* . . ."

There was the crunch of running footsteps down the path. Sarah cried, "Call the police . . ."

"He's not going to shoot. Don't call the police. I've got to ask him . . . Keep Sinbad inside." Jake ran across the porch and, too, disappeared into the impenetrable blackness of the night. She could hear him running along the gravel path. Then both Wells and Jake seemed to have left the path. Suddenly she could hear no footsteps anywhere. There was the slow wash of water below the willows and no other sound.

Jake did not return. Minutes passed. Sinbad whimpered and pushed at her hand and finally settled down with a thud beside her, listening as she was listening for some sound, voices, anything from the night outside. The big house seemed strangely empty; the clock in the hall ticked loudly. Julia must have heard Sinbad's furor. Perhaps she hadn't heard their voices.

Richard Wells. But he had only threatened. If he had intended to shoot, he would have done so then and there. Wouldn't he?

It would be sensible to call the police. Sensible and safe. Jake was their target because Wells obviously thought that he was Arthur. Sometime Arthur had been pointed out to him; somewhere he had seen him or a photograph of him. "Your fat life has been good for you." Bitterly said, grudgingly said, with hatred blazing from Wells's pallid face.

"Robinson is a buddy of mine. We're in this together."

So in one instance at least their suspicion had been fact. Robinson had tried once to coerce Arthur into, as Wells put it, seeing things their way. Failing in this attempt, Robinson had somehow got wind of the meeting in San Francisco, had followed her, thinking she would lead him to Arthur, as she had.

There were things unsaid, implications unspoken, but all too clear. The only puzzling aspect of that short interview was the hatred in Wells's eyes; it was a focused, personal hatred, as if Arthur Travers was a symbol one of the class and kind Wells hated and was determined to destroy.

118

Jake, in Arthur's place, stood now for that hated symbol. He wanted to talk to Wells, alone. Find out, if he could, answers to questions, dangerous answers to dangerous questions. That was why he had told her not to call the police.

State troopers could get to the house in a matter of moments. Jake was wrong; he based too much confidence upon the fact that a man with a gun may not use that gun.

The clock ticked through the silent house. Sinbad lay with his nose at the screen and listened. There was no sound anywhere. She was going to call the state troopers.

First, though, she'd call Sam. Send him to find Jake. Then she'd call the police. Then she'd go to Jake. Wells hadn't shot when she came down and stood beside Jake. Suddenly she thought that a very long time had passed while she stood there, listening to the distant gurgle under the willows, hearing the slow tick of the clock. She ran through the dining room where black windows reflected eerie glimpses of her own white face; she ran through the pantry and into the dark kitchen, and saw from the windows there a remote gleam of light somewhere out in the night. It was a lighted window in the cottage beside the garage.

But Sam was sleeping in the house, in the room above the kitchen. Was Jake out there in the cottage, searching for Wells? There was time and to spare for him to have circled the grounds and entered the gardener's cottage.

As she looked the light went out.

She waited a moment, her hands pressing against the window sill. The light did not come on again; there was only dense blackness everywhere. And it was starting to rain. A few heavy drops tapped upon the window. She felt her way to the kitchen entry and snapped on lights. She called to Sam and he didn't answer. The narrow back stairway led to an upper corridor; the door to Sam's room was at the top of it. She went up the stairway, called Sam and knocked at his door finally, sleepily, Sam replied. He didn't want to get up; he definitely didn't want to venture out into the blackness of the night. She urged. She told him to hurry. At last he said, his voice slow and heavy from sleep, that he'd be down right away. She waited until she heard sounds of motion, then went back down to wait in the lighted kitchen entry. It seemed again a long time before Sam emerged, hair on end, and reluctant, hitching up khaki pants.

And then she had to explain again, and again Sam was reluctant. Eventually he trudged through the kitchen, snapping on lights as he went. They reached the door as Jake came running up on the porch again and into the hall.

"Jake . . ."

Sam relaxed with a sigh.

Jake's shoulders and face were wet with rain. "I found his boat. It's tied at the slip in the boathouse. I can't find him, but he'll come back for his boat. Have you got a flashlight?"

"I'm going to call the police. They'll be here . . ."

"Where's the flashlight?"

Sam woke to life and lumbered to the table at the other end of the hall where they kept flashlights in a drawer. Sarah cried, "But they'll find him, Jake. It'll prove he exists. They'll arrest him. He's an enemy agent. We've got to call them! There was a light in the cottage. He's out there. They'll get him . . ."

Sam pushed a flashlight in Jake's hand. He ran back across the porch again. She whirled around to Sam. "Go with him. Hurry—oh, *hurry* . . ."

Sam hesitated, then went to the fireplace slowly, taking as much time as he could, took the heavy, brass-handled poker in his hand, returned to the door, gave her a reproachful glance, hitched up his pants and finally went out across the porch and, too, vanished into the night. Sinbad growled and thudded after her as she went to the telephone. Jake didn't want the police. He wanted to talk to Wells alone. Jake was wrong.

It seemed to take a long time to rouse the operator. Eventually a distant, drowsy voice answered. "The police—we want the police! This is Mrs. Travers—it's an emergency," Sarah cried. "Hurry . . ."

"The police?"

"The state troopers. Hurry, oh, please hurry . . ."

The girl's voice had quickened. "Yes, Mrs. Travers. Right away—I'll get them there . . ."

She put down the telephone. Julia was coming down the stairs. She had heard Sarah at the telephone. Her face was frightened and white. "What is it? I heard Sinbad, but . . ."

Sarah told her quickly. How long would it take the police to get there? She turned on lights, lights at the front door, lights along the terrace above the driveway. It was raining steadily now, pattering down on the terrace, reflecting the lights. She could see nothing beyond the rain, shot with

120

lights, beyond the glimmering terrace and the blank, empty driveway.

The lights, of course, would warn Wells.

Wherever he was on the grounds he'd see the lights; he'd guess that they had summoned the police. He'd go to the pier for his boat; he'd try to escape. And Jake was down there waiting for him. She snapped out the lights again and ran back along the hall to the opposite door, the door on the porch and the black lake, where Wells would make his escape.

Julia followed her. The rain was turning into a heavy downpour, which sounded like an army marching upon the house, stealthy yet purposeful in the night and then, through the drone of the rain, there was another sound, loud and heavy, rocking the night. It was a revolver shot.

Julia gave a thin, half-scream. Sinbad burst into wild clamor.

Wells had a gun. She had to go to Jake.

Perhaps Julia knew she couldn't stop her. Sarah was dimly aware of Julia crying, "Wait—wait . . ." and of the slam of the door to the coat closet, and of a coat in Julia's hands. Sinbad shot out the door ahead of Sarah and disappeared, barking, toward the boathouse. Somebody was running along the porch from the other end, the kitchen end. It was Sam, panting, waving the poker. "I heard a shot—where . . ."

He was alone. Sarah cried, "Where is he? Where . . ."

"We were at the cottage. We didn't find anybody. He went back to the boathouse—he told me to stay at the cottage . . ."

She was dimly aware of Julia's voice from the porch, behind her. "Go with her, Sam. Hurry—go with her . . ."

Rain fell upon her like an enemy, seeking to obstruct. She couldn't see; the blackness of the night was an enemy, too. Where was the path between the willows? Sam, she thought, was thudding after her—or was it the hard thudding of her own heart? Something brushed her face and she was at the narrow path, willow grown, that led to the boathouse. It was irregular, winding up and down, slippery. The willows seemed to tug at her, telling her to go back. She could see now, dimly, their denser blackness. She knew the path around this heavy thicket and then to the boathouse. She felt gravel again under her feet and the willows seemed to retreat and a dim rectangle of light outlined the door to the boathouse.

Planks rattled as she stepped on the pier. She thought she heard Sam, threshing and blundering through the willows behind her. Sinbad's wild barks off somewhere in the rain and chaos of the night had stopped.

The boathouse was on two levels, a roofed and screened deck above with a little flight of steps leading up to it, and an open slip for boats below. The dim rectangle of light outlined the door to the lower level, at her right. She ran through it. Jake's flashlight streamed out across a rowboat and black, gurgling water, and Jake was leaning over the rowboat at his feet.

Rain drummed down upon the boathouse and upon the lake just beyond the yawning darkness of the open slip. There was a musty smell of dank, wet wood. Jake heard her steps on the little wooden platform that encircled the slip; his flashlight jerked toward her. "*Sarah . . .*"

She pushed the wet strands of hair back from her face. "There was a shot . . ."

"Is Sam there?"

"Yes, he's coming. What . . ."

The flashlight swept in a circle around the boathouse. Its walls were damp, rough wood, with cobwebs which caught the light in an exaggerated tracery of silvery gleams; the water below was black and glanced back lights as it moved and gurgled around two boats, the old utility motorboat and a rowboat, tied snugly in their slips, moving a little with the water. No shadow moved quickly out of sight. Rain beat down on the boathouse and the pier. Jake turned the flashlight down toward another boat at his feet. A third boat, a rowboat, which was tied behind the motorboat, back toward the entrance of the slip.

Then she saw the thing that lay in the rowboat.

It was Richard Wells, huddled down on one side. His great, gaunt shoulders were twisted to one side, his face had now a terrible, an unending pallor. Gradually a spreading patch of wet blackness along his white shirt, below his heart, took on a deeper color.

She was kneeling on the rough wooden platform beside Jake. Jake said, "He's dead. It's murder."

Murder, beat the rain upon the black water beyond. Murder, gurgled the water below them. Murder, whispered the dim shadows of the boathouse.

Jake's hand was on her wrist. It was the only steady thing

in the world. "Go back to the house. Sam will go with you. Call the police."

The musty, cobwebby boathouse steadied a little, too; it ceased to move around her, with cobwebs swaying near.

"Sam will go with you. Call the police. Stay in the house."

She stumbled, getting to her feet and Jake held her. "Hurry!"

"I called the police! Just now—before the shot. I called them . . ."

"All right. *Sam*—" his voice rose and the musty dank walls seemed to hold it and whisper it eerily back again but Sam did not reply. Jake said, "Tell Sam to go to the house with you. Stay there. The police will be there. Send them down here. *Hurry.*"

The sharpness of the command made a demand upon muscles and nerves: it was peremptory, and it was something to do. She was on the pier and planks rattled and rain beat down upon her face. Sam must be somewhere in the murmurous darkness, somewhere among the swaying willows. She was on the path, something brushed her face; her hands groped amid the moving, wet willows with their soft, tentacles, she was running, stumbling, finding her way because she knew the path. Expecting to hear Sam, expecting his lumbering running figure to emerge from the blackness. Sam was not on the path. He had lost himself, she thought vaguely, somewhere amid the confusing, crowding thickets; suddenly those soft wet fingers fell away and she could see lights ahead of her, blocking out the house like a boat at sea, in the night. She ran toward the lights.

Julia was holding the door open. Sam was nowhere. Sinbad, dark as the night, had disappeared, too, become a part of it. The police had not come. Liebchen somewhere was whimpering shrilly. Rain drummed on the porch, and the white pillars gleamed and the rain sent back silvery streaks of reflected lights which made a curtain for the blackness beyond. Where was Sam?

She must send him to the boathouse. Whoever had murdered Wells might still be there, somewhere about the grounds. Jake was their target. She didn't then question why Wells had been shot—Wells, not Jake. She was vaguely aware of Julia's questions and her own answers and of Julia beside her when she turned on lights at the front door again. The driveway and lawn sprang from the blackness. There was a switch which controlled lights over the garage. She touched that too, and the garage and the cottage appeared; the shrubbery made bending, wet black patches, but there was no sight of Sam's running, awkward figure.

She had to go back through the wet blackness of the willows, back to the boathouse. Julia cried, "Don't Sarah —don't . . ."

She was jerking open the drawer of the table, hunting blindly for another flashlight. Julia at the door, peering through the rain screamed suddenly, "*Sam—hurry* . . ."

Sam's shambling, rain-drenched figure jogged into the light, running across the driveway from the woods. "Sam!" Julia called, her voice thin and high above the drum of the rain.

It seemed a long time while they watched him trotting along the driveway, his face wet and white in the lights; he came up on the terrace and into the house, the poker still in his hand. "I got into the woods—I couldn't find . . ."

"He's at the boathouse. Quick, Sam . . ."

Again he didn't want to go. He glanced rather desperately around the house, a haven of shelter and lights. Again eventually he let himself be urged out onto the porch, down off the steps, "He'll never get there," Sarah cried frantically and started after him. Julia had caught up a flashlight and pressed the little button before she thrust it into Sarah's hand. It made a wavering, jerking circle of light spreading out ahead of her, diffused by the rain. Sam saw and waited for her and again Sarah went ahead of him. The flashlight caught silvery gleams from the willows; the boathouse loomed up ahead with its flight of wooden steps clearly outlined in the light. The door to the slip was open, but there was now no light within; it was a black tunnel leading to nowhere. She entered it and turned the flashlight in a quick sweep around the slips. Jake lay flat on the wooden platform. One hand trailed in the water below it. The third rowboat, with its terrible freight, was gone.

Sam was jabbering incoherently, snatching the flashlight from her hand, shooting its rays in nervous glancing circles. She was kneeling on the damp, rough platform, clutching at Jake's wet coat, turning him, pulling up the hand that dangled so helplessly there in the water.

There was a steady pulse in his wrist; he moved a little, moved again in her arms, said something groggily that sounded like, "Where is he . . ." and sat up.

"Jake . . ."

Sam's flashlight had jerked to shine on Jake's face and he winced and put up his hand. "What a wallop!" He felt the back of his head.

"What happened?" Sam cried in a high, quavering voice. "Who did it? Where . . ."

Then Jake saw that the third rowboat was gone. "Give me that light."

Again long rays of light shot out, traveled the boathouse, lingered on the two boats, empty of human presence, softly rocking in the black wash of water below, moved toward the wide black mouth of the slip, caught back gleams of silver from the rain and black emptiness beyond. "What happened?" Sam demanded, squeaking. "What happened?"

"I was leaning over the boat. Trying to find his revolver. Somebody hit me. Have the police come?"

Sam gave a choking gasp. "Who hit you? Where is he?"

Jake was running out to the mouth of the slip, trying to see through the moving curtain of rain.

Sam followed him. The two empty boats moved up and down, up and down.

Nothing really was important except Jake's voice, talking to Sam, explaining to him, Jake's hand moving the flashlight this way and that, Jake's footsteps running past her out into the little cleared space and then up on the pier. Planks rattled. Sam ran after him.

A dead man cannot row a boat. A rowboat, a thing of wood and paint, cannot disappear.

She couldn't stay in the murmurous, haunted blackness of the slip with the empty boats moving and whispering below her. She went out onto the pier. Rain dashed upon her face. Then she saw lights, dancing along the path, shooting upward against the rain. She heard men's voices. The police.

Jake heard them, too; he ran back along the pier, the light jerking ahead of him, the planks rattling. The state trooper, Lieutenant Sharp, came first, a bulky glittering figure in his wet mackintosh. Other men in uniform followed him.

Through the shouts, questions, the shuffling of feet, the drum of the rain, the rattle of the planks below heavy feet, Sarah heard Jake's voice. He wanted one of the troopers to take Mrs. Travers to the house. A man was murdered. Whoever murdered him might still be somewhere in the rain-drenched thickets around them.

A young man, thin and tall with a wet, rosy face detached himself from the others and came to her. He carried a flashlight and courteously held back dripping small branches of willows with their soft, whiplike lash. He left her at the front steps, where Julia stood beside the lighted door, and ran back across the lawn into the path.

There was, then, nothing to do but wait. Wait in the lighted, too empty house, wait while the rain droned down upon it. Julia made Sarah go upstairs, turned on a hot shower, dried Sarah's hair with towels, dropped her drenched, muddy dressing gown and red slippers in a sodden little heap and made her put on warm clothing. Julia dressed, too, and looked oddly neat and self-possessed with her gray hair done up in its smooth French roll and her gray knitted dress and sweater. Julia went into the kitchen and made coffee and made Sarah drink it. Julia lighted the fire which smoked sullenly before it finally caught and blazed, but could not dispel the chill of the house. Eventually one of the troopers came, running, to the house and used the telephone; he went back again down toward the boathouse. Someone had started a motorboat, the old utility boat with its sputtering engine. After what seemed a long time another police car and then another came hurtling through the rain and blackness. More men ran through the rain down toward the pier.

From the door they could see the wavering thin light of the old motorboat chugging along the shore. Some time later another boat appeared, a brighter light, a launch from the village, apparently. It was equipped with a searchlight which sent long beams glancing up and down, back and forth, searching the willows, searching the shoreline. Searching for a rowboat, and a dead man.

After a long time Sinbad returned, emerging like a piece of the night itself, black and dripping. He wanted in. He was wet and muddy and tired and he was also puzzled. He thudded anxiously around the house, going from one room to another, stopping at the doors and windows. Finally he came to the fire and sprawled down on the hearthrug and chewed one foot. Sarah found and extracted a burr. He gave her hand an absent lick and got up to resume his worried, nervous prowl around the house, back and forth. Some time later Sam, too, returned, equally wet and obviously frightened. The police, he said, had sent for more police, and they had got a launch from the village. They had taken out the old utility motorboat, but they couldn't use the speedier launch at the buoy because the engine was still in its winter

126

coat of heavy grease. They hadn't yet found anybody, and they hadn't found the rowboat. He was going to get into dry clothes and make them coffee and sandwiches. He was still clutching the brass-handled poker and took it with him to the kitchen.

The rain drove down steadily. At last a cold gray dawn began to outline deeper black patches of shrubbery, and the fringe of willows began to emerge as a thicker line against the faintly gray area beyond them which was the lake. The lights of the boats circled and circled, disappeared for long intervals and then returned. Men were also searching the woods.

The lake was bleak and gray, the further shore engulfed by rain and invisible, but the willows and the lawn taking on a dismal drenched green, when at last Jake and the constable, the lieutenant and another state trooper came to the house. Sinbad barked furiously when he saw the lieutenant; Sarah dragged him by his collar into the study and shut him in. Jake was white and his black hair was shining with rain; he gave her one troubled, yet somehow reassuring look.

They were all drenched and tired, and the constable and Lieutenant Sharp were angry and suspicious. They had found nothing. There was no rowboat and a rowboat, a cumbersome thing made of wood, cannot vanish. A dead man cannot disappear.

They came to stand before the fire. The constable put his sodden hat on the floor. The lieutenant took his revolver from his wet leather holster, examined it, returned it to the holster, and got out a handkerchief to wipe his shining boots. Julia automatically told Jake to get dry clothes. Sam brought out the enormous platter of sandwiches, his eyes shooting nervously from one to the other; he put it on the low table before the fire and as he went back for coffee, the telephone rang.

Sarah started toward it and the state trooper, Lieutenant Sharp, sprang to action. "I'll get it," he said, his brown young face hard with suspicion, and strode smartly toward the hall, his boots squelching with water. The constable listened; everyone listened. He said, "Yes . . . Yes, well, you can tell me. I'm Lieutenant Sharp. No, no, we haven't found anybody, no rowboat, no murdered man. Nothing . . . Oh . . ." There was a long pause, then he said loudly and clearly and with satisfaction so pronounced that it seemed to ring

127

through the hall, through the long living room and the crackle of fire and the hum of rain outside, "I see. . . . No, he's here, I'll tell him. It's what I suspected from the first."

He came back along the hall; he strode into the living room. His hand was on his gun. He paused with an air of triumph, looking at Jake, looking at Sarah. He spoke, however, to the constable. "That was the county attorney. He had a message from Washington. He told me to tell you Travers was not sent on any mission. They know nothing about it—nothing whatever. So you see—" his bright, suspicious eyes came back to Sarah, to Jake—"it's what I said. They've been lying all the time. They murdered Travers."

14

The fire crackled and shot out sparks. The clear fragrance of coffee floated out from the kitchen.

The lieutenant came a step nearer. "They murdered him. It's as the girl, Miss Bayly, said yesterday. They're trying to get away with his money."

Sarah cried, "But it is true! He told me. It *was* the government! That's why they killed him!"

Jake said, "Have they identified Travers? Until they do, you have no case. There is no evidence implicating Mrs. Travers or me."

Lieutenant Sharp outranked the constable. "There'll be evidence," he snapped. "We'll get that, all right. I'm going to arrest them, Constable."

The constable wiped his thin black hair and sallow face with a muddy handkerchief. He said uncertainly, "I don't know that that's the thing to do."

"Why not?" the lieutenant demanded. Sinbad heard his voice and lunged with a frustrated howl against the study door. The lieutenant glanced rather uneasily over his shoulder, but his hand tightened on his gun. He turned back angrily toward the constable. "They've lied. Travers was not sent anywhere. They've invented this fantastic story for a cover until they can get hold of his money! Dixon had much to gain by Travers' murder. He only needed time. It's all clear . . ."

"What about this man Wells?" the constable said hesitatingly.

The trooper snorted. "Wells! You believe that! I don't. It's another lie. They made it up to provide a—a suspect. Somebody they could blame. He wasn't murdered. The reason we didn't find him, the reason we didn't find a rowboat, is because there wasn't any! Whose word have you got for it? Dixon's and hers! This man—this fellow that works here, Sam —he didn't see any dead man. He didn't see any rowboat. Why? Because there wasn't any."

The constable was suspicious, too; he half-agreed with the lieutenant, he more than half-agreed, but he was too, in a kind of plodding, common-sense way, seeking an answer to his own questions. "What about that bump on Dixon's head? Somebody hit him . . ."

"It didn't kill him, did it? It didn't even hurt him much. He could have given himself a bump like that. The woman —Mrs. Travers—could have done it. Carefully—oh, very carefully," the trooper said, with an ugly grin, "so it wouldn't hurt him much. Who else saw this Wells? Nobody."

It was true. Julia had come down into the hall after he had gone; Sarah had called Sam long after Richard Wells had vanished into the night.

The constable's sallow face was both suspicious and stubborn, "That bullet . . ."

"They shot that bullet—into the house, into the casing of the door, for the same reason. So it would sound real; so it would sound as if it had happened. Nobody except those two claim to have seen this—this Wells. This murdered man! Nobody saw the other fellow they keep talking about. Robinson. Nobody but Mrs. Travers. Why? Because there was no such person."

Jake said very quietly, but thinking hard behind the white, concentrated look in his face. "His name would be on the passenger list of the plane Mrs. Travers took to San Francisco."

The trooper blinked, but recovered. "Sure it might be. She could get hold of a name. There might even have been a man who looks like this man she described. Maybe it gave her the idea. But the rest of it—if you won't make the arrest —I will, Constable. It's my job anyhow . . ."

"Well, well—now, wait a minute. We've got to be careful about this. It's serious . . ."

"Serious," snorted the young trooper. "It's murder! And there's the fellow that murdered him and there's the woman that . . ."

Jake said to the constable. "I'm a lawyer. You cannot charge anybody with Travers' murder until you know he's been murdered."

It dashed the trooper a little. He looked at Jake, looked at the constable, and his wandering glance fell upon the plate of sandwiches near him; he reached down absently, took one and bit into it, largely. But he said, mumbling through the bite, "Hold them now. Arrest them now. Get your evidence—" he swallowed and took another bite—"later."

"You can't," Jake said. "You've got no case. And besides you've forgotten Costellani."

The constable's sallow face jerked toward Jake. Jake said, "It's Costellani's murder that you have to investigate. I was in San Francisco all last week. You don't know exactly when he was murdered, but you do know that it was before Sam got here and after Travers and Lisa Bayly were here at the house. That's between Thursday night and Monday morning. I know that I can provide you with alibis if I need them, to prove to you that I could not have crossed a continent and returned. I'm equally sure that Mrs. Travers could provide alibis for the time of Costellani's death. His murder, of course, may conceivably have no connection with the murder in San Francisco, or with Travers or Wells or any of it. But there could be a connection. It seems reasonable to believe there is."

It stopped them for a moment. The constable shifted uneasily. The lieutenant said at last, derisively, "That's *your* theory! It squares with this story you've fixed up! But the cold fact is that Costellani knew Travers. He'd have given the show away the minute you turned up, posing as Travers . . ." The obvious flaw in his own reasoning struck him then. His voice hesitated and broke off. He gave the constable a guarded glance, and the constable replied to it. "But we believe Costellani *was* murdered last week. If Dixon can furnish alibis . . ." His voice too, trailed into perplexed silence. He wiped his face again and looked hungrily at the sandwiches. Sam came through the dining room and the fragrance of hot coffee preceded him.

Jake said, "So you've got no case, either way you look at it. You can't charge me or Mrs. Travers with Costellani's murder. You can't arrest either of us for Travers' murder when he's not been identified."

The other trooper, with a guarded glance at his superior, shifted nearer the platter and stretched out a hand. He jerked it back however for the lieutenant saw it, stiffened to a sense of authority, swallowed the last of his sandwich with a gulp and snapped, "I'll show you whether we can or not. I'll show you . . ."

"Wait a minute," the constable said. "Maybe you're right, but . . ."

"Certainly I'm right! They've murdered Travers—there's a motive, she'd quarreled with him over Miss Bayly; Travers wanted a divorce, she wouldn't give it to him. Why not? She's got this lawyer here, telling people he's Travers. Why? If she only wanted to get away from Travers and marry Dixon, she'd have agreed to a divorce. Why didn't she? Miss Bayly was right; they want Travers' money. With a power of attorney, they intended to cash in securities, get all the money they can and get away."

"Maybe you're right," the constable said stubbornly, "but I'd like to talk to the county attorney first. I'd like to get the man in San Francisco identified as Travers. I'd like . . ."

"You'd like to give them a chance to get away?"

"No." The constable shook his head gravely. "No—they can't get away. But I'd like to have a solid case."

"That man in San Francisco is Travers. They told you that. Everything points to it, and here's a motive . . ."

"We'll have the identification in a matter of hours. I expected it before now. But I'm in favor of waiting for it."

The lieutenant wavered; he looked hungrily at the sandwiches again, but restrained himself, and squared his wet shoulders and drew himself up with angry dignity. Hunger, however, operated perhaps in their behalf; he wanted and needed his breakfast. He said, "All right, all right. We'll talk to the attorney. But don't try to get away, either of you." He glared fiercely at Sarah and at Jake. "You've got to stay right here, understand?"

He nodded at the other trooper whose hand, again, was stealing irresistibly toward the coffee Sam was pouring. Again the other trooper snapped to attention. "Yes, sir. Yes, Lieutenant . . ."

The constable said nothing, but followed the two troopers. Jake went to the door with them; presently Sarah heard cars starting up, swishing around the driveway and away. There were still men, however, about the place, searching the woods through the rain.

Julia said stiffly, "They said Arthur—they said . . ."

"Yes."

The entire structure had collapsed. The bottom had dropped out. There was no mission.

Sarah went to the window and looked out on the drenched and sullen walk, not seeing it. But from there she couldn't see, either, the frightened knowledge in Julia's white face. She knew as well as Sarah what it meant.

Julia said unsteadily, "Why? Why did Arthur tell you that? Why did he send you and Jake here? Why . . ."

Jake was returning. Sarah turned, and he was walking briskly toward the fire, his head high, his manner cool and confident. He poured himself coffee and took it to the fire and stood there, easily and apparently unperturbed.

Julia's old hands folded and unfolded anxiously. "Jake—what are we going to do?"

"Get at the truth. We've got to."

"I did this," Sarah's voice too was high and uneven. "I dragged you into this. You never really believed Arthur. . . ."

Jake drank some coffee. "I did and I didn't. It sounded logical; it was perfectly possible." He put down his cup and kicked the logs to a stronger blaze. "It's still possible."

"But they said . . ."

"Look at it this way. Suppose Travers was going on a military mission, but as a civilian, naturally. Suppose he was asked to go in an ex-officio capacity. Suppose whoever asked him to go made it as a request, say, a favor. It was to be done secretly; he wasn't to tell anyone about it. If that's true, it might take some time to get in touch with the men who sent him. His name may never have appeared, anywhere. He'd have to have his passport in order and visaed—but it could have been, indeed, it was vital for all that to have been kept strictly within the knowledge of only a few officials. It's possible that there simply hasn't been time to sift it out."

It was possible, of course. A band that seemed to have tightened itself around Sarah's heart relaxed a little. "He said—I'm sure he said that he was flying, under another name."

"Well," Jake said. "There you are. Don't give up the ship yet." He sat down and stretched out his long legs toward the fire.

Julia said slowly, "The F.B.I. does not make mistakes."

"No, they don't. But a thing like this would take some time."

"But suppose it's true! Suppose there was no mission . . ." Sarah began.

Jake looked at her quietly. "We didn't murder Travers, Sarah. The truth exists, somewhere."

"The trooper, the lieutenant said . . ."

"No matter what they say, or what they think, there's no case. Not yet."

"If they identify Arthur . . ."

"Maybe it isn't Travers. I meant that."

"Then—who is the man in San Francisco? Why would Arthur . . . ?"

"Take it easy, Sarah. If Travers was lying there must have been a reason for it. Don't forget Wells and Robinson. If they are not enemy agents, then there must have been some private quarrel, either with Robinson or Wells, or with somebody whom they represented."

The rain beat down upon the porch as if it knew and could tell something of the dark and terrible secret the night had witnessed. The fire sputtered and whispered. Sinbad, relaxed, turned over to stretch his great paws toward the fire and sighed. Richard Wells, now, could never explain anything. Sarah said in a kind of whisper, "Who killed him?"

"If we knew that we'd know the story. One thing, I'm sure that Wells had either known Travers at some time or had seen him, but he hadn't known him well or hadn't seen him for some time. Of course, he could have been shown merely a photograph. But he thought that I was Travers. Another thing is, certainly Travers came up here to meet Robinson. So that definitely links Robinson." He looked at Sarah. "Tell me again everything that Lisa said about Robinson."

There was almost nothing to tell. "She said that she had come here, last week with Arthur. He had come to see Robinson. Later, of course, she denied it, but she was telling the truth at first."

"But she didn't actually see Robinson?"

"She said she didn't. That was before she said that—well, she wouldn't tell the police that you were not Arthur if we—if I saw to it that she was . . ."

"Paid for it," Jake finished. "Why did she come?" He said it thoughtfully, as if questioning himself.

Sarah replied, "I told you. She had read about Costellani She brought the newspaper."

"But she wanted to see Travers?"

"Yes."

"And she tried to blackmail you. I wonder—" Jake said softly—"whether or not she had an idea that she could bring a little pressure on Travers."

"You mean—Arthur murdered Costellani?"

"I didn't say that. Lisa came; she had read about the murder, and she wanted to see Travers. He hadn't phoned her nor tried to see her after she exploded to you. She must have waited, thinking he'd get in touch with her, since she had forced the thing into the open. Then he didn't. She doesn't sound like a woman who gives up easily. She was here the night Robinson was here. Below that smooth manner of hers, she's emotional and impulsive, shrewd in a way—but not very intelligent. If she had been she wouldn't have raged out to put on that act for the police. She'd have gone away to think about it, and she'd have tried to figure some way she could profit. Suppose when she read about Costellani she thought of something she knew which would, say, embarrass Travers. Something he wouldn't have wanted to come out in a murder investigation. Something she could remind him of, delicately, but say, in effect, I'll keep quiet about it, because you're going to marry me. Something like that."

"What?" Julia said, blankly.

"I'd like to find out."

Sarah said, "Lisa wouldn't tell you. She wouldn't tell me . . ."

"She might. If . . ." Jake paused; after a moment he said, "There's another alternative, of course. If Travers *was* murdered, whoever murdered Wells could have done so because Wells knew that he had murdered Travers. Wells's murderer and Travers' murderer could be, might well be the same man. In that case—call him Robinson—in that case Robinson knew that while Wells obviously didn't, tonight, know that Travers had been murdered, Robinson knew that as soon as Wells did discover it, Wells would know, too, that Robinson had murdered him."

Sarah—and Julia erect and ashy-faced in the tall chair, her old hands clutched hard together so the little blue tracery of veins stood out—considered that. Jake got up. "I'm going to change. Wells stayed in this vicinity. He had a rowboat. If the police believed there was such a man they could find out where he was staying and where he got the boat. And that boat's got to be somewhere. Wells's body has got to be somewhere."

Julia said, kneading her hands together, "Could be—I thought of it while they were searching the lake—was there time for the murderer to—the way Costellani . . . ?"

Jake shook his head. "Not enough time. I suggested it to the police. There are concrete blocks back of the boathouse, a little heap of them. But he'd have had to get a rope, fasten the weight, row out into the lake, get the body overboard—and then row somewhere out of sight, scuttle the boat, which wouldn't be easy and would take time, and get away himself before the police got here. Maybe not before they got here, he could have got to some inlet, dragged the boat up into the woods—but it would have taken time to tie a concrete block to the body and get it out into the lake. There simply wasn't time. No—it's somewhere about the lake. It's got to be."

A rowboat, a dead man cannot vanish.

Jake said, "The thing rests with the state police. But the old county attorney seems to have a certain standing. He's reasonable and he listens. The constable and the state police seem to respect his opinion. If I can find any clue to Wells I think he'll listen. I think he'll listen to our side of the thing. I'm going to see him now."

It was still raining when Jake left, taking Sarah's little car, with the top up and rain streaming down the windshield.

After that the house was gloomy and dark. The rain enclosed them like the unending repetition of questions which might have many answers, none of them certain, all of them bringing a whole train of implications, of doubt, of more questions. Once Julia said, trying to knit and merely holding the red yarn in her lap, "How soon do you think we'll hear from San Francisco?"

How soon would they know that the man murdered in the park was Arthur? Or wasn't Arthur? It was another question which had no answer and beat itself over and over again, upon Sarah's consciousness, like the rain. Once, thinking of Lisa, she thought of what Jake had said of her. Emotional and impulsive. Not very intelligent. But shrewd. So shrewd that she had pulled something out of the air, pounced upon it, instinctively. You are in love with this man you call Jake.

It provided the motive for the case against her and against

Jake. It was the entire basis for their case. Suppose it came to a charge of murder. A trial.

The rain stopped about noon, but the sky remained lowering and heavy, reflecting itself in the gray cold lake. Shortly after that Jake returned and Rose Willman came at the same time.

She didn't come with him; she drove up following him in her own small, sleek car—as sleek and neat as Rose. But she had been at the attorney's office. She had driven to the village through the rain from New York that morning to talk to the police; the attorney had wanted to see her, too, and Jake had met her there. She wanted to talk to Sarah.

She took Arthur's chair in the living room. Her small, delicate face was white, her black hair shining and neat below her smart black hat; she wore a black suit, too, with pearls at her slender white throat. Only her red lips and her blazing eyes had color. She was as precisely and sharply efficient, in her own single-minded way, as a small steel blade.

She wasted no time in coming to the point. "The police telephoned to me last night. They wanted me to provide identification for the chief. I was able to give them a name —John Evers; he lives in San Francisco. He knew the chief well." She looked at Sarah, her eyes so unexpectedly passionate in her small dead-white face, and smoothed her neat skirt over her knees. "I think I ought to tell you, Sarah, what I've told the police. This story of a power of attorney is completely false. The chief would never have given you a power of attorney. I know."

Jake was standing before the fire, looking down at Rose. He offered her a cigarette which she refused with one move of her small hand. He said, "Tell Sarah why you say that."

Fire flashed deeply in her eyes. "Because it proves that you and Sarah have lied." There was also a kind of triumph about her. At last she was vindicated; at last it was proved, even if too late, that Arthur's marriage to Sarah had been tragically, terribly wrong.

Jake said, "That's your opinion."

"I *know*," Rose said again. "I know about the chief's will. I've seen it. I'll put it plainly. He knew—he said to me—that Sarah is utterly unable to deal with business affairs. He wished the business that he built up to go on, in the event of his death, automatically. So she could not change it. So she could not touch more than an income which—" her voice caught then—"which he provided. He would never have

136

given her the wide powers of a power of attorney. I've told the police because it was my duty to do so. You've done a wicked, a terrible thing. You did it for money and for this—" her passionate eyes went to Jake "—this man. I came to tell you that. You may as well confess. I'll never give up until you've paid for this." Her voice shook a little then, and hatred blazed from those vehement, feverish eyes.

15

Jake was watching her curiously. He said evenly, "The power of attorney was not signed."

"That would be easy. Copy his signature. Sarah knows it. She would have been able to copy it. Unless—" her eyes shifted to Jake—"unless that was part of your share in this."

Julia cried, shocked, "Rose, Rose, how can you! You know that this is not true. You know Sarah would not . . ."

Rose stood as precisely as if every muscle had its own special message of control from that active, implacable mind. "You wanted her to marry him. She did everything she could to trap him into marriage. He was taken in by that schoolgirl face, that air of honesty. I saw it. I couldn't stop it but I knew. That's in the past. I've waited a long time. I knew that some time the chief would see, sometime he would . . . But I didn't dream of—" she turned her small, deadly white face to Sarah and said—"murder. I can't bring him back. But I'm going to make you pay for it. That's all I came to say."

"Wait," Jake said. "Do you mind answering a few questions?"

"I'll answer anything you like. And I'll answer anything the police want to know."

"Did you know of a man calling himself Robinson?"

"Why?"

"Travers met him. Here. Last week. Did he tell you that he was to meet him? Did you make the appointment?"

"No."

"What about Wells? Did you tell the police that he had talked to you? Did you tell them that his attitude was so threatening that you told Sarah to tell Travers? Did you tell them that you talked to him again yesterday and phoned here, then, urgently warning her to tell Travers to look out?"

For the first time a kind of flicker went over Rose's face. "I told them a man calling himself Wells had telephoned once or twice. Yes."

"What did he say yesterday? What were you afraid he would do?"

She hesitated, but only for an instant. "He asked for the chief. I didn't like his manner. That was all."

"What did he say? Did he threaten Travers?"

"I've told you everything I know."

Jake waited a moment. Then he said quietly, "Did you know that Lisa Bayly intended to marry Travers?"

For a second Rose's precise control slipped. Her small, sleek hand seemed to move forward a little. "Lisa! He wouldn't have married her!"

"That's what she claims."

Rose's long velvety eyelashes shaded her eyes. "I don't believe it," she said at last.

"Well, then. You've seen his will. Who inherits?"

Rose's eyelashes lifted. "His wife! But she'll not get it now! I'll see to that."

She turned and Jake made a quick stride toward her. He caught her little steely wrist and whirled her around. "Who else inherits? Lisa?"

"Lisa!" It was as scornful as an agile little snake sure of the deadly poison of its own venom. "No!"

Jake said quietly, "Do you?"

She was breathing hard. That and the passion of hatred in her eyes were the only signs of emotion. "I'll not tell you. What is it to you? You have no right to ask."

"You do inherit from him, then. How much? You may as well answer. The will has to be probated; there are ways to learn exactly what it provides. How much does his death mean to you?"

A sudden and dreadful change shook Rose. She gave a long, quivering sigh. She leaned back against the table, both hands flat upon it. Her mouth so red, so frankly patterned upon her small white face, made a fumbling motion. "His life meant everything to me. It was my life, too."

"Rose!" Sarah started forward. It was nothing less than the truth.

But Rose drew away. "Don't touch me. How dare you stand here in Arthur's house, you were Arthur's wife—how dare you come here with *him?* You had the chief, but no, it

138

wasn't enough. You wanted—" her eyes blazed at Jake—"you wanted *him*."

"Rose, you must believe me. Arthur told me he was going on a trip. He told me . . ."

Rose straightened her hat, and she turned toward the door.

Jake said, "Wait. You said you'd answer any question. Did you know that Travers had been asked to make this trip?"

"There was no such mission. The police told me."

"He was an expert. His advice was sought by various people interested in the oil industry. Wasn't it?"

Her eyes flashed. "Certainly."

"So it would not be unlikely that it would be sought by government officials too."

"Not unlikely. Everybody knew that he was a great man. Everybody knew . . ." She caught herself. "But he would have told me if he intended to make such a journey. He told me everything." She looked at Sarah. "I've said what I came to say. You're in love with this man. Which of you murdered Arthur, I don't know. Which of you thought of this scheme, I don't know. Your lover, probably. But you fell in with it. You are as guilty as he is. You . . ."

Jake said, in a voice that was suddenly as deadly and implacable as Rose Willman's, "Have you an alibi for the time when Travers was murdered?"

Rose flashed toward him. She caught a rasping breath.

"You knew of the provisions of his will. Sarah didn't. Probably you inherit a large sum. Have you an alibi?"

Her lips had drawn back from even, very small teeth. "I didn't murder him!"

"Can you prove that?"

Her agile mind had had time to operate smoothly as was its custom. She lifted her little black head. "I am not suspected of murder. I don't have to prove anything. But you—" she looked at Jake, she looked at Julia, her eyes swept to Sarah and lingered—"you killed him. And I'll help them prove it." She turned, every muscle again under control. She started toward the hall.

Sarah went after her. "Rose—Rose, you must listen. Rose . . ."

There was no sign that she heard Sarah. Her small, sleek black figure turned into the hall; there was the precise tap of heels toward the door. Sarah cried, "*Rose . . .*" and followed her and Jake said quietly, "Don't Sarah. It's no use."

The front door closed as neatly and precisely as if Arthur himself had closed it. Jake said, "She's hysterical. Don't let it worry you, Sarah."

Julia's ashy face looked pinched and stricken. "Do you really think she might have had something to do with Arthur's murder?"

Jake shook his head. "You can never be sure of what a nature like that will do or won't do. She's got too tight a control; she's got the makings of a genuine hysteric. But—no, I don't think she murdered him. I thought I might be able to shock her into common sense."

Sarah said unsteadily, "She was devoted to Arthur. He really was her life."

Jake lighted another cigarette. "Yes, I think she was. In a way that Lisa could not possibly comprehend. Lisa frankly wanted his money; she wanted to be Mrs. Arthur Travers and she was determined to get her way. But this woman is heartbroken. And dangerous."

"Did she tell all that to the attorney? Did you hear her?" Julia asked.

"Oh, yes. She arrived as I was leaving. I waited. I don't think it counted for too much; her own state of mind discounted her accusation. The business of the power of attorney was the important thing. It would have its weight in —well, in a trial."

There was an instant's silence during which all sorts of pictures suddenly conjured themselves against the rosy glow of the fire. Jake said rather too quickly, "I don't think it will come to that. I do think that Rose Willman knows something. And Lisa. The problem is to get one of them to tell it. If I could work one of them against the other . . ." He paused and thought and said slowly, "But I don't see how."

Julia sighed. "They both hate Sarah. Lisa"—her lips were tight—"Lisa wanted him for his money. She's been after him a long time. I've seen it. Rose is sincerely devoted to him; she has always been that. But both of them—" her faded blue eyes went to Sarah—"both of them hate Sarah because she was his wife."

Jake said soberly, "I think Rose's statement about the power of attorney in fact is more damning than all of Lisa's accusations. Lisa introduced a motive. . . ." He went to the fire and shook ashes off his cigarette, and thus did not look at Sarah when he talked of the motive both women had hurled at him and at Sarah. Your lover, Rose had said. She's

140

in love with him, with Dixon, Lisa had cried. Jake said, "Lisa suggested a motive and a purpose to the police. But it would be easy enough to prove, in fact, I think they saw for themselves that Lisa wanted Travers, so they would take her statements at something less than their content. But Rose and the power of attorney—that's different. I told the county attorney everything Wells said last night, details, everything. The fact is, of course, Wells's threats could be taken two ways—as a personal threat to Travers, or as a threat under orders to stop Travers. He could have been an enemy agent —or he could have been an enemy of Travers. Certainly he thought I was Travers. The only other fact that Wells admitted was his conversation with Robinson. It explained Robinson's meeting Travers here and following him to San Francisco. And Wells admitted that he shot high, into the door, merely to scare Travers. The county attorney listened. He was reasonable and patient about it. I don't know how much he believed. But he did seem to think it possible that Travers had been sent in a sort of private-citizen, ex-officio capacity, and that they hadn't yet managed to reach the men who sent him. He also seemed to think that there was sufficient reason for the police to make a minute search of the vicinity on the chance of finding some sort of evidence about Wells. Also, he said, they are inquiring about the rowboat. So that's promising. I think they'll find something if they really look for it." He came to Sarah, "I'm going to take a look myself. If I can find even partial proof that Wells was staying somewhere near, somewhere so he had access to the lake and the house it would—" his mouth tightened—"it would help. You know the lake. Will you come with me?"

Three hours later they found it, but it was as Jake had said, only partial proof, for there was nothing certain, nothing that could be proved to have belonged to Wells or to anyone, nothing that could be taken to the police and put down on a table to provide positive substantial testimony to the fact of Wells's presence. To Jake and Sarah it was both promising and disappointing. Its only value was a negative one, for if anything in the nature of a clue had existed, it had been removed.

They found a fishing shack where Wells might have stayed.

It was on the other side of the lake, in a wooded cove on the very edge of the water, almost directly across from the Travers house. The wooded shore jutted out to a point and from the rocks below the fishing shack there was a distant view of the long white house and pier, and the willows around the boathouse—not a clear view that gray, overcast day, but a view. From that point, it was perhaps a long mile across the lake to the Travers house.

The lake was irregular, curving in and out in generally a half-moon shape. There was a public highway, curving in and out too, sometimes close to the lake shore, sometimes winding at some distance from it, but completely encircling the lake. Most of the summer houses, with their generous grounds, lay on the south side of the lake, which was the outer rim of the half-moon, and the side which was the more likely to receive the cool northern breeze. Saguache Village lay at the head of the lake, which was one point of the half moon; a smaller cluster of summer cottages, a filling station and a grocery store, marked the opposite, lower tip of the half moon, and the shorter half-circle was wilder, less regular in outline, wooded for the most part down to the water's edge and dotted mainly and sparsely with small cottages and fishing shacks. The woman at the little grocery store gave them their first information.

That was after they had driven to Saguache Village and inquired but without much hope at the rambling summer hotel—where no Richard Wells had stayed—and at the two motor courts on the main highway leading into the village with again no results. It was after they had driven, slowly, all along the south side of the lake, passing one summer place after another, stopping occasionally to inquire whether any guest house or caretaker's cottage had been let. Sarah knew some of the summer residents, not, actually, many of them, but she knew in a general way the arrangement of the various grounds, who might have let a guest house or had one to let. Usually by that time most of the summer people had arrived at the lake. That summer had been cold and started late and many of the houses were not yet occupied. As it happened, she saw no one she knew. And there was no clue or suggestion of Richard Wells. Yet, Jake argued, he must have stayed somewhere not far from the house. A rowboat is neither a swift nor particularly easy method of transport.

And then, when they stopped at the little grocery store and a pleasant-faced woman came bustling from the living rooms at the back of it she knew of the fishing shack. She knew, when Jake asked her, that a rowboat went with the shack. She knew, too, that they were not the first to inquire about it.

142

"Yes, there's a man staying there. He rented it a few days ago from Mrs. Penick—she owns it—and he paid her cash in advance. But she doesn't know his name. I asked her yesterday after a woman came to inquire about him." There was a bright curiosity in her face. "What's he done?"

A woman. Lisa? But when Jake tried to get a description of either of them the friendly little woman shook her head. "It was about noon. There were several people in the store, and my husband talked to her and told her where the shack is."

"Can I talk to your husband?"

She was sorry; her husband had gone to Albany. He wouldn't return till late that night. And she didn't think he'd remember anyway. "So many tourists stop about noon. We're not far from the main highway, you know."

She gave them directions to the shack.

In the car again Sarah said, "Lisa?"

"If she inquired simply for the shack, sounds as if she had some sort of appointment with Wells."

"Why?" Sarah asked.

They found the fishing shack with no difficulty, for the "For Rent" sign was still at the entrance of the narrow track that led through the woods, winding down to the lake. And to the shack.

But there was nothing in the one-room shack that could testify to Richard Wells's short tenancy. There were a few groceries on the table, and someone had slept in the cot at the other side of the barely furnished room. The blankets were thrown back. Someone had started a fire which had smoldered and gone out, in the round black heating stove. There were no clothes, anywhere, and no razor or soap, no papers, not even the remains of cigarettes in the ash trays. And someone had been there before them.

Jake was sure of that. "He'd have had a razor, he'd have had something in the way of shirts. Somebody got here ahead of us." He searched then for evidences of that previous search and the only evidence was a smear of mud and some diffused damp patches around the door—which were too smeared, too blurred in outline to be called footprints.

"The only thing certain is that somebody came here after the rain began. The woman inquired at the store around noon. She could have returned."

"After he was murdered?" Sarah asked, half-whispering. "Maybe."

143

It was a gloomy, dark little shack, cold that day, with an air of desolation that seemed, somehow, sinister. There was the faint odor of kerosene from the little oil stove, and the musty, dank smell of old wood, closed and unaired. Jake examined the fire that had been started in the heating stove and there were only old newspapers, half-burned, kindling and a little coal which had not caught fire.

But when they left the shack and went down to the lake there was no rowboat. That, too, however, was only a negative piece of evidence. There was a cleared strip at the edge of the water around some piling where a boat could have been drawn up and tied. Jake searched through the thick growth along the shore while Sarah waited. It began to rain again as he searched. Perhaps neither of them wanted to go into the musty and gloomy little shack for shelter. Jake found no rowboat. He came back and they got into the car and backed and turned and backed again and followed the narrow little track out to the highway.

It was something, but it wasn't enough. A man who might have been Richard Wells had rented the shack for a week. A man who might have been Richard Wells had taken out the rowboat.

"Fingerprints?" Sarah suggested, watching the windshield wipers swish through the little streams of rain—and then she realized that, of course, fingerprints would provide no evidence, either.

"If the police find Wells's body . . . But it may not have been Wells. It may be somebody out in the rowboat fishing, right now."

"In this weather?"

There was no answer—no answer to anything, she thought. The rain stopped again as they drove along the woods road toward home and through the wide gates. This time the driveway was wet and deserted. There was a trail of blue wood smoke from the great chimney above the living room.

It was then nearly dusk. No one had telephoned, Julia told them. No one had come. The men searching the woods had given up long ago. The lake stretched out into the increasing twilight with no launches, no motorboats continuing what was obviously going to be a more and more perfunctory search for a man the police did not believe had been murdered, a rowboat in which they had still less belief.

They told Julia all there was to tell. The two women listened while Jake telephoned to the old attorney. It was a short conversation and not a promising one. "He says they'll take a look at the shack in the morning. They'll talk to the man in the grocery store, and question him about the woman . . . It may come to nothing."

Julia said bleakly, "Have they heard from the—from San Francisco? Have they identified Arthur?"

Jake shook his head. "If he knew he didn't tell me."

They were tired and conquered by the chill discouragement that sheer fatigue induces. Julia made them go to the fire in the living room and brought a tray with glasses and whisky and soda. Then wearily, every line of her usually indomitable figure sagging, she went upstairs. Sinbad greeted them wearily, too, and sprawled down on the hearthrug again.

Sarah stretched out her cold hands to the fire. Her brown moccasins were wet and muddy from the path around the deserted, sinister little shack. Her suede jacket was damp, with wet patches over the shoulders. She still wore the tweed skirt and sweater she had snatched up long ago, in the night before that cold, gray day had dawned. She brushed back her hair, tousled and damp too, and held out her hands again toward the fire. Jake said behind her, "Let me take your jacket." He drew it gently from her shoulders. He took her hand and pulled the sleeve from it, and then dropped the coat and took her in his arms.

"Sarah." His face was warm against her own. "Sarah . . ." The fire cracked and sighed. He moved her face a little and kissed her. And then held her in his arms, close so he could look down into her eyes. "I don't know how it happened. I don't know when. But you—I love you, Sarah."

Away off somewhere Liebchen burst into shrill, excited little yelps.

Jake's arms made a barrier against all other worlds. He said, "It didn't happen at first. I've never believed in love at first sight or all that. I think I felt just at first—I don't know —sorry for you. I don't know why. You—but then you got between me and everything else. The fact that you were his wife—the fact that you had never so much as seen me before. You got between me and common sense and—you can't love me. I couldn't expect you to love me. But I . . ."

As if she had known it all her life she said, "I do love you."

One of the French windows opened. Sinbad clambered to

his feet with a startled bark. A cold damp current of air sifted across the room. She looked, then. Arthur was standing just inside the French window.

He was standing there quietly, thin and tall in his suavely tailored brown suit, his narrow face immobile, except for a thin, queer smile.

16

Jake's arms held her hard.

Arthur came into the room with delicate, catlike steps that were so typical of Arthur that reality seemed to walk with him—it *was* Arthur.

Jake's arms moved slowly, away from her, so they stood apart.

"Arthur . . ." Sarah's hands reached for the chair near her and held to it. "Arthur, they said . . ."

The faint smile was fixed on Arthur's narrow face; his eyes were hazy and soft—and angry. "What did they say? Aren't you glad to see me, Sarah?"

Jake's voice seemed to come from far away. "Some things have happened, Travers. You'd better know. . . ."

Arthur stood very still. "Yes, I think you'd better tell me." His hazy eyes shifted once to Sarah and then back to Jake.

Jake's black head lifted so his chin looked square and formidable. "Sarah and I—you'll have to know that, too. They told us—the police in San Francisco told us that you had been killed."

"An overstatement." Arthur lifted his arched black eyebrows.

"There's more than that. A man was murdered here last night. His name was Richard Wells."

Arthur never showed surprise; only the arch of his eyebrows, the fixity of his smile witnessed it then. "Here? Where were you when it happened?"

It struck Sarah, queerly, as the wrong question, yet Arthur was never predictable. Jake replied, "We found him. Who was he?"

Arthur shrugged. "I don't know. Did you call the police?"

"Yes. Wells came to see you, Travers. I talked to him."

Arthur said, "Who shot him?"

"I don't know. He knew you."

"Wells knew me! Impossible!"

"He talked to me," Jake said slowly. "He thought I was you. He made threats . . ."

"If he thought you were me, he couldn't have known me very well. Wait, though—I suppose he was one of the men who tried to stop me. He could have called himself by any name. What do the police think about it? They didn't accuse you of shooting him, did they? Surely if you and Sarah were here at the time you'd have a—well, an alibi, wouldn't you?"

"As a matter of fact," Jake said slowly, "I don't have."

"You don't—weren't you here, in the house with Sarah when he was killed?"

"I was looking for Wells. I was going to the pier actually when I heard the shot."

There was a long pause. Then Arthur said, "That's rather bad for you, isn't it? I wouldn't like you to get into any serious trouble, Dixon, you understand that. I employed you. I feel a responsibility. Although," his eyes shifted dreamily to Sarah, "I rather think you have exceeded your duties. But—do the police think you had shot this man?"

"By the time the police got here Wells was gone."

"I don't understand . . ."

"I'll tell you. It's rather a long story. I'll begin at the beginning."

"Yes," Arthur said, "that might be an excellent plan. Just why did you think that I was . . ." He made a delicate motion with his narrow shoulders, went to the table, poured himself a drink, and went to settle himself in his lounge chair; he looked up at Jake. "Why did you think that I had been killed?"

As Jake told it, marshaling the facts in swift order, it was not in fact a long story. Yet it seemed to carry Sarah back to some very distant point in time, when the buzzer had sounded at the door of a hotel suite and when she opened the door and Jake—so like and so very unlike Arthur—had walked into the room. Back to San Francisco, back to a blue twilight, back to a shadowy little park and a policeman who had strolled past and asked Jake what time it was and had a glimpse of his face. Not a distinct glimpse.

147

"Obviously," Arthur said, "he made a mistake."

"There was also a box found near the body. A jeweler's box from Gump's."

Arthur's eyebrows lifted. "From Gump's? I gave Sarah a bracelet." He laughed noiselessly. "So you thought I'd been murdered! No, no, not at all, as you see. The fact is, I had to leave at once. Everything was ready. I couldn't meet you in the park as I planned. I couldn't—" he glanced at Sarah—"I couldn't even allow myself the pleasure of saying good-bye to my wife. I had to go direct to the plane that was waiting for me."

Sarah said unevenly, "Where did you go, Arthur? What was it . . . ?"

"I can't tell you yet. But I may say this, I accomplished the thing I was asked to do. Not without some honor to your husband, my dear. I returned this afternoon, taxied from the station, saw the smoke from the fire here and thought I'd give you a—a pleasant surprise. I didn't expect—however, we'll talk of that later." He sipped from the glass in his narrow elegant hand and smiled at Jake. "Do go on. So you thought I had been murdered."

"Somebody was murdered," Jake said shortly. "In the park. At about the time we were to meet there."

"I gather that there's been no identification of the murdered man."

"No."

Arthur's black eyebrows went up in a slender arch. "Ah, well—some stray. Some thief probably, if he had a box from Gump's. I hope you have followed my instructions about this thing." He leaned forward suddenly, his face alert and cold. "You have not broken the promise you gave me, Sarah. You were not to tell people of this mission . . ."

Jake said, "As a matter of fact we have. The police investigated, they got in touch with Washington. The report was that you were not sent on any mission at all."

The smile was fixed upon Arthur's face. His hazy eyes met Sarah's, and he said after a moment, very softly, "I told you not to tell this. You promised me . . ."

Jake said, "She had to tell it. A friend of yours, Lisa Bayly, came here. She came to see you. The police were here at the time. They didn't find Wells's body last night, but they did see Costellani's."

"Costellani?" There was something cold yet perfunctory in the question.

"I thought," Jake said rather deliberately, "that you might have seen a newspaper."

"No, I—didn't . . . What are you talking about?" Arthur was angry. Sarah knew those hidden signs of anger, the white dents around his mouth, the complete immobility of his head. But he was poised, too, and alert, listening. This time he did not question or interrupt. He did not so much as look at Sarah. Sinbad came and pressed his head down rather anxiously on Sarah's knee and watched Arthur, and Jake's voice went on, deliberately yet concisely, too.

Costellani had been murdered some time during the previous week. A weight tied to his body had worn through the rope during a storm, and the body had washed in to shore. Jake had, during the following police investigation posed as Arthur; no one had questioned it. And then Lisa had come. Jake's voice became even more remote and impersonal, merely stating facts. Lisa had come once before and had gone; this time she had read of Costellani's murder and had come and insisted upon seeing Arthur. So there was nothing to do but tell her the truth. And she had—here Jake hesitated briefly, but continued—she had offered to keep quiet about the masquerade if it was made worth her while to do so. Sarah had refused. Lisa had accused Jake and Sarah of Arthur's murder.

The deadly anger lay still and cold behind Arthur's dreamy eyes, but he smiled a little. "So Lisa said you had murdered me. Why? Oh, obviously because you and Sarah . . ." he chuckled softly.

Jake said flatly, "Her object in coming was to tell Sarah that you had promised to divorce Sarah and marry her. Consequently she was in rather an emotional state."

"So Lisa told you that! Nonsense, of course. I hope you didn't believe her, Sarah."

"Lisa also told Sarah that she had come up here with you last week to meet a man by the name of Robinson. A man Sarah later saw in San Francisco . . ."

"I never heard of him. Lisa is not, as you have already noticed, a very reliable reporter."

"There was a corroborative witness," Jake said. "I talked to Wells. He said that Robinson came here to see you."

"Wells!" Arthur said skeptically and lifted his glass.

"Wells was here, make no mistake about that. Wells and another man."

"Another man! Did you see him?"

"He was here," Jake said shortly. "This is what happened . . ." Two visitors during the night, a shot into the door above Sarah's head.

"Obviously enemy agents." Arthur shrugged.

Wells's second visit, his threats, his murder; the body and rowboat had disappeared. The police had found neither.

"A rather odd set of circumstances," Arthur said softly. "I can see why the police are a little skeptical. I take it you believe this Robinson you talk of killed him."

"Someone else was here. He was in the house. Who is Robinson?"

"I'm sure I don't know, I told you that. One of them, I suppose."

"Lisa . . ."

"Lisa simply wanted to make trouble." The words were gentle and deadly. Suddenly Sarah thought, He'll make Lisa pay for this. Arthur said, "So Costellani was killed! Was there a burglary? Was that why . . ."

Jake said slowly, "There was no burglary at the time Costellani was murdered. There was what could be called a burglary the night before last. Whoever was in the house appears to have taken the bracelet you gave Sarah."

"Really!" Arthur sat up. "Why then it must have been attempted burglary last week. Costellani got in the way and was killed, and the burglar returned. You ought not to have been so careless with the bracelet, Sarah. It was a rather costly trinket to leave lying about. So everything has gone wrong. I asked for secrecy; you have apparently taken the whole world into your confidence. Lisa, the village police . . ."

"Also the state troopers," Jake said.

A flicker of annoyance crossed Arthur's face. "Troopers, too. I suppose they've been as ubiquitous as flies."

"They've been doing what they are paid to do."

Arthur said with an edge, "Newspapers, too?"

"Costellani's murder hasn't been much of a story. At least —not yet."

Arthur's eyebrows lifted. "If a foreign agent killed him it was because he was after me. But it's much more likely it was attempted burglary, and Costellani got in the way, the burglar returned . . ."

"I don't think he killed Wells."

"Wells. Yes, Wells. It's rather curious that they can't find him. They have no—what's the term?—no *corpus delicti.*

Your whole story of Wells must be a little difficult for them to swallow. So the village constabulary, the state troopers . . ."

"And the F.B.I.," Jake said. "Who report that you were sent on no government errand whatever."

Arthur lifted his glass again, sipped from it and said easily, "They didn't get hold of the right men. I went in an unofficial capacity, naturally. And very secretly. I'll tell them the facts now. It's all over and—as I told you, Sarah, not without some honor to me. However, I seem to have returned at the right moment to get you out of rather a mess, Dixon. I'll fix it up immediately with the police." He looked at Sarah and said softly, with that implacable anger hidden. "You found consolation in your widowhood rather soon, my dear. However, I suppose that was to be expected. But in the circumstances—" his dreamy, secretly angry eyes went to Jake— "in the circumstances," he said softly, "you'll want to leave my house at once. Frankly, I want you to get out."

Jake stood square and solid before the fire. "I'm going to talk to you about that, Travers. I don't know how Sarah feels about me. But I—love her and I want to marry her."

There was a silence. Sinbad shifted his head restlessly on Sarah's knee and watched Arthur. Arthur leaned back slowly, smiling again, sipping his drink. "Suppose I didn't suggest a power of attorney, Dixon. Suppose that was your idea."

Jake took a sudden step forward. "That's a lie."

"Perhaps. But if you persist in this—very unlikely course, it's what I'll tell the police. If I had been killed, as you so cheerfully assumed, my wife would have been a very rich woman. It doesn't have a nice sound, does it? A young attorney employed for certain duties, drawing up a power of attorney for my wife—making love to my wife! No—I think you'd better take your pay and leave."

Sam had opened the pantry door. Liebchen shot through the dining room, her little feet eager and sliding on the floors. She got to Arthur and tried to climb onto his lap, wriggling and panting in delight.

Arthur pushed her away with an impatient thrust. He rose. Sam had followed Liebchen. He said, "Mrs. Travers, dinner is . . ." and stopped and goggled at Arthur.

Sarah heard her own voice, "This is Mr. Travers, Sam. He has come home. Is dinner ready? Tell Miss Halsey . . ."

Arthur said, "Is that the new man?"

Sam lumbered toward the hall. Arthur added, "Did *he* see

151

this Wells you talk about? Was he here when the shot was fired?"

"If you mean was he an alibi for me; no, he wasn't. But there was such a man, and he was murdered."

"So you say. Well, now, my dear . . ." A thought seemed to strike Arthur. He turned to Sarah. "You said Miss Halsey? Is your aunt here?"

"I sent for her."

"I see. In fact you followed none of the instructions important to my safety. However—as I say, no harm has been done. Now then, Dixon, you probably did what you thought best. But get out of my house."

Jake stood as if planted on the hearth. "I'll wait till you've talked to the police, Travers."

For a second Arthur seemed to hesitate. Then he said, "Certainly. I am a just man. I am fair. Your position should be clarified. I'll talk to them at once. Please come with me."

He started toward the hall, but Jake came to Sarah and put his hand on her own. "Did you mean that? Just now—before he came. Did you mean it?"

"Yes. Always . . ."

"All right. Things will be all right. I promise you . . ."

Arthur said, from the doorway, his face smiling as if faintly amused, his voice like a cold wind in the room, "Are you coming?"

Jake walked down the long room toward Arthur, who stood and smiled and waited. Arthur led the way into the hall, out of sight, toward the telephone. Jake followed.

But he didn't know Arthur.

Suddenly all the knowledge of five years seemed to sum themselves up in one word and that was fear.

Perhaps always she had been afraid of Arthur, and hadn't analyzed it; perhaps fear had always lain, like a feral but sleeping animal, somewhere within the bars of the past five years.

Liebchen crawled under the sofa. Sarah called her and the little old dog crept out again slowly and came to settle down at her feet—but watched the door where Arthur had disappeared. Arthur was invincible. He didn't love Sarah, yet his pride and anger would work against Jake, arousing Arthur's wiliest, swiftest agility of mind.

She heard his voice at the telephone. She couldn't hear the words, but he used his pleasantest, most convincing tone. There were pauses and then apparently his replies.

152

Fear had been like a thin wire stringing together five years like beads. It was like a band around her throat, suffocating her. She rose and went out the French window across the porch. Sinbad, walking very quietly, was like a blue-gray shadow at her side. The cold, damp air touched her face. She was only aware of a driving need to escape the house, Arthur's house. She walked down the graveled path to the fringe of willows and then down to the boathouse. The pier stretched out over the lake. Wet planks rattled. She went out to the very end of the pier.

In the distance sky met the lake, and the opposite shore was hidden in the thickening dusk. It was already so dark that she could barely see the motorboat tied at the buoy and its wet canvas cover; it seemed, in the tricky dusk, to be riding a little heavily, as if it had shipped water during the rain. The lake was a flat, sullen, gray, barely moving so there was only a slow, reluctant gurgle along the shore. Sinbad nudged at her hand, and turned back toward the house.

She was thankful that Arthur had not died, like that, horribly in the shadows of a park. She hadn't wanted him to die.

But she couldn't stay in his house now that he had returned. The chill from the lake seemed to reach for her heart. Sinbad whimpered and she followed him, past the boathouse with its open black door, through the wet, swishy little branches of willows. In that wet, cold twilight she had, strangely, no plucking of nerves that warned her to listen for a rustle, a footstep in the sodden thickets. But the police had searched everywhere; whoever murdered Richard Wells would be afraid to come back. Besides, Arthur's return automatically removed danger. There would not be another secret visitor in the night. Neither Richard Wells, dead so horribly in some hidden, internecine quarrel, nor his murderer.

And Jake was safe. The dangerous, entangling masquerade was over. She went back across the drenched lawn to the house. As she entered it Sam came hurrying through the dining room. "You rang, Mrs. Travers? The bell . . . Perhaps it was Mr. Travers." Sam, his face red, his small eyes bright with excitement, swerved into the hall. She heard Arthur's voice. "Pack Mr. Dixon's things. He's taking the evening train to New York. Get out the car . . ."

Jake behind him said, "I'll take a taxi."

"I'll call it. Get Mr. Dixon's things down here. The train leaves in fifteen minutes." Arthur was at the telephone; his voice was clear and smooth. A taxi please. Immediately, for the evening train to New York. Yes, here at the Travers place . . .

Arthur turned from the telephone. Jake saw her and started toward her, and she cried, "I'm going too! I'm going with you."

Arthur caught her wrist. "I'll have no hysterical nonsense, Sarah."

Sam was thumping rapidly down the steps. "Here's your bag, Mr. Dixon. Here's your bag."

Arthur released her wrist. "My wife wishes to say goodbye, Dixon. It might be a good plan to go out to the highway and meet the taxi. I'll go with you."

"Maybe I didn't get everything in it, Mr. Dixon. But I got your suit and your shirts and your shaving things." Sam put down Jake's brown leather suitcase and puffed.

Jake said to Sarah, "I'm going now. I'll come back."

"That, I think," Arthur said softly, reckless of Sam's listening ears, which was not like Arthur, "would be very inadvisable." He opened the door. "There's not much time."

Jake was so close to Sarah that she could have touched him; all she had to do was put out her hand. He said, "I'll come back." Then he was gone. He had picked up his bag. Sam was staring after them. Arthur called back to him. "Here's my suitcase, Sam. Take it inside."

Sam brought the small suitcase in from the step where Arthur had left it. Already the two men had crossed the terrace; their figures were crossing the driveway, blocked out in the twilight against the lighter strip of gravel.

She watched until the dusk hid Jake's broad shoulders and black hair, slowly but inexorably, as if he had gone forever from her sight. Sam behind her, said, "Better come in, Mrs. Travers. It's cold." He said, eyeing her excitedly but also kindly, "I think Miss Halsey wants to see you."

She went upstairs and Julia was in bed. She knew that Arthur was back. "Sam told me," she said at her first glimpse of Sarah's face. "But don't you see? It's over now. And the police can't charge you or Jake with murder." She seemed to realize, then, what she failed to say. She pleated the thin blanket cover with unsteady fingers, watching Sarah, and moistened her lips. "I didn't want Arthur to die. I didn't want him to die like that."

There was an ominous bluish shadow around her mouth and in the hollows of her cheeks. Sarah said, alarmed, "I'd better call the doctor."

Julia would have none of it. She was only tired, she said, the day was cold, she'd be all right. "Where is Jake?"

"He's gone. He's taking the night train to New York."

"And then—to San Francisco?"

"I don't know. I suppose—I don't know."

After a long moment, Julia said slowly, "Arthur—I was at fault. You were so young. You thought you loved him, Sarah, but . . ."

But she hadn't. She knew the difference now.

"You thought," Julia said with sudden strength, "that he was what you now know Jake to be." Her eyes went past Sarah out to the blank, black windows; she said in a thin, weaker voice, "I saw it coming. I couldn't have stopped it. I didn't want to stop it. I thought you deserved it . . . What are you going to do?" She closed her eyes weakly. "There's Lisa," Julia said but without conviction. "But I don't think really Arthur wants Lisa. He—I've been thinking so much about it, Sarah. He was on the upward climb when he met you, and he wasn't too certain of himself or—so he wanted a lady for a wife. He had to have a lady, a background . . ." A door slammed below and Arthur called softly, "Sarah! Sarah, come down here."

He knew, of course, that she would have gone to Julia.

Julia said, "I'll be all right. Don't think about me. Go and—" her eyes fluttered open; she said with command—"face him. Don't be afraid. Tell him the truth."

Why not? Arthur was a man, subject to the laws that govern other men. Sarah was living in a civilized world; there were telephones, there were other people. Why not?

Arthur was sitting in the lounge chair beside the fire. Liebchen now was on the chair beside him; he was lifting and stroking her velvety ears. And he was pleased and triumphant.

"Come along, my dear." He glanced at her muddy, wet shoes, her sweater and tweed skirt. "You do look rather draggled. Not quite the welcome I might have expected. Pour me a drink, will you?"

Her hands were unsteady on the decanter; it clattered as she put it down. She took the glass to Arthur and instinctively avoided his touch as he put his slender hand toward it. He saw that and a dancing kind of light came into his eyes. "Sit down, here, near me." He caught her hand and pulled her to a footstool at his feet. "Now then, Sarah, I'm not going to have any high tragedy about this. You are a very unworldly woman. You've always been. So let me tell you something. This young man, Dixon, simply made a play for you. I ought to have expected it, I suppose, but you are such a touch-me-not little person that I—well, I didn't. But now I've got to open your eyes." She made a motion to rise and he said, "No, stay there. I've not finished. I'll make it brief, however. It's not a pleasant subject. There's been some romantic nonsense. I must say I didn't expect to find you in his arms! The cold fact is this: Dixon saw a chance to get a young and not unattractive woman and money. Why shouldn't he jump at it? Well, that's over. I retained him. I'm just. I've paid him off fairly and well. He's gone and probably right now is congratulating himself on getting out of it so easily."

"That's not true."

"Always the idealist, aren't you, Sarah?"

"He said he'd come back."

"What else could he say? He had to make as graceful an exit as he could."

"He'll come back."

"Not," Arthur said silkily, "if he's the prudent young man I think he is. Not—" he sipped delicately at his drink and finished—"not if he knows what's good for him."

There was a latent but assured threat in his soft voice. She must have made some betraying motion of alarm. He said, "I meant what I said about the power of attorney."

"You asked for it. You told him . . ."

"But I didn't sign it. Oh, I asked for it, yes; I told him to prepare it. But the police don't know that and I don't intend to tell them. You don't seem to understand. I'm not going to let you leave me. If you try to—if this young man should try to come back—I intend to go to the police and tell them that this was an attempted fraud on his part. I'll tell them that he took advantage of my absence and his belief that I was dead to try to get hold of my money, through you. It will not be very pleasant for him. I needn't tell you that a flagrant breach of trust is not exactly conducive to success in a lawyer's profession."

"But that isn't true! You told him . . ."

"Whom do you think the police will believe? You and this scheming young man, who made love to my wife—or me?"

A weapon came to her hand. "But you—Lisa . . ."

"Lisa is a beautiful woman," Arthur said smiling again, and certain of himself. "She is excellent company. I wouldn't think of marrying her. There's nothing that you can threaten me with, concerning Lisa."

"I saw the letter you wrote to her. She showed me . . ."

Anger twitched at the corners of his mouth. He saw however, smoothly, "There's nothing in that letter that proves anything. You can't threaten me with that. Now then—this is enough about an unpleasant topic. It's settled." He leaned over and cupped his hand around her throat. "Aren't you glad to see me?"

She rose so quickly that she escaped him. "It's not settled, Arthur. There are too many things. . . ." Too many things. Murder. "What did you tell the constable? What did he say?"

"I told him I had returned. I told him that definitely I was not the man you all assumed—rather quickly and readily— was murdered in San Francisco. You have that to thank me for at least—I gathered they were about to arrest you and your charming young man for murder." He chuckled a little and drank slowly, eyeing her over the rim of the glass.

"Have they—identified the man?"

"No. What does it matter? Some waif, some stray, somebody nobody wants to claim."

"He had the box from Gump's. He was in the park where you told me and Jake to meet you."

"Stop talking of Dixon. That's enough of that. As to the park, I didn't go near it. The box from Gump's—well, really, Sarah, I'm not the only person to patronize a very large jewelry store."

She was tired and bewildered; Arthur was triumphant and sure of himself. Yet it could not have ended like that, all the police investigation, all the unanswered questions. Their case, of course, their point of investigation, was Costellani. "What about Costellani?"

"That I know nothing about. That's their problem. Oh, I'll have to talk to them, thanks to your inability to keep a secret. . . ." He rose and poured himself another drink. She thought, as she had thought at a time which now seemed long ago, in a blue and tranquil twilight at the Top o' the Mark, that it was unlike him to drink, and to drink rapidly. He did so then and a faint wash of color stained his narrow cheeks. He said, "Since you've got the state troopers, even the F.B.I., investigating your little tempest in a teapot, I'll have to talk to them and explain matters. I'm to see the police tomorrow."

"What are you going to tell them?"

He was angry again, and as always hiding it. "I'll tell them the truth, of course. There's nothing to conceal. Any more questions?"

"Yes." She took a long breath; she braced herself against the high, wing chair. "You don't love me. I don't think," she said slowly, "that you ever loved me. So why . . . ?"

"Why don't I let you go? I'll tell you why. Because you are my wife. I am a man of a certain position in life. You happen to be the kind of wife I want. And I intend to keep. Besides, frankly, since you ask for facts—owing to the way you have broadcast this affair—there's bound to be a chance of questions, rumors, all that. If I let you go, you'd go straight to Dixon. You'll feel differently later; but that's the way you feel now. I don't intend to give any talk or rumors a basis. Understand that."

Sam was shambling from one foot to another in the doorway, wadding up his white apron in his hands. "Dinner," he said with a gulp, "is served."

Arthur nodded. As Sam disappeared into the dining room and began to light the candles, Arthur said with a thin smile, "Really, Sarah! Can't you persuade this man to wear proper clothes? Although as to that—" he glanced coldly at her muddy shoes and wrinkled tweed skirt—"I can't say that you are setting a very handsome example. However . . ." He finished his drink rapidly, not like himself. "Shall we go to dinner? I take it Miss Halsey is not able to join us. Too bad. But the doctors told me last winter, after that very long and indeed rather expensive illness of hers that her heart . . . The slightest strain, the smallest nervous anxiety might . . ." He shrugged and put his arm around her and moved toward the dining room.

It was, of course, another threat. Julia. And Jake. She had been wrong when she told herself that there was nothing to fear. Jake's profession—and a scandal. Julia—and her hard-worked heart. There were ways even in a civilized world to induce obedience on the part of a wife.

The dining room was cold and seemed too big. The black night pressed against the glittering window panes; the candle flames stood straight. Arthur sat opposite her across the long table with the candle lights and a deepening light from his unaccustomed drinks touching his hazy eyes to a luminous glow. It deepened as he talked. And he talked of his trip. He couldn't yet, he told her, say exactly where he had gone or what he had done. But he described bits of spectacular scenery, told small incidents. And all the time the glow in his eyes was brighter.

But Costellani had been murdered and she had seen him.

Richard Wells had been murdered, after he had come to see Arthur, and she had seen him.

She said suddenly, breaking into Arthur's conversation, "You'll have to tell the police and the F.B.I. about Wells. And—Robinson. If they are enemy agents . . ."

"I know nothing of either of them, my dear. But of course you are right. Certainly . . . Sam!"

Sam came, hurrying, from the pantry. Arthur sent him for wine and glasses. He poured the wine, red wine which glowed the color of rubies in the sparkling glasses. Red as rubies. Red as blood. He made a toast: "To the present, my dear—and to the future."

There was triumph and elation in his look. There was also a kind of anticipatory excitement, the look of a gambler waiting the run of the wheel. It was the way Arthur looked when he had a big and risky business deal ahead of him, but was sure that he could master it.

He said, glancing at her sweater, her bare arms, "You should have your bracelet, my dear. It was careless of you to leave it about like that. Beautiful women should have beautiful jewels. Drink your wine, Sarah."

She moved her hand toward the glass.

A strange and terrible thought entered her mind and it was that Arthur was a murderer.

The glass of wine went over on the cloth. It spread a quick, red stain outward toward Arthur.

17

Arthur arched his slender black eyebrows. "Claret. Where's the salt?" He took the little silver dish; he emptied it evenly on the wet red stain and waited quietly.

Sarah was standing, her hands pressed down upon the

table, wrinkling up the cloth. "How did you know where I left the bracelet?"

Arthur's sleek black head was very still, very alert and wary. He looked up slowly. "What are you talking about?"

"You knew where it was. You said . . ."

"Sit down! Naturally I assumed that you had not locked it away as you ought to have done."

"Richard Wells—I saw him, I tell you. He was murdered . . ."

"Who else saw him? Your fine young lawyer—and you. Nobody else."

"You knew Robinson! Lisa said you came here to meet Robinson."

"Lisa, I gather, was in a state to say anything that served her purpose. . . ."

"That's why she came back! She'd read about Costellani's murder. She came back to threaten you, she was going to blackmail you."

He rose. "Stop that. You're making a fool of yourself. I didn't realize that your infatuation for this young lawyer, this opportunist, would carry you so far. You are hysterical." The gleam of triumph was gone and in its place was deadly, cold fury.

"I'll not stop. I'll tell the police. I'll tell . . ."

"You have already told the police everything you could tell. . . . *Sam!*"

Sam peered in through the half-opened pantry door. Arthur said, "Clear the table. Mrs. Travers is not well. She's going to bed." He came around the table and put his arm, tight and hard around her. "Come, my dear," he said for Sam's ears. "All this has been very difficult for you. A great nervous strain. I don't want you to become ill, like your aunt. Come with me."

She drew away from him, and, because Sam was there, Arthur said lightly, "You are very tired. I'm so sorry." Suddenly he was all smiles, all tender solicitude.

But in the hall, at the foot of the stairway he said, "You have asked preposterous questions. You have suggested outrageous things. You are infatuated with this young fool. I'll see that it stops. I expect you by morning to have come to a more sensible conclusion."

She pulled away from his hand and ran up the stairs, past Julia's closed door, and into her own room.

She was going to Jake. He'd got the train, so he'd be in

New York soon. She'd drive. She'd hurry. If he planned to take the night plane she might reach him in time. She'd go to the airport; if he wasn't there then she'd—well, she'd inquire about trains. Somehow, somewhere, she'd find him.

She was moving about the room, pulling a suitcase out from a cupboard, picking up a dress, putting it down. Arthur would never let her go out of the house, taking a suitcase with her. It didn't matter; she wouldn't take a suitcase.

Julia was still here.

But he couldn't do anything to Julia—there wasn't anything he could do, was there?

There wasn't really anything he could do to Jake.

Wrongly using his legal knowledge, so Arthur would accuse him; abusing the confidence and trust placed in him. Not a nice thing for a lawyer.

But she couldn't stay in the house with a murderer.

Exactly why do you accuse your husband? Why do you say that he is a murderer? It was as if a voice had spoken to her, an authoritative voice—the constable or the old attorney. Why?

The bracelet—yes, the bracelet. Arthur had spoken as if he had known where she had left it, so therefore it suggested that he had taken it from the handbag where his own hands had placed it—and thus had entered the house. If then Arthur had been the second, furtive visitor of the night when Wells had come too (knocking at the door as if he were expected—by Arthur?), if Arthur had been that second visitor, he might have returned the previous night as secretly—and murdered Richard Wells. Why would Arthur have murdered Richard Wells? A man he said he knew nothing about.

She must think it out slowly. She had been wrong to attack Arthur, like that, without thinking first.

The talk Wells had had with Jake was threatening, of course; there had been a hatred in his pallid face and blazing eyes which had seemed personal and deep. He had said nothing that he might not have said had he been an enemy emissary, sent to prevent Arthur's giving his expert services to his own country and thus against the country or the political theory Wells represented. But suppose there had been in fact a quarrel between Arthur and Wells which could end only in Wells's murder.

But Arthur *had* gone at a government request. He had talked to the police; he had said with satisfaction that some honor had accrued because of his accomplishment, and he

161

had shown no reluctance, nothing but prompt willingness to substantiate his claims and to back them up with the very highest authority.

That fact automatically replied to every question.

So therefore she had leaped blindly to a conclusion which the facts themselves denied. It was entirely a matter of her own frightened instinct and it was wrong.

The truth was that she had leaped to the conclusion, not that Arthur was a murderer, but that he had the capacity for murder. It was perhaps latent, but it was there.

Even allowing for her own fine-drawn nerves and frightened imagination, she was sure of that. And she could not stay in his house.

But she was going to. She was then horrified at her own precipitate impulse to follow Jake. It would only add immeasurably to the weight of an attack upon Jake. Arthur had meant his threat about the power of attorney. She put away her suitcase.

She must see to Julia. She went into the hall quietly so Arthur would not hear her and question her. Julia's door was closed; probably she was asleep. The house was quiet. The hall below was lighted but she heard or saw nothing of Arthur. Sinbad came soberly up the steps and nudged at her hand and followed her back into her room. Sinbad was accustomed to Arthur, but had never been in any sense Arthur's dog.

It was late. The rain began again some time after that, pattering down upon the roof of the porch outside her windows.

Once in the night Sinbad roused and went to the window and growled softly. After awhile it struck her that Jake might have returned and might be on the porch below. She went to the window. Sinbad pressed against her knees and growled again and listened, but Sarah could hear only the steady drone of the rain. She was convinced at last that no one was on the porch or anywhere in the murmurous darkness. But Sinbad remained at the window for half an hour or so before he came back and sprawled down near the door with a long sigh. If there were other sounds in the night Sarah did not hear them.

The next morning Rose Willman came.

That was about noon, a sullen, chill day with blue mists around the willows and the woods. Julia was better; the frightening blue shadows in her face had almost gone, but she remained in bed, pretending nevertheless that she was only tired. When Sarah went downstairs, dreading it, Sam told her that Mr. Travers had had breakfast and had gone to the village, taking the car. He had gone, she knew, to talk to the police.

The house was dark and gloomy in spite of lights and it seemed too big, too empty. As a rule during a summer weekend the lake was lively with boats, and the piers that dotted it were gay with people in bright bathing suits. That day, because of the chill air and overcast sky, the lake was deserted.

Once it occurred to Sarah that perhaps in fact Jake had not gone. Perhaps he had merely taxied to the village, to the hotel; perhaps he intended to stay in the vicinity until he could see her again. She telephoned to the small taxicab office and inquired cautiously. Had the taxi which had gone to the Travers place last night reached the evening train in time for their guest? A cheery voice assured her that it had. "I was driving myself, Mrs. Travers. We didn't waste much time, I'll tell you. But we made the train."

So Jake had really gone.

About noon Arthur returned and at first glance she knew that his errand had been successful.

He took off his raincoat, folded it neatly across a chair and came toward her, rubbing his hands together, his black hair sleek and shining above his narrow temples and a smug pleasure in his smile.

"You were still asleep when I went to the village. I've seen the police."

He opened the cigarette box that stood on the table before the sofa; the silver winked in the light from the lamp beside her. "Everything is satisfactorily settled."

"What do you mean?"

His slender brows arched as he settled himself in the lounge chair. "What do you suppose I mean? I told them the facts of the situation. I explained that your young friend had been retained by me, and why. Obviously I am thoroughly alive, so there's no San Francisco murder for them to concern themselves with. There'll be an inquest into Costellani's death. That's tomorrow. I'll be a witness, but only because he was in my employ. There's nothing that I know about it. I settled in their minds the tempest in a teapot that you and young Dixon raised. They seemed relieved. Although one of the troopers, a lieutenant, seemed a little disappointed at the way their fine case of nothing was washed out. However, that's done. They'll not trouble you any further."

She had to question him, although it was like walking over thin ice, with danger signs ahead. "What about Wells?"

He shook ashes neatly from his cigarette. "That's a problem for the F.B.I. If, that is, they discover his body or anything like evidence concerning him. I've told the police the facts, easily substantiated. My duty in that direction is done." He eyed her. "I told the police that you were not well. They wished you to appear at the inquest, inasmuch as you found Costellani's body. I wasn't sure that you'd be able to, and they were very understanding about it, I must say."

"I am able to appear."

"I am the best judge of that, my dear. Besides they already have your testimony. All they have to do is read it into the record. Your testimony and Dixon's. Although they were rather annoyed with me for letting Dixon leave. But it isn't really important."

He smoked and leaned his head back against the cushions of the chair. "You were a very silly girl last night, you know. Come here."

He drew the footstool near him and she went quickly to the big wing chair opposite him, across the hearthrug. A flicker of that secret anger touched the corners of his mouth. "I might have been angry last night. You all but accused me of—" he shrugged, "—of theft. As if I would steal a bracelet I had given you! And I didn't like the tone of your questions. However I realize you were not quite yourself. This infatuation of yours . . . By the way, it occurred to me that Dixon suggested your questions. Did he? What else has he suggested? What exactly does he think he knows?"

Then she saw clearly his intention. He had sent Jake away too quickly, too hurriedly; he now wanted to know what Jake believed and what Jake intended to do.

18

Opposed to that was the concrete fact that Arthur's entire story was true. It was substantiated and it had convinced the police. So what had Arthur to fear from Jake?

But in spite of these facts her dark imaginings of the night returned. Whether or not he had murdered, he had the secret, ruthless capacity for murder. She had to reply so she said slowly, "Everything was altered when we believed that you had been killed and we had no message, no communication about it. Your dispatch case was empty. We looked there, too . . ."

"Yes," he said softly. "Another breach of trust. So he questioned my veracity. What else?"

She said with a catch in her breath, "I told him that I believed you."

The doorbell rang then and Rose Willman came.

For an instant Sarah thought, It's Jake. Arthur rose and went into the hall with his wary, catlike footsteps. He opened the door and said warmly, "Rose!"

Rose's voice was as clear as Arthur's, but for once trembling and uneven. She was not, however, surprised. Rose had been told that Arthur was alive and at home. Who had told her? The police?

"I drove up from town. I had to see you for myself. They said . . ." Her voice faltered. Arthur said, "My dear Rose! It wasn't true. I'm perfectly well and as you see very much alive. It was very cruel to tell you . . ."

"I've got to talk to you. Alone."

There was the slightest, smallest pause. Then Arthur said smoothly, "Certainly." Again the door opened and there was the slight sound of movement. It closed heavily again and silence came upon the house.

Sarah was halfway to the door before she realized what she had to do and why it was so vitally important. By the time she reached the door they had disappeared. They were not in Rose's little car, or on the terrace, or strolling across the lawn. She snatched a raincoat from the hall closet and ran back to a window on the lake side of the house. Presently she saw them, Rose, small and sleek as a blackbird, walking beside Arthur across the lawn. The two figures vanished into the narrow willow-grown path leading to the boathouse. Sarah went after them.

She closed in Sinbad who would have accompanied her. When she reached the path she entered it cautiously, but Rose and Arthur had gone on ahead. She could hear the light swish of willows and the murmur of Arthur's voice.

They went to the boathouse. She heard their steps on the wooden stairs to the upper deck of the boathouse. She heard the muffled creak of a chair as if Arthur had dragged it forward.

She didn't hear their entire conversation. It took some time to edge through the willows, skirt the cleared space by flattening herself against the boathouse itself, enter the dusky, brownish interior of the boat slips, where the two boats rocked lazily in the gloom and the smell of fish and wet wood lay stagnant over everything.

But once there she could hear their voices directly above her. Rose was talking. ". . . that was this morning early. Dixon saw Lisa and she is going to make trouble for you."

"What did Dixon say to her?"

"He told her that you hadn't been murdered—oh, Arthur, they said . . . Why didn't you telephone to me?"

Arthur's voice was perfunctory and rather impatient.

"I'm sorry, Rose. I intended to. Go on. What did Dixon tell her?"

There was a little pause, then Rose said obediently, "He told her that you had said that you had no intention of marrying her. That's true, isn't it?"

"Of course. Lisa? Go on."

"I knew you wouldn't marry her. She didn't care about you, it was only . . ."

"You needn't explain Lisa to me. *What did Dixon say?*"

"He told her that. Then he said that she knew something of the gardener, Costellani. He told her that she would be an accessory after the fact if she didn't tell the police everything she knew. . . . Does she know anything?"

"What could she know? Don't be absurd, Rose. Then what? Why did Lisa come to you?"

"Because," Rose said precisely, "she intends to make you marry her."

"Nonsense."

"She said she wanted you to know—these were her words exactly—that she had refused to tell Dixon anything. But I was to tell you that."

"That's not all."

"No. I'd better tell you exactly. She can make trouble for you. Whether it's true or not. She said that she came up here last week with you. That was Thursday night. You came, she said, to meet a man called Robinson. The police asked me about him. I'd never heard of him and I told them so."

"Of course."

"Then, she said, you and she arrived here and waited.

166

Robinson didn't turn up and the gardener—Costellani—fixed a little supper for you. Then someone came to the door and rang. You said, "There's Robinson," and made her leave by the kitchen door and go for a drive. She said she did and as she left she looked back from the driveway and—and you were in the hall with somebody she couldn't see and Costellani was standing just outside the front door and he seemed to be listening. She said that."

"That's nothing."

"She said—" Rose seemed to take a breath and Sarah could almost see her vehement eyes searching Arthur's face— "she said that she went for the drive, and that when she returned it was dark. She said the house was dark and the door closed. She rang and waited and went around to the kitchen door and there were no lights there, either, and the door was locked. She thought of the garage and the gardener's cottage and went there. Costellani wasn't there. She couldn't find you. She came back to the car and waited and then—then she said you came from around the house, this end of it, from—from the pier."

"She couldn't have known that. She couldn't have seen . . ."

Rose hurried now. "She said you were nervous and unlike yourself. She said you got in the car and the car started, that you told the driver to hurry. She said you got your breath, it was as if you'd been running or—or doing something very difficult, something that required physical effort. And that—that she lighted a cigarette and your hands were—she said there was dirt—and blood around the fingernails."

It could have happened like that. Blood on his hands, dirt from the concrete block and the rope which had later worn through. Costellani, listening on the terrace, pressed against the house at the side of the door. Arthur finding him there, after Robinson had gone.

Arthur said sharply, "Wait. I heard something . . ."

Sarah heard his footsteps, crossing above her head, toward the steps. There was a long silence except for the water lapping against the boat, whispering against the pier. Had she moved; had he heard it?

Arthur's footsteps went back toward Rose. "Nothing. . . . What else did she say?"

Rose made a curiously oblique reply. "It was the next day, Friday, that you phoned to me and told me that Costellani was going away, he was going to see his daughter who was sick, and I was to get a new man for a month to take his place. I did. I got a new man, Sam Cleetch, from the employment agency. I sent him up here and he arrived Monday. Costellani was gone. The police asked me if Costellani had left a message at the office. They'd been told that."

"What did you say?"

"There wasn't any record of a message. I thought then that you'd been killed. I told them . . ."

"You said I had told you Costellani was leaving?"

"Yes. I didn't realize . . . I'd do anything for you. But I didn't know . . ."

"It doesn't matter. You could discover a message—something forgotten by one of the office girls. If necessary."

"Yes. Yes, I can do that. But Lisa can make trouble, Chief, if she tells the police all this."

"If she'd decided to tell them she wouldn't have come to you."

"She's going to tell them unless you buy her off, somehow."

"She can't expect to bludgeon me into marriage with that."

Rose said, "Lisa is a stupid woman. But she's dangerous, too."

"I don't think so. Why did she talk to you instead of me? She was afraid . . ."

Rose's voice had an unexpected throb. "That's why she came to me. She is afraid."

Arthur laughed softly, "Of *me?*"

"She wanted me to tell you. It's her gamble, Chief."

There was a shuffle of footsteps, then a long pause. Finally Rose said with that deep throb in her voice, "I didn't understand why you married Sarah. It was very hard for me. But Lisa—I can't stand that!"

"I'm not going to marry Lisa. It's always been you, Rose, except I—I didn't know it. Until too late. We'll stop Lisa."

"How? Tell me," Rose said, "what to do."

I'd do anything for you, she had said, with the ring of simple truth in her clear voice. Murder?

Arthur said, "I'll see her."

"She is dangerous. Be careful. You can't afford . . ." Rose was thinking murder, too. Arthur said suddenly, "You do believe in me, don't you? You don't think I'd have killed Costellani?"

Rose said with that clear, cold simplicity of truth, "I don't care."

168

"Rose . . ." There was another long pause. Then Rose said, "Be careful. If Sarah suspects you . . ."

"Sarah," Arthur said, "is infatuated with this young lawyer. This is the story, Rose. I was sent to do a job for the government. It was secret and confidential. I couldn't tell even you, Rose, and I tell you everything."

"Yes."

"Dixon took advantage of the situation. But whatever he has suggested to Sarah, or whatever she thinks she knows—" Arthur chuckled a little—"a wife's testimony against her husband is not admissible in this state."

"Has she questioned you?"

"Only about things that Dixon suggested to her. She'll get over it. I've got her so she can't do anything. If she tries it, I'll smash this young man like that!"

"You can't get rid of her now. You can't afford . . ." Rose said precisely, "you can't afford that, either. Just now."

How alike they were, in all their mental processes! It was as if Rose had placed herself with utter, unswerving devotion in Arthur's mould.

Arthur said, "There is nothing Sarah can do. And as to Lisa—you said Dixon is still in New York. What is he planning to do?"

"I don't know."

"Where's he staying?"

"I don't know. I ought to have asked but—he was in New York this morning." Her voice took on a quicker, anxious note. "Is there anything he *can* do?"

"N-no. No. I've fixed him with the police. They'll not credit anything he knows or thinks he knows. No." Arthur seemed to think and then said firmly, "There's not a thing. Remember, Sarah is here. He'll not risk Sarah . . ."

Rose seemed to move quickly toward Arthur. "You *can't.* It's too—it's too dangerous!"

Arthur said with a little laugh, "Darling Rose. Trust me. What did you tell Lisa?"

"I told her she was a fool. I told her she had no proof of any of her claims. I told her nobody would believe her—you least of all. I told her that she'd gambled and lost. Everything. You and—everything."

Arthur said cuttingly, "That was a mistake. She'll turn to Dixon." Rose must have made some beseeching motion, for he said quickly, "But she can't hurt me. None of it is true.

169

I'll see her before she can do anything. Dear Rose . . . Dear Rose . . ."

The boats rocked up and down at Sarah's feet. There was a shuffle of footsteps over her head. They were coming down the steps.

Sarah flattened herself back against the damp, cobwebby wall. A plank rattled as they stepped on the pier. But Arthur did not cross and look up into the boathouse, for Rose said very clearly, almost in Sarah's ears, "I'd better tell you. I saw Wells. Night before last. I had to."

"*What?*"

"He had inquired for you and I didn't like his manner. That was when he first telephoned and said that you had returned from San Francisco. That was before they told me that you—that you'd been murdered. Then he telephoned again. He said I was to tell you that you couldn't get away from him. He was threatening and—I still believed that you were here, and I thought I'd better see him and find out what he wanted. So I did."

"You saw Wells!"

The woman who had inquired for directions to the fishing shack. Rose, not Lisa. Rose in her zealous devotion to Arthur. She said, "I made an appointment with him. I came and he told me the story and I'd do anything for you."

There was an instant's complete, utter silence. Then Arthur said, "*You* . . ."

19

The planks rattled to their footsteps and there was the light swish of willows. Then there was only the murmur of Rose's voice and the gurgle of the black water which gradually became the only sound. They were going back to the house.

What had Rose meant?

I'd do anything for you. Murder? A woman can hold a gun, take careful aim, pull a trigger. A woman couldn't have rowed a boat out into the dark lake. A woman couldn't have disposed of the boat—or the freight it bore.

Rose's little but resolute figure, clad in black, walking

170

neatly through the blackness of the night. I'd do anything for you.

Sarah had to get back to the house. If she followed them Arthur would see her. She'd go through the woods. Return by the woods road. Say she'd been for a walk, say anything.

Jake was still in New York. He had seen Lisa, and she had seen Rose. He had tried to pit them against each other. He had not succeeded.

She was stumbling through the wet woods, her breath painful in her throat when it occurred to her that there was no evidence.

Whatever Lisa had seen or guessed, Arthur wouldn't let her tell it. Rose would never turn against Arthur.

And Arthur was in the clear. There had been no faltering, no hesitation, no question in the assurances he had given Rose.

A wet branch of shrubbery brushed her face and she pushed it aside and stopped to take a breath. She realized then that she'd been running toward the highway. It was an instinctive, blundering flight. But Jake would come back. That meant to the lake, to the house, to her.

She pushed the wet strands of her hair back from her forehead. A car was going rapidly along the woods road. That was Rose, going back to New York. She couldn't see the little winding road; it was ahead of her and to the right, screened by the shrubbery. Rose couldn't see her.

The sound of the car slackened, seemed to turn into the highway, speeded up again. And another car came suddenly into the woods road.

She waited while it shot along the winding road, too fast for the curves, scarcely checking as it reached the highway.

She knew that that was Arthur and that he was going to Lisa.

Lisa was no match for Rose. No match for Arthur.

Arthur had gone to Lisa.

Sam confirmed it. He was coming down the stairs with Julia's lunch tray. Mr. Travers had gone to New York, he said, but would return that night. He eyed Sarah's wet hair, her muddy brown pumps curiously.

She telephoned to Lisa, and Lisa did not answer. She didn't know what she could have said, she knew only that she had to warn Lisa.

A few minutes later she tried again and again there was

no answer. Sam served her lunch and hovered around her while she pretended to eat. She said, "Thank you, Sam. You've stayed here in spite of everything and helped . . ."

He shuffled from one foot to the other, turned red, mumbled something to the effect that Miss Halsey was a nice lady, ". . . and so are you, ma'am," he said, and bolted for the pantry.

But as she thought of the conversation between Rose and Arthur she began to see that many implications yet very few facts emerged from it, and nothing that could be offered as evidence.

She could tell the constable that Lisa Bayly had claimed to know something of Costellani's murder. Lisa would—after Arthur had seen her—deny it. She could tell them that Rose Willman had seen Wells and talked to him the night Wells was murdered. Rose would deny it.

The whole premise of her terrible debate still rested upon one thing. If Arthur had not in fact been sent on a government mission, if he had in fact evolved the whole scheme in order to give himself time and cover to settle a private quarrel—then he could have murdered Costellani who might have known too much of his meeting with Robinson. He could have murdered Wells. But Arthur had willingly offered proof to the police, to everyone, of his absence and the reason for it.

Sometime later she tried again to telephone to Lisa; still no one answered. Jake must return—he would return. But minutes and hours ticked away and the telephone did not ring and Jake did not come back.

She couldn't talk to Julia, who lay with frightening gray shadows in her face and stared at nothing. She was driven by an urgent need to act and there was nothing that she could do. Once, however, thinking of Richard Wells, she thought of a gun. Arthur's gun, which had not been in the house when the police searched for it. She made another search, this time in Arthur's room, listening for his return. His small suitcase had been unpacked; there was nothing in it. She didn't find the gun that he must have taken to San Francisco with him.

She had not expected to find the bracelet and she didn't. And there was the lake where a gun would sink without a trace. Whoever murdered Wells had had a simple and quick means of disposing of that particular evidence. It occurred to her then that the problem of Wells's disappearance was not so much where, as why.

Was it to induce doubt on the part of the police, doubt that murder had actually occurred—or was there some other reason?

By late afternoon the sky cleared and the sun came out, brilliant and hot, soaking up moisture from the drenched earth. A few boats appeared on the lake. Her skirt and sweater began to feel hot and sticky, so she changed to a thin cotton dress. It happened to be a dress as dark green as the willows at night. She brushed up her short brown hair and the red lights in it made the white face that looked. back at her from the mirror seem whiter still, with shadows around her eyes. Her sense of an urgent need for action was stronger and there was still nothing she could do.

What was happening in Lisa's apartment in New York? The clock in the hall was striking when she tried again to reach Lisa. This time there was a queer feeling of emptiness in that distant room where the telephone rang and rang and no one answered it.

The house was growing dusky with the approach of night. She whistled to Sinbad, who came sleepily to accompany her. She couldn't walk down toward the lake where the body of a man had moved and loosened itself and washed to shore, where a rowboat and another man had vanished and yet must exist somewhere along its wooded shores, or in its secret depths. She went out the front door. Roses, beaten by the rain, hung in languid crimson clusters. She crossed to the road that wound through the woods. Sinbad trudged beside her. Nothing moved in the woods, but all her dark questions went with her, an obstinate, pursuing company.

She reached the highway. Still no car came speeding along the road, Jake driving it. The highway was deserted, stretching away in a curve past the woods, toward the village. The mail box stood, white and ghostly in the gathering twilight at one side of the road. A sudden thought struck her; perhaps Jake had written to her. She opened the mail box before she remembered that it was Sunday, and that even if he had written a letter it could not have been delivered. She had not thought of mail during the entire week; anyhow, most letters went to the apartments in town. There was a little bundle of advertisements in the box, and on top a letter addressed simply "Mrs. Travers." It had no stamp and no

173

postmark, but looked as dull as an advertisement. She took the little accumulation of circulars and started back to the house. She walked faster; she didn't like the sudden shadows in the woods which pressed closely on both sides. Yet Sinbad heard and saw nothing as he trudged contentedly beside her. She emerged from the road and the lights of the house shown across the lawn.

When she entered the hall she put the little bundle of mail down on the table. Only then it struck her that the letter addressed to her, without stamp and postmark, might have come from Jake. He might have returned; he might have sought that means of communication with her. She tore open the letter.

Perhaps thirty seconds later the revolving circle of questions stopped. All its confusing integrants fell into a definite, clear pattern.

The letter was written by Richard Wells—who had been murdered, who couldn't therefore explain anything and yet supplied every answer. It was written as if hurriedly, with a pencil, on stationery which bore at the top of it "Arthur Travers, Woods Drive, Saguache Lake." The words seemed to spring at her from the white page. *Dear Mrs. Travers, I'm writing this in your gardener's cottage. You love your husband; that's clear. I told you to urge him to do what he must do. I could see that he hasn't told you. You know my name. I have been in prison. He defended me a long time ago, when I was convicted for embezzlement. They could prove embezzlement, but they never got the money because I gave it to him. I trusted him. He promised to see to it for me until I was let out. I was taking a chance with him, but I couldn't stash the money away. I might lose if he double-crossed me but I'd certainly lose if I didn't get the money into somebody's care. He's made a fortune with it, and it's mine. I have no legal recourse, but believe me, I'll kill him if he doesn't settle. Now talk to him. Tell him you know all about it. You love him, I could see it. If he denies it here is proof for you.*

The sprawling signature was as clear as the letter: *Richard Wells.* And there was an enclosure, a note in Arthur's neat, fine handwriting. *I've found your hideout. Don't come to the house. Meet me tomorrow night. Three miles north of Woodsbridge, that's five miles west of Saguache on the main highway, there's a motor court. I'll watch for you there and follow your car. Turn right off the main highway—there's a road there and a bridge. Wait for me at the bridge. I'll leave this on the table.* There was no signature. It wasn't necessary.

Arthur, too, had found the fishing shack. But Wells hadn't gone to meet him. He had been afraid of a trap. He'd preferred to see Arthur in his own house, with other people within view and earshot.

How long had it been since he had seen Arthur! He had said to Jake, "Your fat life has been good for you."

That was the quarrel; that was the motive; the unknown quantity was resolved in a clear equation. Arthur had employed all his brilliance, all his gift for the devious, all that he knew of the strings with which to manipulate people toward one purpose. That was to provide himself with an alibi while he sought out and murdered Richard Wells whose stolen money had built Arthur's fortune.

Costellani's murder had been in a sense an improvisation, an accident as the discovery of his body had been in a sense an accident.

And Robinson—a buddy of mine, Wells had said, we're in this together—Robinson, who had emerged so briefly and importantly and then disappeared, Robinson might be— must be, it seemed to Sarah, as that equation fell into its clear and terrible terms, the man in San Francisco, murdered in the misty darkness of the park.

A car was coming along the driveway.

She hadn't heard its approach. She sensed it only when gravel spattered as the car stopped; Arthur's tall figure was springing across the terrace. He opened the door, saw her and stopped.

"Sarah, what is the matter with you? What . . ."

She moved blindly, stumbling. She ran up the stairway and into her room and locked the door.

Her breath hurt in her throat, her heart pounded all over her body. And then, she realized that the letter was not in her hand. She had dropped it somewhere, somehow in the blind panic of flight.

She realized too, then, that she ought to have taken Julia and left the house before the door of escape was closed.

20

Arthur had the letter. He had both letters. He was reading them. He knew that she knew.

She didn't hear his approach. She saw the door knob turn and turn. Arthur said, "Sarah, come out here. Sarah . . ."

There was the telephone. It stood on the little table across the room.

Arthur said softly, "If you are thinking of the telephone, don't. I've cut it off—just to keep you from making a fool of yourself. I've burned these two scraps of paper. You have no proof of anything."

He went away. She didn't hear his footsteps. She couldn't hear anything. But he must have gone.

So there was no proof. Arthur had won again. She went, nevertheless, to the telephone and it was completely, utterly silent.

What was he going to do now?

He couldn't keep her in the house forever. She'd wait, she'd watch, she'd escape. Besides, Julia; Julia would rouse and wonder. Julia would inquire.

What could Julia do against Arthur?

A long time later she heard the answer to that. There was a stir in the hall, and Arthur's voice said clearly, full of solicitude, "How are you feeling, Miss Halsey? I'd stay there if I were you. Sarah's gone to bed with a headache . . ."

There was the murmur of Julia's voice. Then a door closed and Arthur's light, precise footsteps crossed the hall. He wouldn't hurt Julia. He couldn't afford too much inquiry.

Rose had said it. Arthur had tacitly agreed.

But she'd been wrong to tell herself—how long ago?—that she was living in a civilized world. Murder inhabited that world, too.

Sam would inquire! There was nothing Sam could do either. Arthur would tell him with that gentle solicitude that Mrs. Travers wasn't well; Mrs. Travers mustn't be disturbed. Night was closing down upon the house, and the waiting secret depths of the lake.

It was about then that she began to pace the room, back and forth, but lightly so Arthur could not hear.

She knew exactly what had happened.

The ambiguity of Wells's talk with Jake was no longer unclear. It meant only one thing. Wells had embezzled; Arthur, then a young lawyer, had defended him. Wells was convicted, but the money wasn't found. Because he couldn't use the stolen money himself he had entrusted it to Arthur and Arthur had used it as a basis for his own spectacular success. Then Wells was released, embittered; he felt himself the investor, the entrepreneur. Some time—in prison, perhaps? —he had known Robinson. Robinson, knowing Wells's bitterness, had tried to intercede, had tried to keep Wells from meeting Arthur, had tried to arrange a settlement which would suit Wells—and had failed.

And Arthur, thinking himself invincible, believing in his luck, had worked out a devious, careful plan. He had gone to San Francisco. Why? But he had gone to Jake, and the resemblance perhaps had suggested its value as an alibi for Arthur. Robinson, still intent on keeping Wells from seeing Arthur, had followed her in order to discover Arthur. And he had found him. That, too, must have been swift, improvised and necessary.

And then Arthur must have returned almost at once, on the next night's plane, for two visitors had come to the house, Wells, who had knocked and fired into the door meaning to threaten Arthur; Arthur, who had entered the house. Why?

The answer to that was clear. Because he had to find Wells. He had to decoy him from the house. That was the whole basis of his scheme; he had to lure Wells from the house and from the vicinity of the house. He had failed there. Wells would not be trapped. And time was running short.

That night Arthur had escaped, taking her bracelet. Why? To suggest that Costellani's murder was the result of an attempted burglary the week before? And Arthur later had found Wells's hide-out, the fishing shack, and suggested a meeting with him at a secluded place. Wells, seeing the danger, had rejected it, had insisted on their meeting taking place in Arthur's house, because he was afraid of Arthur, and because his only recourse was the threat of murder.

Wells had stayed persistently at the lake. Arthur's plan had gone wrong there. It had gone wrong when a wind tossed the lake and wore through a rope; it had gone wrong when Lisa had exploded it to the police; it had gone wrong in so many ways, yet at each fault in the shaking structure Arthur had acted swiftly to cement it into a convincing whole.

There was no proof against him.

Arthur had won.

He had convinced the police that he had in fact been sent away on the mission he claimed. There was no gun. There was no body to be identified as Richard Wells. There was no evidence. And there was no proof.

She thought of Lisa, but whatever had been done that afternoon, or how it had been done, Arthur had won.

She thought of Rose. But if Rose had killed Wells, she had acted in that dark twinship with Arthur, because of Arthur, merely the precise and resolute tool of Arthur's hand.

His only purpose had been to murder Wells.

He must have thought it was a safe, a perfect plan. It had sounded so real, so plausible. It was like Arthur to seize upon a real and existing condition, and turn it to his own purposes.

And then, exactly at that instant he was working out another devious, careful plan to encircle her, entrap her, make it impossible for her to talk. With the telephone cut off, with night thick and heavy upon the lake and the winding little road through the woods.

He'd have to do it quickly. Before morning.

But it wouldn't be—it couldn't be—murder. Could it? His life—or hers. It could be accident, it could be something that would appear to be suicide.

Jake would know. But he was in New York. There was no way to reach him.

The night already was endless; she looked at the little luminous face of her bedside clock. It was only a little after ten and the night stretched before her. How could Arthur start in progress the plan he must have, by now, evolved? When?

It was a long time after that that something struck sharply against the black screen of one of the windows. She thought, at first, vaguely, that it was a moth, hurtling against the screen. Then she realized that there was a sharp staccato note like a pebble, gravel from the path, striking the screen.

She went to the window. The porch was a black pocket. Jake whispered from it, "Sarah . . ."

Her heart literally turned over. *"Jake . . ."* She could

178

see now the outlines of his figure; she could see the oval of his face. But she knew it was Jake, not Arthur.

"Sarah, lock the door to your room. Stay there."

"No—no, Jake, I'm coming down. I've got to see you."

"Stay there. No matter what happens."

"Wait, I've got to tell you—you don't know . . ."

He had gone. There was no sound, no movement, nothing in the blackness except the slow lap of the water against the shore which she could not see. But it was Jake.

No matter what happens. What was going to happen? What was happening then, while she waited and listened and heard nothing?

She had to warn Jake. She had to tell him that then, that very minute, Arthur was working out some plan, setting it in motion.

When at last she heard an alien sound, something apart from the slow quiet wash of the lake, it was a rather curious one, for it was a kind of rustle, a brushing of shrubbery but not close to the porch, farther away, and then a kind of deep splash, far out in the blackness that was the lake. As if some heavy object, a rock, had been dropped into the lake.

Almost immediately Jake came back. She heard his footsteps, very light from the pocket of blackness below that was the porch; his figure, his face took vague shape. "It's Jake," he whispered. "Come down. Come down here . . ."

"I'm coming—wait . . ."

She whirled away from the window, across the room. She unlocked the door, carefully, slowly; she opened it and thrust back Sinbad and shut him in. The hall was dimly lighted from the stairwell and the hall below. Arthur was somewhere down there. She turned, avoiding the shaft of light. A narrow corridor led past closed rooms to the kitchen stairs. She passed the door to the room Sam was using and there was a faint light below it; she went down the kitchen stairs, past the little flower room where once Liebchen had been closed in—so she wouldn't follow Arthur, Sarah thought clearly, Arthur who had let himself into the house with his own key, in order to meet Wells at the opposite door, and lead him, somehow, away from the house. The kitchen door was not locked; she opened it and slid out into the night. No one, she was sure, had seen or heard her. She ran then, around the house, toward the porch. A white pillar gleamed, ghostly, ahead of her. Jake was standing beside it and moved toward her. "Jake," she whispered, and his face came more distinctly out of the darkness. And she whirled wildly as Arthur caught her by the wrist. "So that brought you out. I thought it would. You'll never see Jake again."

But it had been Jake. It had been Jake the first time, telling her to lock the door. It had been Arthur who had said, Come down.

Then the sense of his words struck her.

He said, "Don't look for Jake. He won't come back. Now then, I'm going to tell you what you've got to do."

"What have you done?" she cried. "What have you done?"

He drew her away from the house, down toward the willows, across the grass. "You read Wells's letter. But who will believe you? Don't try to get away!" his hold tightened. "You've got to be made to understand. I didn't go on a government mission; nobody but you would have believed me. Since you have taken the whole world into your confidence . . . Are you listening?" He gave a savage kind of shake to her arm and went on, "What I really told the police this morning was that there was no such mission. I had to admit that. But then I told them that you and Dixon had invented that story in order to cover yourselves. I told them that I had to be absent for a time, you knew of it, and that you brought your young man here, passed him off as me because of the resemblance. I let them draw their own conclusions about the power of attorney, about everything. I said that I had got rid of Dixon and I preferred not to make any sort of charges, because I didn't want the thing noised about, in the newspapers. I said that you had come to your senses, I said that I preferred to have the whole thing forgotten—it wasn't the first time an adventurer, a handsome young man, had made love to a woman whose husband had money and had tried to get his fingers on the money. They believed me. Why shouldn't they? *You* had told them this story of a government mission, not I. *You* have involved yourself so completely, you and Dixon, that there is no hope now of inducing them to believe anything you might tell them. Understand that, first. Now then—there is no proof of anything you know or think you know. None."

"Where is he? What have you done? *Where is he?*" The rustling of the willows, the deep heavy sound from the lake! She whispered, "You murdered him . . . I heard . . ."

"That was a—a rock I tossed in the lake. I knew you'd be curious and come down . . ."

"You murdered him . . ."

"Stop that." He caught both wrists hard. "Don't try to get away from me." He was shaking her again, queerly. "There is nothing—nothing that you can do. If you try it—I'll kill you too."

He wouldn't. He couldn't afford it. There would be inquiry. He couldn't.

He could. The knowledge itself drained all strength away from her.

Arthur's grip on her wrists relaxed as he felt her physical surrender.

So she jerked away from him and ran headlong, blindly, into the darkness, toward the lake.

21

Arthur, taken by surprise, seemed to move backward. Then she heard his pursuit.

She veered desperately in another direction, any direction.

Arthur had gone on down toward the lake. She could hear him there.

Suddenly she knew that she had reached the path to the boathouse; willows brushed her face. All at once the boathouse was a black bulk among them. Then she heard him along the path behind her. There was a rowboat in the slip. The lake was so black he couldn't see a rowboat, moving away from the slip; she could lose herself in that blackness. He'd never think of a boat.

She was inside the boathouse on her knees; her hand encountered a rope. She knew the loop; she felt the rough rope slide in her hand.

Arthur was searching along the path, slowly, among the willows. She could barely hear the swish and movement of branches. He thought she was hiding there, crouched in some dark thicket.

Her skirt tangled around her knees. The boat was below her, rocking a little. It tipped awkwardly as she stepped into it. Oars.

She found one oar. She followed it to the oarlock. Arthur

181

stepped upon the pier. She pushed against the slip, with hard thrusts inching the boat backward. Arthur was going up the steps to the deck above.

It was dimly lighter. Fresh air struck her face. The pier made a vaguely lighter streak out into blackness. She was free of the boathouse and Arthur was above, searching, moving about the deck. "Sarah—I see you now . . ." A chair moved. There must be another oar in the boat.

There wasn't. Never mind—get away. One oar. He'd heard the splash in the water. No matter how carefully she dipped the oar he'd hear it, he'd hear the rasp of the oarlock.

A long, slow ripple moved the boat back over the way she had come, back toward the boathouse.

She lifted the oar, she fought the ripple. It carried the boat around the open slip, gently and inexorably toward the shore, but on the side away from the pier, into the deep obscurity behind the boathouse. Willows again softly touched her face.

The water was shallow, the bottom sandy; she felt the boat graze that sandy bottom. She reached up and caught willow branches.

She held them, kneeling in the boat, staying its progress. It moved and came to a slow stop, sliding into the sand. The tough branches of willows gave her leverage against the wash of the water.

Arthur had not heard her.

He couldn't have heard, because there was nothing to hear; the gurgle of water in the boathouse, against the shore, had covered other sounds. Hadn't it? The black bulk of the boathouse stood between her and the pier and Arthur.

But he had come down from the deck, for then she heard him again on the pier. A plank rattled dully, and then another and another quickly. He was running.

He was running not toward the end of the pier, but back again. He had reached the path, for the sound of footsteps on the pier had ceased. He was going back to the house.

He wasn't. He was coming into the willows, thrusting them aside, running, stumbling once, around the boathouse toward her.

The path there diverged upward away from the water. He did not follow it; he plunged down, sliding, along the bank, tearing through the underbrush, suddenly stopping.

Then she heard it, too. Somebody was walking along the pier. Several people were walking there cautiously, but the betraying planks rattled. They were going out to the end of the pier.

A twig snapped along the bank above her.

They were doing something out at the end of the pier; there was a murmur of voices. Someone slid into the water. Someone was swimming.

She could hear the steady, purposeful strokes, the tiny splash of water.

Somehow she knew that Arthur, too, was listening for the steady, purposeful sound of the swimmer. Then she realized that the man in the water was swimming toward the motorboat, tied to the buoy.

The faint dip and splash went on, less distinct, but she knew when he reached the motorboat. She heard him climb into it. Somehow he had carried a flashlight with him in that short swim, its rays glanced out over black water, jerked and steadied, downward. He had thrust aside the canvas cover; she could see the hump it made. Suddenly all the night and everything within it listened, everything except the lake, for it already knew.

The faint light vanished. Someone was swimming again, quickly this time, not so cautiously, splashing. He reached the pier, for there was a shuffle of movements as if hands went down to hoist him upon the pier.

They were not so cautious now. "Find anything?" a man's voice cried.

Another voice replied, a familiar voice; it was the young trooper, gasping from his rapid swim. "He was there, all right. The only place we didn't look. There's blood-stains . . ."

Jake, she thought; Jake. Her body was as cold and still as the lake, only her hands had a stubborn life of their own, gripping the tough willows.

There was a movement on the bank.

Suddenly the men's voices were reckless and loud, but jumbled; she could not distinguish words. Out of it the young trooper said distinctly, "Where's my pants? . . ." They were walking back along the pier. They were now on the other side of the boathouse; there appeared to be a council there, murmured voices, a shuffle of feet upon the pier. A ripple washed in and pushed against the boat. She levered herself against the slow tug of the water. She heard steps on the deck of the boathouse; they were going up there, had gone up there, were moving with attempted stealth and their feet were clumsy and loud and hollow. A chair shifted and somebody said, "Damn it to hell . . ."

"Not so loud." That was the constable.

"Damned near broke my leg."

The trooper cried, "What are we waiting here for? We've got the case. He killed Wells, got the body in the boat after he knocked out Dixon, scuttled the rowboat. Last night he tied a weight on the body, rowed it out and heaved it into the lake. Dixon said he saw it. There's bloodstains . . ."

She heard and did not hear what they said, but some part of her mind told her that here was a new fact, something she had not known. They were talking of Wells and his body had been in the motorboat. Wells, not Jake.

Another voice emerged clearly; it was the old attorney. "Dixon shot this at me fast. Did you say he got it from the newspaper files in Baton Rouge?" The constable replied, jerkily as if pausing to listen, "Wells was an embezzler, Travers defended him. Wells was convicted but the money disappeared . . ." "Travers had money, got himself started, got into business . . ." That was the state trooper.

The old attorney said, "Bloodstains in the boat, but we'll never find the body. We can't drag the lake."

No one had looked in the motorboat—riding a little heavily, as if it had shipped water during the rain. They'd said, hadn't they, that Jake had witnessed a dreadful transfer? But that was the night before. They didn't know, how could they have known, that Arthur had murdered Jake?

Then voices were businesslike. "The rowboat will turn up somewhere. Besides, the woman's turned state's evidence. We'll get him for Costellani's murder. And maybe for Robinson's out there in San Francisco . . ."

"The police out there aren't sure yet; they've got to check fingerprints with the prison. And even if he is Robinson, as Dixon thinks, there's no evidence. I doubt if you can get him for that. Costellani—that's different. With the woman's testimony . . ."

What woman, Sarah thought. There was a cautious sliding of branches along the bank above her. Arthur knew that she was there. He had seen the dim outline of the rowboat. There was a cautious movement almost beside her, a subdued splash of water, and the boat moved and tipped and swirled around, and at the same time she heard another voice shouting, "Sharp—Harris, she's gone . . ."

It was Jake.

She knew that and life surged back into her body and she screamed and fought the blackness, fought to find the oar, fought to hold the boat against the weight that tipped and swirled it. And all at once the boat was free, and moving, drifting away from the willows.

There were men running, shouting; there were flashlights, jerking and gleaming along the shore. The young state trooper waded out and caught at the boat. And then Jake came plunging down the bank, splashing through the shallow water.

Sarah saw him; she felt his arms. She felt the boat swerve as they lifted her out of it. Men were searching the shore, searching the woods. There were troopers everywhere: they were in the little path jolting against her, shouting at Jake. They were running across the lawn, silhouetted against lights from the house, which was like a ship at sea, blazing with lights. Sinbad was barking wildly somewhere. Julia was on the porch, full in the light, with the wicker chairs looking strange and gay in their bright covers. Then Sarah was in one of the wicker chairs and Jake was kneeling beside her. The sounds of that pursuit had gone further away, deeper into the woods.

Julia said something that sounded like a sob; Jake's black head was so near she could touch it; she did touch it; she put her hand on his face. "I thought—" she began—"I was afraid . . ."

"It's all over, Sarah. Travers . . ."

The old attorney was there, too, standing beside them. "I guess that ties it up."

Jake said, "You'd better know. I got hold of Lisa this afternoon. She's at the troopers' headquarters; she's turned state's evidence. I scared her. Convinced her Travers did it and I had proof. Told her she'd be an accessory after the fact."

Lisa, who cared more than anything for her own safety. There were things Sarah had to tell them and all she could do was look at Jake. He was talking; the attorney was talking. She began to comprehend their talk. They knew everything: they knew why Wells was murdered. They were saying again that Jake had seen the grim, secret transfer of Wells's body the night before, from the motorboat (where nobody had thought of looking for him because they were hunting for a rowboat, hidden along the wooded shore) to the hidden depths of the lake. They were saying that Jake had gone to the train in the village, had got on the train and then, when the taxicab had left, got off again, hired a car at the little garage and came back secretly to watch the house. "Travers got me out of the way in a hurry. I knew there was something he had to do. I saw it from the willows, heard it; saw him get some concrete blocks and row out to the motorboat. There wasn't time to call the police then. I had to watch. I went then to find where Travers must have stayed, all this time. It had to be somewhere in the vicinity. I found it. A motor court near Woodsbridge; they said a man who looked like me had stayed there since Wednesday. I knew that I was on the trail. But still there was no proof, so I went to see Lisa Bayly and she wouldn't talk; I went to see Rose Willman and she wouldn't talk. Then I checked the newspaper files at Baton Rouge, by telephone; it took a long time, but I found the story. The point was that the money was never found and Travers turned up with enough money to buy some oil leases and go on from there . . ."

"Funny Wells would trust the money to Travers."

"There was a letter . . ." Sarah thought she said it aloud but she couldn't have; they went on. Jake had guessed the truth. "What would Wells do with it? He was headed for prison. They had probably a verbal agreement. Maybe there was nobody else Wells could trust, nowhere he could hide the money safely. He might lose either way, but with Travers entrusted with the money he had a chance. When I'd got the story of Wells I went back to Lisa. She had seen me, she'd said, somewhere."

"That gave Travers the idea for his scheme. Yes . . ."

"I was to be his alibi," Jake said. "That's why he went to San Francisco. Lisa knew it. She and Travers had seen me; it was a newsreel, an amateur tennis match. They commented on the resemblance between us. That was several weeks ago. When Travers decided to murder Wells he remembered it. He traced me to San Francisco; that was simple. He must have intended to decoy Wells from this vicinity, but he was held to the lake because Wells wouldn't leave. But Travers' first question, when he came back, was about my alibi. He didn't know then that my alibi wouldn't be his alibi because the police knew that I wasn't Travers."

How deviously and adroitly Arthur had manipulated Jake and herself, and circumstances! The crime he intended was never to be traced to him because he had an alibi. Jake said, "It boomeranged because he'd had to get rid of Costellani who, Lisa said, had listened to his first meeting with Robinson and had heard too much. And because Wells refused to be lured away from the house. I knew that if Travers' real purpose was a private and deadly quarrel with Wells, then I knew—after Wells was murdered, that Travers would return. Besides, time was running short. The week he had allowed himself for murder was nearly gone. He did return—but Wells's body had to be somewhere. So I came back. . . ."

The attorney said slowly, "Travers denied it all this morning. But if it hadn't gone wrong, if you hadn't found Costellani . . ." He said suddenly to Sarah, "Travers told us that you and Dixon . . ."

"I know."

"And you see—well, I'm an old man. I've seen life and the way people—and I knew there was something in the air between you and Dixon," he said simply. "So when Travers told us this morning that there was nothing to the story you told about his absence, he was so—so reasonable about it, you see, convincing—I believed him."

Revolver shots blasted the night. Distant shots, heavy, following each other in such rapid succession that the shocking waves of sound met and mingled. It was then very quiet, except for the frightened twittering of birds. Except for a burst of barks from Sinbad inside the house. The attorney was running down across the lawn. Jake started after him and then came back. As if the night told them, as if the woods whispered it, she knew and Jake knew what had happened.

Jake said, queerly, his face white, "If that's it, it's better . . ."

Two troopers came from the woods, running. They met the attorney. There was the staccato of quick words, and then again they were running toward the porch. Jake said, "Go in the house, Sarah. I'll tell you later."

The tramp of footsteps over the porch, along the hall. Voices at the telephone. Sinbad barking furiously upstairs. Sam's excited red face peering at Sarah and at Julia where they sat together on the sofa in the living room. More voices; more footsteps. The roar of cars along the driveway. There were things she must tell them. But it didn't matter now—they knew.

The constable's voice came clearly from the hall. "We'll get the Willman woman, she knows something."

187

Rose who had said, his life was my life. Somebody had to tell Rose.

The men's voices in the hall went on, mingled; they were telephoning again. Another car came with a roar along the driveway and stopped. Julia saw her hands and said something about bandages and went away.

Stillness settled down upon the house. Jake came to her, then. "It's all right. They've gone. There won't be a trial—there'll be an inquest."

She whispered, "Rose . . ."

"The attorney talked to her. She'd seen Wells. Wells telephoned again to the office and she made an appointment with him, here at the lake. She met him. He told her the story. She—she says she's going away. I think she knew, she must have guessed . . ."

"She guessed . . ." There was so much to tell. Yet they knew.

Jake said, "There'll be an inquest. We'll stay here for that. And after that . . ."

Julia had let out Sinbad. He charged down the room and upon Sarah. Jake said, "We'll take Julia and Sinbad. Little Liebchen."

"Take them . . ."

"There's a place I know in the High Sierras. It's not far from San Francisco. Sunshine and pines. Time passes quickly there. Peace and—and sometimes happiness . . ."

Sinbad put his black head on her lap. She felt the sunshine; she heard the murmur of the pines, the promise lay already, sturdy and strong in her heart.

Mystery . . . Intrigue
. . . Suspense

__**BAD COMPANY**
by Liza Cody   (B30-738, $2.95)

Abducted by a motorcycle gang, Anna discovers she has shaken an unsteady balance in the London underworld—and now must fight for her life.

__**DUPE**
by Liza Cody   (B32-241, $2.95)

Anna Lee is the private investigator called in to placate the parents of Dierdre Jackson. Anna finds motives and murder as she probes the unsavory world of the London film industry where Dierdre sought glamour and found duplicity . . . and death.

__**STALKER**
by Liza Cody   (B32-807, $3.95)

In a peaceful village, Anna finds a corpse with a bolt from a crossbow piercing its side. In an unfamiliar world of city princes and country poachers, she pursues the Stalker.